Deadly Sins— Deadly Secrets

Sylvia Dickey Smith

L & L Dreamspell
Spring, Texas

Cover and Interior Design by L & L Dreamspell

Copyright © 2007 Sylvia Dickey Smith. All rights reserved. No part of this publication may be reproduced, stored in a retrieval system or transmitted in any form or by any means, electronic, mechanical, photocopying, recording or otherwise without the prior written permission of the copyright holder, except for brief quotations used in a review.

This is a work of fiction, and is produced from the author's imagination. People, places and things mentioned in this novel are used in a fictional manner.

ISBN: 978-1-60318-018-4

Library of Congress Control Number: 2007932506

Visit us on the web at www.lldreamspell.com

Published by L & L Dreamspell
Printed in the United States of America

DEDICATION

To Bill, my partner in crime—and in life.
I love you *this* much!

ACKNOWLEDGEMENTS

I must begin by thanking my husband, Bill, for helping me make the time to do all that is necessary, not only to write, but also to sell what I write. Thanks for doing all those home chores (except the ironing and the cooking!) that make all this possible. I promise I'll get to that stack of ironing one of these days! You give a whole new meaning to the word soul-mate.

A special thanks goes to Marlin Merrell for taking my publisher/graphic designer, Linda Houle, and I out to the Sabine Lighthouse to snap pictures for the book cover. A true facilitator in that effort was Sharon Patton who borrowed her friend's boat and shuttled us across Sabine Lake to the site, and to my niece, Karyn Trantham, for volunteering Sharon's services. Karyn also freely gave of her knowledge of locations in Orange, the roles and actions of paramedics, and the response paramedics receive from a grateful community.

Continuing gratitude goes to my publishers, L&L Dreamspell. Lisa Smith, the fiction editor, does a fantastic job of interior design and editing. She spends hours searching for just the right fonts and symbols to match the story line and doesn't stop until she finds the perfect fit. Plus, she is so very patient with all my last minute edits and changes, cheers me on, makes excellent suggestions when I'm stuck, and maintains the neatest sense of humor throughout. She makes me want to write books faster just so I have an excuse to email her. Linda Houle, the other "L" of the fabulous L&L duo, designed the book cover and sent out advance copies and media releases, and published the work in Mobi-pocket, e-book and book trailer. But who would expect their graphic designer to don borrowed rubber boots, ride out on a boat, tromp through swamp water and reeds up to her waist while watching out for snakes and alligators, to reach a pre-Civil War built, and said-to-be-haunted, lighthouse to snap pictures for the cover of this book? Linda did, and that was after she spent the day before attending my book launch party, snapping pictures and meeting all my long-lost relatives and friends. I could not ask for a more skilled, supportive and encouraging publishing duo. A duo that raises the bar for other publishers.

Special thanks goes to my step-daughter, Robin Agnew, for her patience and willingness to read through my final draft, helping me catch errors that should have been caught long before.

Special recognition goes to the fantastic band, Three-legged Dawg, who not only played at the book launch of my first book, but also shares their pack-howling music in this one.

And a special thanks to all the folks who have read Dance on His Grave and taken the time to tell me what you thought of Sid Smart and the gang. Your keen anticipation for the next book in the Third Eye mystery series has kept me pounding away at the keyboard!

👁   👁   👁

**The answer for which I search
is right before my eyes.
When I think I don't see it,
what I do see is simply the other side
of that for which I search.**

One

Sunday morning

A menacing vortex surrounded Ned Durwood as though Satan himself tried to claim his reward, but then managed only one last shuddering breath before banishment back from whence he'd come.

Regardless, hell's horrors still filled the room.

Abe and Cherrie Collins lay sprawled across the bed in their own blood. Abe's hairy arms crumpled to his chest against a t-shirt and blue boxers, both now coated bright red. Cherrie lay beside her husband, her skirt yanked up to her waist exposing short thick thighs shoved into pantyhose, now laddered with runs.

Ned Durwood waited, hoping against hope that Abe and Cherrie were not as dead as they looked—certain that they were. The stench of excrement and slit-open intestines sickened him. He forced the bile back down his throat, willing himself not to throw up.

Get out of here, cried a voice in his head.

He hurled the butcher knife across the room, turned, and skidded out of the bedroom like the Foul Fiend from Gehenna snapped at his heels.

Down the short hallway, to the kitchen, through the back door.

Outside, the cold temperature raised goose bumps on his damp skin. He shivered as he pulled a dingy handkerchief out of his back pocket, stopping just long enough to wipe the doorknob clean before he charged across the large cedar deck.

Mid-way across, the fact hit him. Oh God—the knife…

He stopped, half-turned toward the house. He had to go back and clean it, else they'd know he'd been there—have evidence to…

Fear clamped his feet to the deck while rational thinking urged him back inside to wipe his fingerprints from the knife handle. As time warped, stopped, then sped up again, Ned heard the pounding of a judge's gavel in his head. But when tires crunched on the oyster-shell driveway beside the house, the spell broke, and Ned realized it had only been the sound of his heartbeat pounding in his ears.

He realized, however, someone had driven up to the front of the house, and they'd find the bodies and the knife.

Tucking his head between his shoulders, he fled down the steps and into the backyard, feet moving faster than the drumbeat in his chest. He retraced his path through the soupy fog to the railroad tracks behind the house.

But the sight of the couple still burned behind his eyes, and half-blinded by the image, Ned didn't see the train—stopped dead on the tracks—until he almost ran into it.

"Dammit." Pungent creosote vapors from the railroad ties tickled his nose. He swiped it with the back of his hand and looked farther down the tracks, not believing his rotten luck.

Then he saw his escape route—two of the boxcars sat unhitched, with just enough space between the couplings for him to slip through. Ned sprinted down the tracks toward the opening, breathing hard, feet skidding on the gravel. He stumbled, regained his footing and pushed harder, faster.

At last, he stepped between the unbuckled boxcars, but as he did, a rumble startled him. He stopped, jerked his head to listen. There it was again, a slight jolt, then another.

Just as he recognized the sound, the couplings on the two boxcars banged shut. The two parts of the train became one again, and the movement smashed Ned in half.

👁   👁   👁

Blue peeled off his clothes in the kitchen and stuffed them into a black plastic bag, relieved Ella had already left for church.

Bare-ass naked, he slipped into the garage and dumped the bag into the trashcan, glad tomorrow was collection day. Beneath mounds of refuse at the landfill, the soiled clothes might as well be on another planet.

Upstairs, he turned on the shower and adjusted the temperature to one notch below scalding and stepped inside. While the hot water pounded on his head he prayed that the heat burned iniquity from his soul.

But when he stepped out and towel-dried his reddened skin, flashes of the early morning horror returned as real as ever. He'd never meant to go that far—to—to…

He tossed the towel to the floor, went into his bedroom closet and selected a charcoal-gray suit. Then, pushing the early-morning images to the back of his mind while he dressed, he focused his thoughts on the upcoming worship service. He could pull this off, all he had to do was ask God's help.

Decked out in dark suit and white shirt, he looked in the mirror one last time, admiring the man who smiled back at him. He did a three-quarter turn, glanced back at his reflection, and clicked his heels. Perfect. Folks said he looked like a preacher—dammit, he did, a good-looking one at that.

Straightening his dark red tie one last time, he headed out the door into the cool morning air, righteousness hastening his steps across the early-spring grass. A sudden gust of wind blew his jacket open and as he glanced down to button it, he saw dew-soaked grass clinging to his freshly polished Cole Hahn shoes. Shit. He was going to be late. He'd never been late for church before.

He pulled a handkerchief out of his back pocket and swiped the grass off of his expensive new shoes. To be honest, he'd bought them because they looked like something a famous television evangelist might wear, but give him a few more years, and he'd be in their league anyway.

Tucking his handkerchief in his back pocket, he strode up the sidewalk to the church. Just as he reached the door, a hand grabbed his shoulder, and for an instant he feared he'd been caught.

"Can I talk to you a minute before you go inside?" a deep voice asked.

Blue turned, relieved to see it was only Clarence Clark. He glanced back toward the building as the clarion bells pealed. "Clarence, good morning. What can I do for you?"

Blue shook the proffered hand of the pot-bellied man, both relieved and irritated at the interruption. He'd hoped for a few minutes to collect his thoughts, to pray. Frustration itched around the starched collar of his dress shirt.

"Sorry to bother you, but I'm heading up a fundraiser to restore the old lighthouse out at Sabine Pass. I know you've opposed the restoration before. Just wanted to see where you stood on it now. With you fighting it, I doubt we'll make much headway."

A flood of childhood memories washed over Blue. They always did—every time anyone mentioned the lighthouse. He thought he'd killed any plans of restoration the last time they tried. "I can't support the project, Clarence. I've told you that before. My mind's made up, and I'm not going to change it."

"But you know the place is a historical landmark. I can't understand why you oppose the repair." The man rubbed the back of his neck. "Makes *no* sense to me."

"Well, it does to me," Blue snapped. "Now if you'll excuse me, Clarence, I'm rather busy at the moment."

Blue snatched open the door, slipped inside and closed it behind him, leaving the other man standing with his hands on his hips.

He glanced at his watch and listened. *Amazing Grace* resonated from the sanctuary. Good, he had a few more minutes.

Easing to his knees, he bowed his head and prayed for forgiveness.

But his mind wandered from God to events earlier that morning. What would the congregation think if they knew what he'd been doing while they sat in Sunday School?

Regardless of whether they knew the truth or not, God did. But maybe righteousness sometimes strayed from its usual path. After all, there was no law that said it couldn't. Even Abraham had been ordered to kill his own son. Maybe what he had done had indeed been God's will—else why would he have done it?

"Amen." With that, Blue closed his mind to all doubt.

He rose to his feet, dusted off his pants legs and sat at his desk. Shoulders high and proud, he flipped open his Bible to Ezekiel, Chapter Seven.

While he scanned the scripture, he kept an eye on the clock. When the hands on the timepiece jumped another couple minutes, he closed the book, stood and squared his tie, walked through the sanctuary door and stepped onto the platform.

The Very Reverend Humble Bluett—Blue to his friends, and Brother Blue to his congregation—sat on the preacher's bench, crossed his legs and straightened the crease down the front of his trouser leg, and then scrutinized his congregation.

Once again, Ian Meade, the professor from Lamar University, sat on the back row flaunting his full head of wavy dark hair and blue eyes. Blue felt himself hardening, so he shifted in his seat and adjusted his trousers, forcing his eyes and thoughts away from the man's chiseled good looks. If it weren't for God's grace, he, the most reverend Brother Blue, would long ago have burned in the flames of hell.

After the collection, the congregation stood and sang the Doxology, a short praise hymn rendered—after the collection of the money—in every Baptist church he'd ever attended, which was legion.

When the congregation sat, a young woman strode to the pulpit and sang the special music. *"I'm pressing on the upward way..."* she declared, hands folded in prayer, eyes focused on the ornate ceiling. At the conclusion of the song several men in the congregation voiced a hearty "Amen" while the woman reclaimed her seat in the choir loft behind Blue.

The sanctuary grew quiet except for a fussy child and the thud of a hymn book dropped in the rack.

Blue waited.

The room grew quieter still.

This was the moment Blue lived for, this in-between time, when the whole congregation waited, hushed eagerness settling them down even more. Many times he'd wished this feeling could be captured on DVD. Perhaps by replaying it, the persistent shadows of doubt resident within him might be banished.

Blue stood, cleared his throat and stepped to the pulpit. He tugged on his tie, jutted his chin, and opened his Bible.

The Gift slid down from Heaven.

"Let he who is without sin cast the first stone," his voice boomed. Two women on the front row stopped whispering and sat up straight. So did the child in the rear. The stillness grew deeper. If it hadn't been for plush burgundy carpet, a pin would have sounded like a cannon ball when it hit the floor.

Once again, he held them in the palms of his hands.

But only by the grace of God, he reminded himself.

Two

Sunday night, a week later.

What started out as an ordinary drive back to Orange after a pleasant weekend away, grew more and more treacherous. Sid felt stupid. Why had she let the man at the truck stop talk her into locating the owner of the lost, half-frozen dog, in the midst of a freak ice storm?

The man had described how he thought the dog's owner might live five miles further, in the house off to the right of the highway. Furthermore, he'd been certain she'd recognize the barn behind the house, for someone had painted large turquoise balls on the side.

Unsure whether the man knew what he was talking about, or not, it was obvious he wanted nothing to do with the dog, and she couldn't just drive off and leave the poor animal outside freezing to death.

Driving in the fast-moving, unseasonably late winter storm created a knot in her chest, and the tinny sound of sleet pinging against the Xterra only increased the anxiety. She shivered and adjusted the heater to full blast. In the seat across from her, the whining, hyper-vigilant dog looked first at her, and then out the icy windshield, as if he too, searched for the weirdly painted barn.

He had some retriever in him, she decided, Chesapeake, and maybe something else. His short hair lay in tight damp swirls, and he smelled like—well—wet dog.

Ice storms were rare in southeast Texas, especially this time of year. The front had barreled in from the north late that afternoon, and by sundown the temperature had plummeted. Now, she passed only an occasional vehicle as a thick layer of sleet accumulated on the road in front of her, the yellow line barely showing through the icy layer.

"I'm not going to lie to you, buddy. This weather doesn't look good. But I'm going to do my best to find your owner. If we can't, then I promise I won't leave you stranded outside in the cold."

The dog cocked his head and looked at her as though unsure whether or not she was a promise-keeper. Then he dragged his attention back to the road.

"It's okay, buddy, you're not the only one wanting to get home safe and sound. We'll be okay."

But her words tempted fate. Just as she spoke, headlights looking like icy halos topped a hill and veered into her path. Panic thumped in her throat.

She gripped the steering wheel and braced to head towards the ditch, but in the split second before she did, the driver inched back across the road. She exhaled a chest full of air and heard the dog do so as well.

"Oh, wow, we gotta keep breathing, Dog. And I better keep my eyes on the road while you look for your house."

A couple miles later, with no other cars in sight, Sid couldn't resist stealing another glance over at the squirming dog. It seemed he didn't like looking out the side windows, for when he did, he scrambled around in the seat and hunkered down as if something was out there waiting to get him. Occasionally he glanced through the rear window, but seemed much more comfortable peering through the front windshield with its wipers struggling against the icy drag.

"Something out there scaring you, boy?" She took another quick peek at the dog. "Do you see your house? Are we getting close?"

The dog chuffed, scratching around in his seat, his nails doing lord knew what to her black leather upholstery. He scooted up, his nose almost touching the windshield, eyes straight ahead.

Something told Sid the dog wasn't lost. If not, had he run away from an abusive owner? Was his nervousness over the possibility of her finding his house?

"We'll go a little further, buddy, but if we don't find something soon, I'm going to have to turn back. The roads are getting too treacherous." He whined and stole a quick look at her before turning his eyes back to the road, ears cocked. "It's okay. If we don't find it tonight, we'll come back soon as the weather clears."

Woof. He screwed around in the seat, looked out the passenger side window, his body quivering.

"I'm telling you the truth, sweetheart. The ice will melt as soon as the sun hits it tomorrow. We can come back then." She felt silly defending her actions and discussing the weather with a dog.

A quarter mile further she spied what looked like a driveway and geared down, hoping to see a house and weird-painted barn, and if not, at least she could turn around and head home. Easing to the shoulder, her wheels crunched on the icy gravel, slid a little, then came back under control as she crept into a right turn and found herself on a one-lane, unpaved road. Following her high beams down a long, barbed-wire fence, a white farmhouse glowed in the crystal night, but the windows offered no light from inside.

The dog saw the house just as she did; he turned and barked at her, his eyes pleading like a child in pain.

"So this is it, huh? But where's the barn?"

Sid inched the Xterra up the long drive to the house, hoping there would be room to turn around. Relieved when she reached the wide front yard, she threw the gear in park.

The dog gave another woof and propped his legs on the dash, scratching at the window, panting hard.

"Is this your house, buddy? Okay, let's go check it out." She grabbed a flashlight from the console and opened her door to sleet-like needles hitting her in the face and falling down her collar. Swiping her cheeks as she got out, she turned to close the door, but the dog leapt across the console and bounded out into the freezing rain. "In a hurry, huh?" The wind grabbed her words and flung them back in her face.

She switched on the flashlight and trudged toward the house, the dog several feet ahead. Not as convinced as he, that this was the right place, she flashed the light around the area until the beam spotlighted a building she hadn't seen from the road. A little behind the house on her right sat a light-colored barn with what looked like turquoise balls on its side. Yep. This was his home.

The dog beat her to the house, and in one easy bound, leapt onto the wide front porch and slid across. By the time Sid got to him he clawed against the door, whimpering, desperate to get inside.

Sid knocked and waited.

Only the wind howled around the corner.

She knocked harder, and then rammed her freezing hands down in her coat pocket and waited. What did she do if no one answered? Or if someone did, and they didn't want the dog?

"Buddy, there's no one here. I'm heading back to the car," she called out above the wind. "You can come with me if you want." Her words sounded big, but she knew she'd never leave the poor dog outside in this weather.

She stepped off the porch, hoping he would follow, but instead, he grew more frantic, clawing at the door like a mad-dog.

It was obvious he wasn't leaving, and she couldn't stay. Maybe the door was unlocked. If so, she could just put him inside and leave. When the owner came home, they'd find him hungry, but warm. She could even come back tomorrow and check on him.

She turned back to the dog who now stood stiff-legged, crouched low, a deep growl in his throat.

"Okay, okay, you've convinced me." She strode back up the steps. "Let's see if it's unlocked." She turned the knob, and the door squeaked open to a pitch-black void.

No sooner had she shined the flashlight inside than the dog charged in and slid across the floor into the dark recesses of the room.

Sid stuck her hand around the doorframe and felt until she found a light switch. Instant relief flooded her when the light clicked on. But when she turned, the relief lurched into sadness.

Across the small sitting room, an elderly woman, dressed in a long-sleeved print house dress and apron, lay slumped in a rocking chair, arms dangling over the sides. An unopened pill bottle lay in her lap.

Sid walked over to feel the woman's pulse, but the instant she laid her fingers on the woman's hard, cold body, she knew the poor soul was dead.

Without making a sound, the dog crept over to a dining table, reached underneath a chair and caught a small squeeze-toy between his teeth. The rubber-ducky quacked once.

Spell-bound, Sid watched the dog crawl across the green and yellow linoleum towards the old woman. Then, with the tenderness of a mother with her newborn child, he rested the toy in the old woman's lap, eased to the floor and rested his chin on her bare, misshaped, arthritic feet. A soft whine from the guy broke Sid's heart.

👁   👁   👁

The sun came up bright and warm, melting the sleet quicker than it had accumulated. By the time the Trinity County sheriff's deputies released the body—and Sid—the roadways were dry. She headed out the door, the dog loping along beside her with his tongue hanging out, content it seemed, now that his loved one had been found.

"What about the dog?" Sid asked the deputy. "Are you taking him to the humane society?"

"Yeah, we'll take 'im. But we don't have no society. All we have is the pound. They'll keep him for awhile."

"A while? You mean they won't place him with a family?"

"Oh, sure, they will—if one comes up."

"What if one doesn't?"

"They treat animals very humanely, ma'am. You don't have to worry."

She knew what he meant, but the thought of animals treated anyway other than that bothered her, bothered her a lot. "What if I took him?"

While the deputy scratched his chin and eyed the dog, Sid imagined herself tripping over the animal in her small apartment. But before she could take back the offer, the deputy agreed. "Sure, 'less some family member comes and claims him. I've got your name and address, so if you want to take him, go ahead."

The man's *if you want to,* sounded more like *y-ont* to, but she understood what he meant, and that said something about her adjustment to the local dialect.

"Okay, buddy, looks like we're stuck with each other for now." She scratched behind the dog's ears with both hands. "Come on, let's go." She headed to her car, the dog at her heel. "My place is small, but it's warm and dry. I just wish I knew what your name was. You've suffered enough loss, shouldn't have to lose your name, too."

The words were no sooner out of her mouth than the dog slid to a stop, skittering gravel in his wake. He looked up at her, tail wagging. Seems like every time she looked at him, he was sliding on, or into, something. "Slider," she volunteered out loud.

The tail wagged faster.

"No kidding? Is that it? Slider?"

The dog slurped in his tongue and woofed up at her.

"Well I'll be damned. Okay, then, Slider it is." She opened the car door and the dog jumped in.

Three

The next morning.

Sid and a freshly bathed Slider tramped down the weathered stairs outside her one-room apartment. A gust of wind groaned through pine boughs and ruffled their hair. The gray, overcast day matched Sid's spirit as she passed Sophia's darkened kitchen window. The *For Sale* sign in the front yard wobbled in the breeze. "I sure do miss Sophia, Slider. The two of you would have gotten along well. She had a stroke a few weeks ago, and…" She wasn't sure why she explained her landlady's health condition to the dog, but then it dawned on her, she loved the resonance inside her head and on her tongue when she said *Sophia*.

Slider regarded her, tail wagging like a metronome, then he pranced around her like a show pony at the fair. Soon as he completed his business, Sid chided herself for not bringing a couple of baggies to clean up after him, promising herself she'd do better the next time.

A half hour later, the two bounded upstairs for breakfast. Sid collected a container of plain, non-fat yogurt from the fridge, and a plastic container of homemade granola from her tiny pantry. Next, she opened the bag of dog food purchased the night before. "Here, boy, let's eat." She filled the red plastic bowl with Slider's food and sat it on the floor.

Slider schlepped over, tail between his legs, took one sniff, then sat back on his haunches and whined up at her. His left ear bent towards the floor, the other reached for the ceiling.

"You pathetic creature. Don't tell me you dislike dog food."

The dog shuddered, and with a furrowed brow, looked at her as if she were crazy.

"But that's all we've got right now."

He whined some more, scooting his butt around on the linoleum floor.

"Look, fellow, you didn't tell me you were a finicky eater."

He yawned and looked around the room with disinterest.

"Tough noogies, what do you want, yogurt and granola?"

Slider licked his chops.

"It figures. That's too bad, this is *my* breakfast." She pointed to her own bowl, "and that is yours." She pointed at the rejected bowl on the floor.

Slider walked over, sniffed at the dog food again, then looked up at her as if she'd tried to convince him strychnine was edible.

"You gotta be kidding."

Damned if it didn't look like the dog grinned.

"Oh, all right, here." Relenting, she spooned a few tablespoons of yogurt on top of the dog food, which Slider licked off while waltzing around the bowl in a manner reminiscent of the Bolshoi ballet.

"Okay, so you've got great table manners, but I want to make one thing clear, bud, if I don't get a new client soon, we're both going to be eating this dog food, so you better get over being a finicky eater." Slider cut his eyes over to her, but never missed a beat in his dance around the dog nuggets.

After breakfast, although the chore seemed useless, she straightened the old blanket she'd put on the floor the night before, a blanket the dog hadn't touched. Instead, he'd headed to the over-stuffed chair in the corner. After crawling in and making a couple tight turns, he'd rolled on his back and flopped his head off the front end of the seat cushion. Then, with all four legs straight up in the air, he soon fell into a deep, loud, snore.

Exhausted, she'd covered her head with a pillow and let him stay there.

"I hope you have a big bladder. I'll try to come by mid-day and let you *stretch your legs*; that's the best I can do right now." She switched on the television for company, rubbed under his chin, and headed out.

It still seemed impossible that her brother had left her his private eye business, even arranging a mentor—George Léger—to help her learn the business. The day after the reading of the will she'd driven to Orange and met the big Cajun. She smiled now just thinking about him.

Her husband Sam—ex-husband, she still had to remind herself—had thought she'd lost her mind when he'd heard about Warren's will and what she planned to do. Of course he'd already decided she'd lost what few marbles he'd assigned her, the day she left him, and that was before Warren had even died.

She turned onto Division Street and pulled nose-first into the parking space alongside meddlesome Aunt Annie's maroon Olds.

When Sid stepped inside the office, Annie stood with her back to the door. Her cherry-red pants brought a whole new definition to the word 'stretched,' and the hot-pink top almost blinded Sid.

"Oh, I didn't hear you come in." Annie negotiated to her desk, newspaper under her arm, and steaming coffee cup in her hand. "Seaport's ready, and I already checked the message machine. We didn't have none."

"That's too bad, if we don't get a new case soon, we're both going to be out on the streets." Sid headed for the coffeemaker while, behind her, Annie rattled the newspaper.

It had taken Sid a while to grow accustomed to the local brand of coffee, but after more cups than she dared count, both at George Léger's office, and here, she had developed a taste for the strong brew.

"Siddie, your name's in the paper," Annie squealed, the pitch of her voice bordering on glass-breaking. In one fluid motion, she stood and shoved her chair back. "Why didn't you tell me you were out in that freak ice storm last night, and that you found a dead woman?"

Sid started explaining the details one more time while Annie sat enraptured.

"Yep, it says here," Annie interrupted before Sid half-finished her account, "the coroner thinks she died from a heart attack while trying to open a bottle of nitroglycerin pills found in her lap."

Sid drank her coffee and waited for her aunt to run down.

"What'd she look like?" Annie fidgeted. "Was her eyes open, blank-looking, like I seen on T.V.?"

Sid laughed off the question with, "Sweetheart, you've seen way too much television."

"I have not—them detective shows are teachin' me how to do this job."

"What job? Office Manager?" Okay Sid, that was tacky.

"Wait, look here." Annie folded the paper in half. "It also says you took the old woman's dog home." She shot a glance at Chesterfield, her orange-colored, king-of-the-hill cat. He'd been stretched out on the hearth, soaking up the warmth from the fire until he heard a dog mentioned. Now on his feet, he arched his back and hissed.

"His name's Slider, and yes, he's at my apartment. So far, we're getting along great." She started to mention the dog's snoring problem, but bit her tongue.

"You really shouldn't keep him, sweetie. That'll make it difficult for me and Chesterfield when you move in with us."

That prediction turned Sid to stone. Annie kept insisting Sid move in with her, and Sid kept swearing that she'd sleep atop a bed of fire ants first, but she didn't dare say that to her dad's favorite sister. Instead, she offered, "Slider's a little persnickety, but actually he's well-behaved."

Annie had just given her another reason to keep the dog. She anchored that decision to a will often referred to as stubborn.

"Yeah, but when you…"

The phone rang, and both women reached to answer, but Annie snatched it up before Sid got halfway there.

"The Third Eye." Pride in her position swelled Annie's chest to twice its size. "Yes, Ms. Smart is here, may I tell her who's calling, please?"

"Hold on." Annie held the phone to her chest. Pointing at the device, she whispered, "It's some old man, says his name is Dempsey Durwood." Her eyes grew wider. "Ain't that the same last name as that fellow the train cut in half last week? I'll bet this is his pappy. It's been in all the news." Shaking with excitement, Annie scanned down the front page of the newspaper, and then shoved it toward Sid. "Look, see here, they're still writing about it in the paper. Everyone says the guy murdered that couple, then killed his self."

Four

Late that afternoon.

Following the old man's directions, Sid pulled into the mud-rutted driveway of a weathered house crouched at river's edge. Across the yard an old man, Dempsey she figured, stood under a shed fiddling with a box of rusty tools. He looked up as she parked then headed toward her. "Nice to meet you ma'am, thanks for coming." He wiped a gnarled hand on rust-dusted overalls and stuck it out at Sid. "Come on in where we can sit and talk."

Inside, he scraped a ladder-back chair across the plank flooring. The chair bottom was made of black-and-white cowhide stretched across a wooden frame, hair still attached. "Here, take a seat Ms. Smart. Pardon me, and I'll make us a cuppa *black-Joe*. Just make ya self to home. I'll be back directly."

"Take your time Mr. Durwood," Sid called after him as he disappeared into the back of the house. She cringed as she sat on the hair-chair. Twiddling her thumbs, she glanced around the room. "I hope I'm not too early. I wasn't sure how long it would take me to find your place."

"Don't make me no never mind," Dempsey called from the kitchen amidst banging pots and rattling dishes. "I got all the time in the world. Don't do much no way but sleep, eat, and drown a worm ever now and then."

The room smelled like an old man—medicinal and musty. She pulled a tissue from her pants pocket, rubbed her nose, and tossed the tissue into an overflowing wastebasket.

An old-looking coon dog ambled in from another room, his brown back as dusty as the furniture. Retired, Sid figured, from late night carousing with tricky raccoons.

When he sprawled beside a wooden rocking chair, his floppy ears dangled to the floor.

She thought of Slider and wondered how he was doing, locked inside all day. If Sophia were home, she'd take him out for a potty break, but…

The vertical slats of the chair began to dig into Sid's back. She squirmed into a different position, but at length gave up and eased to her feet, keeping an eye on the dog in case she startled him.

She needn't have worried. He didn't raise an eyelid.

She browsed around the small room viewing Mr. Durwood's few possessions. She stopped at an old sideboard, swiped her fingers across the dusty surface, and then picked up a daguerreotype photo of a white-haired woman—taken in the early 1900s, Sid guessed, from the way the woman was dressed.

The subject sat encased in black, from the high-neck of her dress to the full, long sleeves. Her black-gloved hands lay in her lap; one clasped the handle of a black purse, the other, a fan. Black net swept across the top of the woman's dark hat and down both sides of her outfit like a macabre bridal veil.

This woman was one serious piece of somber. Not one iota of frivolity showed anywhere. Was she in mourning, or was it her Sunday best at a time when black fit the religious color of the day? Despite the outfit, however, the woman's eyes were what defined her, what caught Sid. Hollow, but at the same time, like a smile waited just long enough for the shutter to snap. As if they had survived so much grief, all that remained was only a curious laughter at life.

Sid smiled back at the woman. In another hundred years, today's fashions would probably look as odd as those the woman wore in the photo.

With the picture still in her hand, the wooden frame flashed from warm to ice-cold. Startled by the sudden change, Sid dropped it on the sideboard and stepped back, staring at her beet-red hands. She'd felt the same hard coldness before—the day she'd touched Warren, dead in his casket.

A logical reason explained her frigid hands. She'd been chilled coming in from outside.

But if that was it, why did her face feel so hot?

Shuddering, she hustled back to her chair. "It's just a picture," she whispered to the dog.

He raised one eyelid. Closed it.

At last, Mr. Durwood shuffled through the doorway negotiating a tray with two cups and a pot of steaming coffee. He'd changed into a clean pair of overalls and a green-plaid flannel shirt. Instead of the muddy brogans, now his shoes looked like Sunday's best, spit-polished black leather.

"Here, let me help you." Sid took the tray and placed it on a table while he limped over to the rocking chair.

"Go ahead, drink your coffee, never mind me for now." He motioned to her while working to contain a mouthful of tobacco juice that dribbled out on his chin.

Sid's stomach roiled. Desperate to move the conversation forward before her stomach embarrassed her, she poured herself a meager half-cup of the black, thick-looking liquid and returned to her chair. "So, Mr. Durwood, you need a private detective?"

Durwood rocked, reached down and fluffed the coon dog's ears. The animal groaned and shifted while dust particles floated in a sunbeam above its head. The old man snorted away tears and wiped a hand across his eyes. He leaned over and lifted a rusted tin can from the floor, spat in it, and sat it back down. Then he examined the shine on first one shoe, and then the other.

Sid waited, fidgeting, hoping her stomach settled down.

"My son Ned graduated first in his senior class. Never caused me a lick a trouble. That red hair got him teased a lot, but he just ignored 'em—went on 'bout his business." Durwood rubbed behind the dog's ears again. The dog moaned and melted even deeper into the floor. This time, a fly took flight off the dog and buzzed against the windowpane, desperate for escape.

"What's your dog's name?"

"I call him Whiz." Durwood chuckled. "Earned the name as a pup, he did, and he ain't done much better since, if'n you know what I mean."

Sid tried to chuckle along with Durwood, but ended up choking back a gag reflex after he spit the whole cud of tobacco into the coffee can and wiped his mouth on his shirtsleeve. A quick glance at the photograph on the sideboard took her mind off her stomach, and onto the hairs standing at attention on the back of her neck. Who was the woman? Had Sid imagined the coldness?

"My boy didn't kill them people—that Abe and Cherrie Collins. He went there to talk about some work they wanted him to do."

"Yes sir." Her body tensed. "I read about it in the paper." But she had no idea whether his son killed the couple or not. "How can I help, Mr. Durwood?"

"Folks round here just call me Dempsey." He waved his hand at her and rocked, getting more mileage out of a rocking chair than anyone she'd ever seen. "Buried him Friday, you know."

"Yes sir. I'm sure sorry. It must be tough losing a son."

He nodded. Grief deepened the lines around his eyes. "You have a son, Ms. Smart?"

"A son and a daughter. Chad and Christine are both grown now, and pretty independent."

"That's nice." Twisting his hands, now lying in his lap, he stared at the floor for a long while before speaking again. "They say he did it—say he stabbed them people to death. Ned didn't do no such thing. He couldn't—" Dempsey choked, "I know my boy. He might a been a little different than some folks, a little sissified you know, but he never did kill nobody. A man knows that sort a thing about his son. Don't you think?"

"Yes sir. All I know about the case is what I've read, that the police found your son's fingerprints on the murder weapon and something about a shoe print."

Dempsey slumped in his chair, legs sprawled out in front of him like useless appendages. He'd moved his arms back up on the rocking chair. "They ain't said for sure Ned did it, not yet they ain't, but they're gonna. When the sheriff came by here last night he told me they had it all wrapped up nice and neat like, wadn't even gonna send it to the county attorney."

Sid stiffened with the mention of the county prosecutor—Ben Hillerman—the same guy she'd dated for awhile, the same guy that had suddenly stopped calling, or even returning her calls. Irritated her every time she thought about it. Now, she leaned forward in her chair, forcing her mind back to the present. "That seems like fast crime-solving. What's the sheriff's hurry?"

"Beats me." Dempsey rocked, staring at the floor. "Thing about it is, they blame it on Ned, and with him dead and all, there ain't no way he can prove he ain't done it."

"Where do I come in?"

"I talked to my lawyer. Marv Bledsoe's his name. Thought maybe he could clear Ned, or at least his name. But he said since Ned was dead, and they think he killed his self there on that train track, there weren't much he could do. Said I should hire a private detective, that he weren't much good at that sorta thing. So that's where you come in."

Dempsey grew quiet, fidgeted in his chair, inspected his shoes again. "I ain't got a lot of money, Ma'am, but I got a little saved up. I figure there's more than one way to skin a squirrel."

He raised his head and looked at Sid. "I read in the paper what you did for them gals from outta town…"

A vision of her first two clients flashed behind Sid's eyes. She'd learned a lot on that case—mainly to trust herself.

"I said to me self—I want that woman for my boy. We got to prove that sheriff wrong, that's what we gotta do. Just 'cause Ned was a homo don't make him bad. Don't make him no killer. Besides, I want someone mature like yourself, someone who's a survivor. Don't have much faith in them young folk today."

Dempsey choked again.

Sid cast her eyes to the floor, allowing the heartbroken father his grief.

He cleared his throat, coughed into his fist. Humor mingled with the sorrow and crackled his voice. "What you did for them gals, that's what I like—a woman with a backbone. That's why I called you 'stead of some other detective. Besides, you women have that intuition thing goin' on."

Sid wasn't too sure about that, but let the comment drop. "You said Abe and Cherrie Collins wanted Ned to do some work for them. What kind of work did he do? And do you have any proof that he had an appointment with them?"

"No'm."

"Even a piece of paper with their names written on it—anything?"

Dempsey looked up through crusted eyelids. "I been through all his stuff, but I didn't find no papers like that. Anyways, you asked what Ned done did. Well, he called his self a artist. Used pieces a junk metal to make them big critters for the backyard, and then he sold 'em over at First Monday in Canton—at Winnie Trade Days too, over in Winnie. Called it yard art, he did. Made enough to stay alive, but you know how these young folks are, they spend it fast as they make it."

The old guy had wound himself around Sid's heart, but a nagging feeling told her the investigation wasn't going to end like Dempsey wanted. From what Annie had read to her from the newspaper, his son sounded guilty.

She stood, wishing she had the balls, or the ovaries, or whatever part of anatomy she needed, to refuse the case. Just as she did, her cell phone rang. Excusing herself, she pulled the phone out of her jacket pocket and flipped up the cover. A familiar voice screeched, "Siddie?"

Annie and hysteria created a natural symbiosis.

"The rudest man just called and swore you was late making your car payment." Annie's chest rattled and wheezed over the phone. "I told him either he lied or his staff did, because my niece always pays her bills on time."

Humiliation stung Sid's cheeks as she flipped the phone closed and glanced over at Dempsey who busied himself swiping the toe of one shoe on the back leg of his overalls. The man offered cash, whether his son murdered the couple or not. And who knew, maybe he wasn't guilty; maybe someone else killed them, maybe Ned's only guilt was bad timing.

"Okay, Dempsey, I'll take your case. Not sure what we'll find, but let's give it a go."

Dempsey didn't hesitate when she'd quoted her fee. Instead, he simply handed her a coffee-stained envelope—or at least she hoped it was coffee—filled with greenbacks, probably from underneath a mattress.

Sid said goodbye and stepped outside into fading sunlight shimmying off of the muddled dun backwater of the Neches River. An old boat, paint peeling, lay propped against the house.

Sid backed her vehicle around and headed into town.

But she couldn't get her mind off the woman in the picture on Dempsey's sideboard. Who was she? Maybe she would ask Dempsey when she came back with a report.

Poor old man, son dead, no wife to make sure he kept himself clean—or stopped chewing tobacco. When Sid had been a preacher's wife, labels and ascriptions of sin had seemed simple, hard-line, no room for negotiation—or humanity. Perhaps truth wasn't as easily prescribed as she'd been taught. She liked Dempsey. She hoped Ned was innocent, but if he was, what had the sheriff missed?

Five

Sid drove back into town excited about the case. It would not only help pay her bills, but also occupy her days. Too much free time and she'd sink into another of her *what if* funks. What if she hadn't left Sam, what if she hadn't inherited a private eye business? What if...?

She pushed a CD of soft music into the player and drove toward her upstairs apartment over Sophia's house. She missed the old crone and wondered how she was doing since the stroke, reminding herself to visit her landlady at the assisted living center. From what Sophia's family had said, they had several interested buyers. When the house sold, Sid's lease would be null and void. Dang it, she'd just moved out of the parsonage in Houston a few months ago, and soon she'd have to move again. So far, nothing had surfaced within her price range, but she'd keep that fact from Annie as long as possible.

The first quarter moon hung low in front of her, looking like she'd drive right into it if she went far enough. Sid loved this time of year, when the days grew longer, when life that had rested underground during the cold winter, now stirred, anticipating energetic spring days.

A flashing blue light in her rearview mirror decimated Sid's reverie. She'd noticed the cross atop the steeple of the Baptist church before, but she'd never realized it was neon—much less blue and flickering.

To some people, the age-old symbol of execution broadcast

hope, new life—redemption, but not to Sid, not anymore. Now the cross appeared as a bi-polar expression of her own religious wounds. Regardless, much like a kid playing a road trip game counting McDonalds, or service stations, or drugstores, she still watched for Baptist churches every time she went into a new town, for they were as ubiquitous as the others.

Who pastored this one—and whose idea was it to light up the night sky with a symbol of execution? Curious, she swung the car around and drove back to the white building with the cerulean glow. The parking lot sat empty this time of night.

Steeling her emotions against the resistant tear that rolled down her cheek, she gripped the wheel and squinted in the evening light. Of course the sign didn't list her ex-husband, Reverend Samuel Smart, as Pastor. Instead, it read Rev. Humble Bluett, D.D.

Fitting name.

She shuddered against old memories, some pleasant, and some not so, that rushed around her heart. How many years would she feel both the tug and, at the same time, the inexpressible freedom of release from a prison of her own making—inadvertent, powerful, and debilitating.

Glassy-eyed, she stared until her eyes forced closure, and then she roused and drove home, thankful and sad, and then eager when she remembered that Slider waited for her. She wondered how he'd done on his first day alone in her apartment.

※ ※ ※

The next morning, after taking Slider for his walk and coating his dry dog food with plain, fat free yogurt, Sid headed to the sheriff's office and obtained a copy of the crime report on the murders of Abe and Cherrie Collins, and the train accident that caused Ned's death.

It in hand, she sat in her car and flipped through the report. Just like Dempsey had said, charges against Ned were based on his fingerprints on the murder weapon—a butcher knife identified as belonging to the Collins couple. A witness statement by neighbor, Jack Agnes, described how he'd seen Ned in the Collins' backyard the morning of the murders.

Sid pulled out her Blue Tooth, looped it over her ear and tucked the cell phone in her lap. Double-checking the crime report for Jack Agnes's address, she pulled a city map out of the car pocket, reviewed it, and then headed out. Half-way there, she flipped open the cell phone and dialed her office.

Annie answered on the first ring.

"Good morning Annie, just checking in. I'm going to be out and about this morning. You have my cell number."

"Morning Siddie, yes, I got here bright and early." Annie's voice blasted through the earpiece. "You just go about your business. I have everything under control."

She thought she did, but Sid wasn't convinced.

When she reached the address listed as that of Jack Agnes, she pulled into the gravel driveway. In the wide front yard a man in blue jeans and tee shirt, with the sleeves ripped out, leaned under the hood of a beat-up truck.

She got out of her car and headed toward him. "Mr. Agnes?"

The grease-stained man turned his head her way. When he saw Sid, irritation flicked across his face. He pulled himself out from under the hood and shoved a Houston Astros cap to the back of his head. "Holy mother of God, when is it going to stop? Let me guess, you're either a plain-clothes cop or a reporter, and you come to talk about the murders." He snatched a red work rag from the fender and wiped his hands, then tossed the rag back on the truck in disgust.

"Ma'am, I done told the deputies all I know. How the hell is a guy supposed to get a job done with all this shit going on?" He sucked through his teeth as he turned back under the hood. "I've made all the statements I'm gonna make. Go the hell away."

"I'm not a cop or a reporter, I'm a detective working for Dempsey Durwood. He believes his son is innocent. He's hired me to clear Ned's name."

The man stood back from the truck, grabbed a bottle of water off the fender and swigged. Then he tilted his head back and splashed his unshaven face, wiping the drips with the bottom of his T-shirt. Tan muscles rippled with his movements.

Sarcastic eyes surveyed Sid top to bottom then back up. "Well, you don't look like a private detective, that's all I got to say," he spit out. "If Dempsey hired you, he's a bigger fool than I thought. Hell, what'd he want, a grandmother?"

Her arm twitched, eager to punch the man in the face. Instead, she ran her fingers through her close-cropped hair. "Don't discount me, Mr. Agnes." She looked him in the eye. "Seems to me the sheriff needs to take a closer look at your alibi, and I'll just bet I can make that happen." She spun on her heels.

"What do you want from me?" His boots crunched on the gravel driveway as he stepped closer to her. His voice was gruff, condescending. Sid detested men like that. Still, a trickle of fear edged underneath her skin.

In her previous life as a minister's wife, she'd been taught to disapprove extraneous vulgarities, but at the moment nothing other than profanity fit. She swung around and stood solid, her hands on her hips and her face inches from his. "I don't give a good goddamn if you think I look like Grandma Moses, Mr. Agnes. The fact is, a couple died, Ned Durwood is accused, and he can't defend himself. Either you tell me what you know, or I will make your life a living hell." She pushed the threat through gritted teeth, knowing it held no substance, hoping he'd think it did.

A mosquito hawk glided between them.

"Like what?" he asked.

"Like what do you know?"

"I told the sheriff what I know. Go read the report. Get a damn copy and read it."

Sid stared him in the eye, raised her hand that held the report, then turned and walked to her car.

"And you might check with that preacher, Bluett, over at the

Baptist Church," he snarled the words at her. She heard his footsteps, knew he was at her heels.

Her heart sounded like a sledgehammer pounding in her ears. She jerked open the door and slid in, but when she tried to pull it shut, Agnes held the door handle. "Look lady. I don't want to get involved in all this mess." He hesitated, stuttered. "I—I served time before."

"For what?"

"Kid stuff." He ducked his head and scuffed the toe of his work boot into the gravel. "Me and some other guys—oh hell, it don't matter none what it was, when you got a record, they always come see you first."

"What about the preacher?" The title on her tongue made her heart skip a beat, jerking her right back to her years of *being* the preacher's wife, amazed at how the more she tried to forget the past, the stronger the memory grew.

"I ain't going there." Jack Agnes shook his head and pushed the palm of one hand toward her. "He's supposed to be a man of God—whatever that means—and I sure as hell don't want God pissed off at me. You just check it out, I tell you."

Sid climbed out of the car and slammed the door shut. "Mr. Agnes, I'm not trying to get you in trouble with God, or anyone else. Mr. Durwood hired me to find out who killed your neighbors, and why. If you didn't, you don't have to worry." God, she hoped that was true. "But you need to tell me what you know. All of it."

He motioned her to the front steps. They both sat.

"I don't know who killed them. That's no lie."

"But you know something."

"I know something." He nodded and rested his thick arms on his thighs, grease-stained hands dangling between his legs.

"I'd left the house and gone down to the Shell Station to get a pack of cigs and a Sunday paper. Must a been gone an hour or so—saw a couple of buddies and got to talking. When I got home, I went to the kitchen, poured me a cup of coffee, and sat at the table with the paper. Then I look up and see Ned hurrying across the backyard towards the tracks. I didn't take no mind to it, just figured he was taking a short cut or something, you know?"

Sid didn't acknowledge the question tacked on at the end of his sentence. Rather, she sat without saying a word, hoping to force more information.

Sure enough, after a long awkward pause, the guy continued. "Something strange going on in that house though, I do know that." Agnes pulled off the ball cap and twirled it in his hands. "Saw the preacher in and out lots of times."

"Keep talking."

Jack Agnes glanced next door at the Collins place, wiped his arm across his forehead. "My opinion? I think the Collins' were killed to shut them up about something."

"Go on."

"Lately, they were arguing a lot. Couple of times I heard 'em yelling, but I never could tell what it was all about. Heard one of 'em mention shell mounds one time. Never did figure out what that was all about."

"Shell mounds?"

"Yeah, there's piles of shell mounds along the swamps and rivers where them flat-head Indians lived way before white men settled."

"Did you mention any of this to the deputies?"

He nodded. "Sheriff Bonin just blew me off. They had the man what did it, he said. Seemed awful eager to hang it on Ned, my sense was."

"Why would he do that?"

"Beats me, excepting Ned was dead. Guess they figured they could save taxpayer money, and then give themselves raises. They didn't do it so they could cut our taxes, that's for damn sure." Jack spit on the ground then glanced from the spittle over to his truck. "You asked me what I knew, and I told you. Now, if you'll kindly leave me be so I can finish my rings job."

She thanked him, got in her car, and backed out, but as she

drove away, she glanced in her rearview mirror long enough to see Jack Agnes go inside and shut the door.

Odd that he'd do that, since he'd been so eager to get back to his truck.

Accelerating, she sped by the Collins residence where yellow crime scene tape made the house look like it had been lassoed and held hostage by an angry hemp rope.

Figuring what-the-hell, she slammed on the brakes, reversed, and parked alongside a ditch filled with dark green elephant ear plants.

The soggy ground squished inside her shoes and between her toes when she stepped out of the car and tiptoed alongside the ditch. By the time she reached the house, doubt consumed her. She hesitated, looked around, shrugged, and then scooted underneath the tape.

A black cat scatted off the porch as Sid walked up the steps passing old newspapers still in their wrappers. Adrenalin feeding a head-rush, but still feeling as guilty as sin, she opened the screen and tried the doorknob. The door was locked.

For some reason, she wasn't even sure what, she had to get inside that house. She'd already broken the law by crossing under the tape, but surely the sheriff's office had completed their investigation of the crime scene. What damage could she do by just looking? Besides, no one would know.

Ignoring her well-trained *do-right-be-good* conscious, she sucked in a deep breath and headed to the back of the house just as a train barreled down the railroad tracks. She thought of Ned.

When she reached the back door and found it locked as well, relief and regret battled inside her—relief that the locked door prevented her from breaking the law, and regret, for the very same reason.

But she had to see inside the house.

That's when she noticed someone had left the kitchen window ajar. Renewed excitement tingled up her backbone. She'd be hidden by the shrubs, no one could see her, not even Jack Agnes should he still be inside his house.

She scanned the backyard and noticed a trash heap behind the garage. Jogging over, she collected an empty paint can and dumped the rainwater out—wiggle tails and all—and set it beneath the window. Then, after checking the neighborhood again, she kicked and clawed her way through the opening, glad she'd worn pants so as not to expose her nether-regions to God-an'-everybody. Arms, hands, torso, and finally her legs got through the window. With a loud oomph she landed on her belly near the kitchen table.

Feeling more like a criminal than a private eye, she lifted her now-yanked-out shirttail and wiped her fingerprints off of the windowsill, reminding herself to do the same thing with the paint can when she left.

This was incredulous. Here she stood, illegally, she reminded herself, in the middle of a murder scene. She'd never done anything so outrageous. Hands on her hips, she looked around the bright yellow kitchen and snickered.

But what if she got caught? That thought sent her adrenalin through the roof.

She'd never felt so alive.

A glance around revealed nothing out of the ordinary, nothing except a couple bloody footprints leading to the back door. Ned's, the sheriff's report had said.

Skirting them, Sid tiptoed across the room as if she'd awaken the dead, and pushed open a swinging door that led to a living room furnished with a rattan sofa and two side chairs. Fish trap tables on either side of the sofa sported bamboo lamps, their shades askew. On one of the glass-top tables a Bible lay open to the *Book of Acts*. Someone had used a black ink pen to underline scripture and write a date in the margin, the name *Bro. Blue*, and what looked like a sermon title, *Jesus Wants To Be Your Best Friend*.

Shuddering, she wondered how the hell the reverend knew what Jesus wanted, and how a person even did what the hackneyed sermon title suggested. She'd grown to hate religious clichés—for they'd become nothing more than manipulative devices used to instill obedience in robotic believers. Her fingers itched to close the book, but she resisted, for she'd promised herself she'd touch nothing.

She slipped out of the living room and down the hall. The first bedroom, evidently for guests, sat neat and tidy. The next room held a sewing machine and cutting table. Ruby-colored scraps of fabric and thread lay scattered throughout the room as if the seamstress had stopped mid-project.

Only one room left. The one she feared the most. Somber now, she eased down the hall, tension building in her belly. One peek around the door, that's all she needed. Just one look and she'd leave.

But the one look froze her in place, froze her amidst the images of terror still in the middle of the Collins bedroom. The bed, dresser, easy chair—all period pieces—made the room look normal—normal except for dried blood stains on the walls, the mirror, and the floor. Someone had pulled the bloody sheets off the bed—but no amount of soap could clean that mattress.

Aware Sid held her breath, she tried to inhale, but the air felt cluttered with non-living particles—particles that obstructed her airway, squeezed her chest in a vise. With slow, cautious steps, she backed out of the room with a sense she'd escaped hell.

Back in the living room she didn't feel as threatened. She swiped her top lip clean of sweat and scanned family photos on the walls and knick knacks on a rattan bookcase. Whatnots, mystery, romance, devotional books, Sunday School Quarterly's, Bibles, old high school annuals, things found in the home of an average family. But evidently there was something out-of-the ordinary happening in this couple's home. Something that led to two acts of brutal murder. Had it been Ned? Jack? Someone else?

A smudge on the front door facing caught her eye, but as she stepped that way the cell phone in her pants pocket vibrated against her leg. Startled, but relieved she hadn't been caught, she snatched it out and flipped it open.

"Siddie, I got bad news, honey." Excitement in her aunt's voice belied the warning. Sid held her breath.

"Your apartment locater just called and said there was nothing in your price range that would be available by the end of the week. If she had more time, she could find you something, but right now things don't look good. Honey, why didn't you tell me you were having to move out of your apartment?" Annie ran out of breath, paused and sucked in another mouthful while Sid held her own, fearing Annie's next words.

"I was thinking—what say you move in with me? I've got plenty bedrooms. You could have your own room, run of the kitchen, and all. It'd be like we were roommates. The only problem I see is Chesterfield and—and—that dog—what's-his-name."

"Slider." Annie's mental block to the dog's name irritated the hell out of Sid. Good lord, she'd be chicken poop if she ever forgot Chesterfield's.

Annie droned on, sounding pitiful, begging. Not just begging, but in her own manipulative way—demanding. "You're moving in with me. That settles it. Okay?"

Damn. So much for fire ant beds.

"Who the hell do you think you are, and who gave you permission to be in here?"

The harsh words slung at Sid from out of nowhere caused her to flip the phone shut and swing around toward the speaker. If it weren't for the silver badge that came up in her face, and the strong hands that caught her by the elbows, she'd have been flat on the floor.

Glaring down at her stood a broad-shouldered man wearing a tan uniform, maybe six two, late fifties, with a thick head of dark brown hair. A scar across his right eyebrow added to his rugged good-looks.

"I said who the hell are you?" He released her and laid one hand atop a pistol strapped in his duty belt.

"Sidra Smart." *Ace detective* she almost said, but this guy looked like he'd been born not only handsome, but humorless. Sid stuck out her hand, glancing at the word SHERIFF on the badge pinned to his shirt and BONIN on the name tag.

After an awkward pause, she explained. "I'm the new owner of The Third Eye. You know—private investigations? I went by your office earlier, but missed you. Mr. Durwood hired me to find out who killed Abe and Cherrie Collins, clear his son's name. I just wanted to take a look at the scene. I didn't touch anything."

"Got any ID?"

"Sure." Sid showed him her temporary license.

"Humph." The sheriff shrugged. "You the sister?"

"Warren's? Yes. He left the business to me."

"So I heard. How'd you get in here?"

"The front door."

"You're lying. I locked it myself."

"Look, Sheriff, I'm sorry. I didn't mean to do anything wrong. I just wanted to see where the couple was murdered." She forced a saccharine smile.

The man stood stone-faced. "That ain't allowed. You can't go 'round barging into crime scenes, and don't tell me you didn't know that."

Staring slack-jawed at the man, a million responses charged through her brain, but instead of saying anything, she spun on her heels and walked out. The screen door slammed her in the butt.

Half-way to her car, she turned and looked back at the house. What was he doing here? She understood they'd finished their investigation. Curiosity pushed her to peek through the front window. Sheriff Bonin stood at the bookshelf holding a large, open book. He licked a fingertip, tore out a page, and tucked it in his pocket.

Six

Still puzzling over the sheriff's actions, Sid headed back to the Third Eye to check in with Annie, and to look up the address of Marv Bledsoe—Mr. Durwood's lawyer. She hoped he could fill in some of the blanks regarding the case against Ned Durwood like why he might slaughter the couple who wanted to commission his work.

Inside the office, Annie stood at a file cabinet digging through file folders.

"Hey, Annie," Sid called out as she breezed in and headed to the desk, "you sure are busy. What's going on?"

"I'm working my way through Warren's files to see if someone might've owed him money."

"Good thinking. Let me know what you find." She pulled out the phone book and thumbed through the yellow pages. "Well, I'll be," she stuck her finger down on the page, "Marv Bledsoe's office is just down the block."

Annie looked up, brushing a sprig of hennaed hair off her face. "You headin' out again? I'll probably be gone when you get back. I'm gonna go get some boxes to move you."

👁   👁   👁

Marv Bledsoe's office faced the courthouse, catty corner from Farmer's Mercantile. As Sid approached, she glanced through the glass-top door. A blonde-headed girl sat at the front desk chomping gum and talking on the phone. Hands freed by a headset, the young woman peered into a pink mirror propped on her desk and applied layer upon layer of mascara.

Sid swung the door open and walked in.

The girl glanced at Sid, rolled her eyes at the interruption, and kept talking and applying, until her hand slipped. The wand slid across her face and bumped up the side of her nose. Glowering at Sid, she sucked through her teeth and spoke into the headset. "Let me call you right back. *Someone's* come in. Uh-huh. Really? Oh, okay, yeah, well I guess I can talk a little longer; what'd he say about me?" The girl grabbed a tissue with her free hand, stretched her eyes wide, and dabbed the black smudge from her nose. "He didn't. Really? He said that? Oh God—about me?" The young woman giggled and swung the chair around, her back to Sid.

Sid checked her watch. Then she shuffled her feet and cleared her throat while the perspiration on her face turned to steam.

Okay, she'd waited long enough. She cleared her throat one more time and tried to interrupt the giggly phone conversation with, "Excuse me? I need to see Mr. Bledsoe."

The receptionist placed one hand over the microphone. "Can't you see I'm on the phone?" She slung the irritated question over her shoulder. "If you'll just wait a *sec*, I'll be with right with you."

Sid waited another couple of minutes while the silly conversation droned on, then she leaned over the desk and deftly punched the Off button on the phone. With words as sweet and thick as honey on the tip of a spoon, she cooed, "Sweetie, I don't give a rat's ass who you're talking to, or what the hell he said about you. I need to speak to Mr. Bledsoe. Now."

The chair swung around. The flushed girl lowered her eyelashes in a long, dismissive blink, but when she tried to open them, lashes of one eye stuck together. She pried them loose with long chartreuse fingernails. "He's not here!"

"Why couldn't you have said so when I came in?" Sid tightened her fists instead of slapping the sarcastic look off the girl's face.

The blonde shoved her chair away from the desk, stood, and

with exaggerated emphasis said, "I was on the *phone*." She straightened a tight orange skirt, tucked in a wandering bra strap, then prissed to the ladies room and slammed the door.

Done with the niceties, Sid marched in the direction of what she assumed was Marv Bledsoe's office, turned the doorknob and walked in. A mop of reddish-gray hair stuck up above the back of a chair facing the window, blinds closed.

"Mr. Bledsoe?"

"Shit." At first the voice stuttered then grew angry-sounding. "I told you to lock the damn door and don't come in." A burly man swung the chair around, and when he saw Sid, jumped up and out of it in one fluid movement. The redhead astraddle his lap hit the floor hard.

Sid watched, her mouth hanging open, as the two rearranged pants and buttons and belts and zippers.

"Who the hell are you? And how the hell did you get in here?" The man demanded.

Sid backed toward the exit, mortified by the snort that escaped her lips.

Telephone Girl rushed in, breathless. "Mr. Bledsoe, I told her you weren't here," she whined, "just like you told me to. When I turned my back, she just barged right in." Saliva sputtered out of her mouth. She swiped it with the back of her hand, leaving streaks of blood-red lipstick across her face.

Floor Girl, now on her feet, snatched a pair of red lace panties off the desk, jammed them in her bra and stumbled out of Marv's office, and through the front door, spike heels pinging off the tile floor.

"I-I, I'm Sidra Smart—Mr. Durwood—he—this young lady—phone calls—boyfriends—" Sid tried explaining herself, but when that failed, she took a deep breath, collected her composure and turned toward the door. "Forget it, I'll come back later."

"Wait just a minute," the man pleaded, evidently getting the picture of what had transpired in the lobby.

Sid swung around in time to see him grab Telephone Girl's

elbow and march her past Sid, into the lobby.

Now alone in Marv's office, Sid inched to the door and watched him stand beside the receptionist while she crammed her things, makeup mirror and all, into a gigantic bag and sling it over her shoulder. Then he escorted her out. The floor vibrated under Sid's feet when he slammed the door shut behind the blonde.

Head down, eyes diverted, Marv strode back into his office. "Excuse me a minute," he said, and then mumbled something about stupidity on his way through a door Sid assumed led to his private bathroom.

After a couple minutes, he walked back into his office straightening his tie. "I am so embarrassed, Ms. Smart. I must apologize for my behavior and that of my staff's." He rolled his chair back up to his desk and sat.

Sid eased into a chair across the room and attempted a prim and proper expression. But, despite her efforts, her lips kept curling into a smile. She squeezed them tight, dug her thumbnail into her finger, but the more she squeezed her lips, and gouged her finger, the more the laughter inside her built. A snicker slipped out, and she slammed her hand against her mouth.

Oh God, she couldn't laugh—that would make the whole thing worse. She forced a swallow down her throat. "I met—I met with—with Mr. Durwood. He said…"

Awkwardness sucked all the air out of the room.

"Oh, Mr. Durwood?" Marv finally asked, squirming, "Dempsey Durwood? Then you came—you must be here about…"

His butt squeaked against the leather chair. She guessed he heard it too, because he stopped, cleared his throat, and shuffled papers on his desk.

She might have contained herself if it hadn't been for an infernal tube of lipstick that rolled across his desk and plopped to the floor. Sid felt his eyes track the tube, as did hers, while it slowly traveled across the ceramic tile sounding more like a metal utility pole than a tube of lipstick.

That did it.

Laughter—loud, unladylike, and sidesplitting—spewed from her mouth. She glanced at Marv as she grabbed her sides, humiliated by her behavior.

His eyes avoided hers, but his lips twitched. He pulled them tighter.

In between convulsions she sputtered, "You—you should have seen her face when—when she hit the floor. And you…"

Marv snickered at first, then his belly quivered, and soon he fell back into his chair laughing, as hysterical as Sid. Gasping for breath, he muttered, "Me? You looked like you had glass eyeballs three sizes too big. You didn't know whether to come on in or run and hide." He slammed both hands down on the desk, shoulders heaving.

Sid bent double, wrapped her arms tighter around the pain in her belly.

When both of them were spent from hysterics, she dug in her handbag for a tissue while Marv walked toward her, wiping his nose on a handkerchief.

"Shall we start over?" He stuck out a hand the size of a baseball mitt. "Good morning, I'm Marv Bledsoe."

Sid stood and offered him her hand.

"Have a seat, Ms. Smart. You did say Smart, didn't you?"

Sid nodded.

"How I can be of help?" His eyes twinkled at her.

Sid wiped hers again. "You already have. That's the best laugh I've had in I don't remember when—I'm exhausted. Give me a minute." She fanned her face with both hands.

Marv collected two empty glasses off his desk; the rim of one glowed with red lipstick. He stuck both of them in a sink at the wet bar, then pulled two fresh tumblers off a shelf. Without asking, he poured a shot of Southern Comfort in each cocktail glass, plopped in a couple of ice cubes, and handed one drink to Sid.

"I feel really bad about this, Ms. Smart." He sipped on the

other drink. "The girl at the front was sent over, just today, from the temp service. My regular secretary's off sick."

Sid waited, sipping.

"Now, the other one—no excuses, I just yielded to invitation. My wife left me a few months ago..." He raised his hand and then let it flop on the desk.

Closing the awkward silence, Sid spoke. "I wanted to talk with you about the Collins murders. Mr. Durwood hired me to prove his son didn't kill them. Since you're his lawyer, he thought you might have some information to get me started."

Marv shook his head. "Not real sure about whether Ned killed the couple or not. But you're right, Dempsey's convinced he didn't. I guess most parents don't want to believe their child can commit murder."

"I wouldn't."

"Well, I don't have any, but if I did..." Marv rubbed his chin. "I do know this—the sheriff's a stubborn man. When he thinks he has an iron-clad case, he won't budge unless something forces him to."

"What do you think happened, Mr. Bledsoe? Do you think Ned killed those folks?"

"No, I don't see Ned doing something like that. I've known him since we were kids. He's a peaceable kind of guy, or was. Only passion I know he had was his art."

"Know anything about Jack Agnes?"

"Jack? He's a breed all his own, but I doubt he made up seeing Ned earlier that morning. Bunch of us hung out as kids, Jack, Ned, some others. Then suddenly, the group broke up. I never did understand why. Just kid stuff, I reckon."

Sid stood and walked over to the window, glanced out and then turned toward Marv. "What about shell mounds, Mr. Bledsoe?"

"Shell mounds?" Marv frowned at first, and then his face went expressionless. She wasn't sure if he tried to cover a lack of interest, or the flip side of that. "I don't know anything about them other than they're out there."

"Where?"

"Oh, around the swamp areas. Several of them still left. Most of 'em have been bull-dozed down, and that's a shame. But they're just leftovers from earlier civilizations. We used to play around them. That's all I know." Marv held out his hands, palms up. "I've got an appointment in a few minutes, but if there's anything else I can help you with, give me a call."

👁   👁   👁

By the time Sid got to her apartment, Annie had popped the lock on the door and packed up Sid's few belongings. Slider cowered in the corner.

Annie must have gone home first, for she had changed into black tights, tennis shoes and tube socks, and a full, long-sleeved purple top that stopped just above her knees. Bright red splotches of rouge colored each cheek, and her teased red hair stood four inches above her forehead. She must also have brought dinner, for the aroma of roast duck filled the one-room apartment, driving Slider mad.

"I didn't think you'd mind." Annie swung her arm around the room, showing all she'd accomplished. "We had to get you packed up and moved. The office was quiet, so I just transferred the calls to my cell phone, and then went by the house to change clothes and collect boxes. I've saved them for just such an event." She looked at Sid with an expression that said, see, you can't do without me.

"Did Slider give you any trouble?" The dog looked up at Sid and whined. "Why is he sitting in the corner?"

Annie flitted around the room, humming and cleaning. "Well, for one thing, I told him what I expected of him, now that the two of you were moving in with me. How I keep a spotless house and won't have a dog messing it up. That he'll eat in the kitchen and no where else—and about Chessy."

Enough to make anyone cower. Sid knelt and put her arm

around Slider. "Come on, bud, don't let the old bitty get to you," she whispered in his ear. "We can survive this. It'll be you and me against her and *king cat.*"

The hour was late by the time Sid and Annie finished dinner and loaded their cars. Annie shoved the last box in the back seat of Sid's Xterra, alongside the dog, and slammed the door. "You must've left a lot of stuff behind when you moved from the parsonage," she called across the top of the car. "What'd you do with the rest, put it in storage?"

"Yeah, at this place in Houston," Sid explained as she switched on the engine. "We'll see you back at your house."

Yeah, she'd stored the household effects, but she'd fled the title of *preacher's wife*—without a doubt, the hardest job in the world. For when she'd taken off the role's mask, she'd discovered a crippled little girl, abandoned, faceless, soul-less.

But now she felt herself coming alive again.

Seven

A noise startled Sid awake. She bolted upright in bed.

The shadows of a huge sycamore tree outside her window danced in the moonlight, reminding her she'd moved in with Annie, and this was her first night in a strange bed. Her heart sank.

But what had awakened her, and where was Slider? Had he made the sound? No, there he was in front of the window, looking at her, ears pricked. An uneasy whine issued from the back of his throat.

The swish started again.

"It's okay buddy, just lay down and go back to sleep. It's nothing." She wasn't sure which of them needed the most reassurance, herself, or the dog. He picked a spot where the polished hardwood floor glowed with moonlight, turned a couple of times, and then slid down on his belly, hackles raised.

Hyper-alert herself, she eased under the blanket, admonishing herself about nighttime and strange noises in old houses.

Then she saw it.

A long, narrow strip of what looked like white crinoline floated overhead, looping in on itself, over and over. But like an eye floater, when Sid tried to look directly at the loop, the twisting circle scooted outside her vision. When she looked away, there it was again. Her heart floated too, right up to her throat. She tried to swallow, but couldn't.

Surely the moonlight peeking through the lace-curtained

window toyed with her senses.

"Do you see it, boy?" She asked, her voice a mere whisper.

No sooner had Sid uttered the question than Slider bounded on the bed and crawled beneath the covers, quivering. Never before had Sid shared her bed with a big, terrified dog, but now the company felt mighty good, frightened or not.

The swishing sound continued. Like the rustle of brocade petticoats sweeping over a floor, or leather rubbing against leather, or maybe both in concert. While neither ugly nor menacing, the sound wasn't particularly human either. Sid lay frozen, hoping she'd dreamed it, certain she hadn't.

She sat up, gathering boldness to her like the blanket she held to her chest. "Who is it? What do you want?" Head cocked, she waited.

No answer came.

She switched on the bedside lamp, and the white loop disappeared. The room looked just as it had before she slept: the braided rug on the hardwood floor, her bag in the corner, books piled on the window seat.

Unsure what else to do, she flipped off the light, lay back on her pillow and squeezed her eyes shut.

But when she opened them again, a transparent-looking diminutive young woman stood at the foot of the bed, her hands resting on the iron bedstead. When she smiled at Sid something around her mouth looked familiar, and the wisdom behind her eyes looked like she knew things Sid didn't. Her hair, pulled in a topknot, glowed like burnished metal. With ease that comes from years of practice, the woman raised her hand over her head and poked in a loose hairpin.

"Hey." Sid yelled. "Who the hell are you? What do you want?"

The woman floated away from the bed and vanished in a dark corner.

For a brief second, Sid saw a boy being shoved, falling, hitting his head on a rock. Then he lay still, very still. "Holy Shit."

She scratched her scalp with her fingernails, hoping the pain would awaken her.

"That was a dream—it had to be," she whispered. Her racing brain told her that it was the strangeness of the old house that made her believe she'd seen a ghost. Light and shadow played wicked tricks in old houses that creaked and shifted on their foundations.

She thought of packing her bag and running to her car, but that'd be foolish. She was a grown woman, and ghosts didn't exist. Years before, Sam had told her so. Still, her body quivered, refusing the logic forced upon it by her mind.

She had a choice, go downstairs and sleep where the rooms were cold, or sleep here in her warm bed, but with the light on.

She turned the lamp back on and curled into the fetal position, but resisted the urge to suck her thumb.

Relieved when dawn broke, she crawled out from between the warm blankets into a chilly room, Slider right behind her.

"Morning, bud." She scratched the yawning dog's curly, red head. "A lot of help you were last night. We both must have had too much of Annie's roasted duck." She slid her feet into fuzzy slippers. "Now about Annie, don't let her get to you, she's not as bad as she'd like you to think. Before long you'll have her eating out of your—paw."

Slider wriggled, looked her in the eye and whined.

"I'll bet you need to get outside."

He looked out the window at a blustery March morning, then back at her, rolling his dark, languid eyes.

"Don't tell me you're a cold-natured fur-butt. Well, you at least have to go pee. Come on, the fresh air will do us both good."

She pulled on a pair of warm-ups, ran her hands through her pinking-shear-cropped hair, and tucked her wallet in the zipper pocket of the jacket. Downstairs, she grabbed the leash and they stepped out into the gentle first-light of morning. Tall pines and oaks along the street speckled the ground with shadows as a full moon relinquished its soft yellow glow to the red-balled sun.

No boy lay on the ground, head banged against a rock.

Slider padded happily alongside her, tail wagging, taking in his new neighborhood.

"Uh huh. I see." She laughed at the dog's change in attitude about the walk. "You just need to be convinced, then you're up for a walk, eh? What a wishy-wash."

They'd gone a few blocks when lights from windows of a one-story white frame house spilled out onto the sidewalk. The structure looked like those common in the forties or fifties, but this one had been freshly remodeled into a homey-looking café called The Bread Box.

"Hey, Slider, I'm going to stop in and get a bite to eat. If you'll wait outside like a good boy, I'll bring you something tasty." She looped the leash over the branch of a small shrub.

The dog cocked his head first one way then another.

"See? Don't you feel guilty for your evil thoughts when I fed you dog food?" She put quotes around the last two words.

She headed to the front door of the café that crouched in the shadows of two huge sweet gum trees. Light from the windows made the inside look warm and inviting. That is, until she recognized the man sitting near the window on the left. Ben Hillerman. She wanted to turn around and head back home, but before she could, he motioned her in.

Since he'd stopped calling her she'd drawn a line through his name in her address book. For that had been fine with her. After Sam, she'd had men enough for a lifetime.

After looking back at Slider she willed herself up the steps and through the door.

Just as she entered the lobby, however, Ben walked over and planted a kiss on her cheek. "How're you doing, Sid? It's been a while." He grinned down at her, his hand on her arm.

She hoped her cynical smile didn't reveal the pounding in her chest. "It has been a while. I'm fine, thanks. Still getting over the chicken hatchery thing."

It had taken weeks before she'd felt an ease-up of the horror she'd experienced during her first case. Sometimes she still awoke from a deep, troubled sleep, her heart in her throat. "How about you? What have you been up to?" She knew her voice sounded stiff, but didn't try to soften it. Nor did she allow herself to ask why he'd quit calling her, or even answering her phone calls.

"Oh, same ole six and seven." He rubbed his jaw. "Say, I read in the newspaper about you finding that dead woman up in Trinity County. That must've been something."

"An experience to remember, that's for sure." She'd have at least washed her face and smeared on a little lipstick had she known she'd run into Ben, as it was, she must look a mess.

"Join me for breakfast—tell me about it." He held a hand out toward his table.

While Sid hesitated, the hostess hovered in the background.

Oh, to hell with it. "Sure. I'll join you."

Ben led the way to his table. The awkward silence that ensued was finally broken when the server came to take Sid's order.

"Half-burnt bacon, half-raw scrambled eggs, burnt whole wheat toast, coffee, no cream." The waitress scribbled down the order without question. "Oh, and a side of sausage." Slider would never forgive her if she broke her promise, plus, she had no idea if yogurt was healthy for a dog's digestive system.

"Burnt? That's an odd order," Ben raised his eyebrows. "Is that how you normally cook your breakfast?"

Sid shrugged, fighting off the memories of their *perfect* first dinner at Esther's Cajun Seafood restaurant across the big bridge.

"Now." Ben tucked his napkin back in his lap. "Why in the world were you driving in a freak ice storm?"

"I certainly earned that implication in your question. It was indeed a dumb thing to do. I'd spent the weekend visiting an old high school friend."

"A woman I hope—not that I'm entitled." Ben busied his hands spreading red currant jelly on a biscuit.

Ignoring the remark, she picked up a packet of sugar and fiddled it back and forth between her fingers. "Neither of us had checked the weather, so the storm caught me by surprise on the way home." She dumped the sugar in her coffee and stirred, took a sip, then began recounting the tale, ending with how she'd brought the dog home. After that she ran out of conversational topics. No way in hell would she bring up the fact he hadn't returned her calls, or that her friend was female.

The silence between them grew, so, desperate, Sid latched onto her experience in the middle of the night. "You believe in ghosts?"

Ben strangled on a mouthful of coffee. Pounding his chest with his fist, he swallowed hard, coughed, swallowed again. "That's a wake-up question for sure, and not the one I expected." He chortled. "I don't know if I do or not. Why do you ask, did you see one?"

"That, or I have a vivid imagination."

"Where?"

"I had to move from my apartment over Sophia's house. You knew she had to go into a nursing home?"

He nodded.

So he did keep up with her.

"I moved into an old house over on Pine Street with my Aunt Annie. It was built in the mid-nineteenth century."

"Pine Street? You don't mean the old Dorman house?" Ben leaned towards her.

Sid shrugged. "No clue."

"Big white two-story? With one of those black-faced-jockey statues dressed in a red jacket in the front yard? On the corner of Pine and Walnut?"

Sid nodded. She hated the statue and the racism it represented. One day the dang thing would simply disappear, and Annie would never know Sid had *disposed* of it at the garbage dump.

"Well, I'll be damned. So what they say is true."

"What?"

"Ever since I was a kid, I've heard people call the house *ghost active*."

Coffee sputtered out of Sid's closed lips, onto her plate, and down on the white linen tablecloth. "Sorry about that." She wiped up her mess and tucked her napkin back in her lap.

"Well, I don't mean to offend, but you do look like you've just seen one."

"A ghost? I guess you might say that."

Ben laughed at her.

"Easy enough to laugh now that the sun's up. Okay, does that mean I'm not crazy? I couldn't figure out if I'd lost my marbles, or was just dreaming. My mind tells me that's nonsense. There's no such thing. When you're dead, you're dead. You can't come back and haunt some house, regardless of how old it is." Sid paused, deep in thought. "But whatever it was, it sure scared the hell out of me. I shook for hours. Hardly slept after that. I kept opening my eyes looking for her. Not to mention the boy."

"People have been seeing things in that house for years. Your aunt must have bought the house for a damn good price. It's been on the market forever. No one locally will touch it. You might talk with Bobbie Jean, over at the Heritage Museum. She's studied the history of the place, and is kind of a specialist on our local ghosts."

After they finished that topic, their conversation ran as empty as their plates, and dang it, her stomach still hadn't stopped churning. The only way to stop it was to ask the question she'd avoided. She sucked in a deep breath and blurted it out. "Why did you stop calling or returning my calls?"

Startled, Ben paused, looked at her like he wished he and the floor would be gobbled up by a sinkhole. "I should have, Sid. The one thing I promised you was straight talk. Direct. Now I've shot that to hell." He looked her in the eye. "*God,* how I've missed you. Running into you this morning has just…"

"I didn't go anywhere, dammit, you did." Her fist hit the table rattling the silverware, Ben, and everyone else in the room.

He squirmed in his chair, pulled on his tie, and cleared his throat. "Sid—I—I owe you an explanation, you see…"

"You don't owe me anything."

"…I've had problems with my daughter. You never met her, but she was real close to her mom. When she found out about you and me dating, she threw a fit. Swore if I married you I'd never see her or my grandson again."

"Married?" An activity she'd given up. "Who's talking about marriage?"

He stared at Sid, surprise in his eyes. "Well… No one, I suppose. I guess she—she just expected it to lead there. I guess I did, too."

Sid shook her head.

"I screwed up, Sid. Forgive me."

Sid snatched the side order of sausage off her plate and tucked it into a takeout container while the server collected their plates and left.

"Say something, Sid. Tell me what a jerk I've been."

"You have every right to call or not. I shouldn't have questioned that. I'm just sorry you let your daughter control your life." She inspected her container of sausage, making sure it closed properly.

"You've got to understand, Sid. Irene's death devastated my whole family. She was sick for so long—and while the cancer ate away at her body it seemed like it…"

"Bonded your family closer."

"Yes. Absolutely. Since she died, it's like—like—everyone keeps fighting to make the family stay the same."

"Can it do that?" She tucked her hands in her lap and pressed the palms flat into her thighs to steady them. So Ben's not calling was about him, not her.

"Stay the same? Evidently not. Maybe that's impossible."

"Seems to me it is. But that doesn't have to mean it's less—just different."

The room seemed frozen, like someone pushed the pause

button on a DVD player. In the background Sid heard laughter, idle chit chat.

Ben stirred, asked, "How'd your kids handle your divorce? Did they have problems with it? With you leaving?"

Sure they had. Christine and Chad still floundered over Sid and Sam's divorce, trying to make sense of their own lives, of their past, but Sid had no intention of sharing her own pain with Ben, much less her children's. Maybe after thicker scar tissue had formed, she could talk to him about it, but since it had only been six months or so, the tear in her heart was still raw and bleeding—not as often and not as much, but bleeding, nonetheless. She shuddered, and looked over at Ben, who still waited for her answer. "Since Sam and I divorced my kids have had to try to find a new sense of home. I have, too. They think they wouldn't have lost home had it not been for the divorce. But I'm not sure that's true."

The feeling in her heart was even more complex than the words tumbling in her head. Words that attempted to describe a sense so innate it defied packaging in tidy word-bundles.

"Go on." Ben nudged, his eyes penetrating hers.

"A sense of home—you know. We always lose it, sometimes just sooner than others. I lost it when my dad died, even though I was grown and my mom was still alive." She remembered how different home had felt then. Mom alone in the house, with no requirement for meals at a certain time of day, discarding Dad's clothes and possessions, starting over without him. Yes, her home had changed then. It felt broken, incomplete, not like home anymore.

Now, her kids felt the same way.

"Maybe as we grow up and become adults, that's one of the steps we must take to create our own home, losing that sense of the first one." Unshed tears tightened Sid's voice.

In some ways, many ways perhaps, she had become an adult in her fifties. Now her children must find their own way to adulthood. Was it possible that her father—her *dead* father—felt guilty for dying and breaking up their home—just as she did now with the divorce?

"May I call you?" Ben stood, his eyes sparkling with moisture.

She nodded, fighting the moisture in her own.

Then he turned and walked away.

She sat for a moment, certain her knees would buckle if she tried to stand. When the flutter in her chest slowed, she paid her tab and walked outside.

Slider bounded over, drool dripping off his dangling tongue. She unwrapped the sausage and tried to lay it on the ground, but the dog gobbled it up before it hit the horizontal surface.

Always keep your promise to a dog.

👁   👁   👁

By the time Sid and Slider walked back home Annie had left for the office, and thankfully, she had taken the cat with her. "Looks like you got the house all to yourself today, fur-butt." She chucked him under the chin. "You behave yourself, and I'll bring you home something good for supper. Maybe some unhealthy fast-food french fries—you like those?"

Slider barked in anticipation, his wagging tail knocking against a table leg.

She turned her ring around to the inside of her hand as a reminder to pick up the fries, and then headed to the Heritage House. Maybe the woman Ben said was an expert on old houses and local ghosts could explain what Sid had seen floating at the foot of her bed. At this point, anything would help.

A museum operated by a local association, the house looked like a typical upper-middle-class home from the turn-of-the-century through the 1940's. The building had two stories, with balustrade porches, five fireplaces and a slate roof.

A small bell jangled as Sid opened the front door and stepped inside where she was greeted by two friendly docents talking with other visitors. One of the women wore *Bobbie Jean* on her name tag. After introducing herself, Sid explained where she lived and that she was looking for information about the old home on Pine Street.

Bobbie Jean pushed her straight brown hair out her face then gathered Sid by the arm and sat her down at a corner table away from the other visitors. "You live in the Pine Street house, you say?" Her words were soft—half-whispered. "I couldn't believe it when I heard someone actually bought that place. When did you move in?"

"I moved in yesterday, my aunt, a couple months ago. Why?

"Why? The place is haunted, that's why. By a woman named Kate Dorman. History is, old Kate and her husband built that place in Sabine Pass in the mid 1800s. Named it Catfish Hotel—it was both a restaurant and a hotel. Steamboat captains docked on the backside of the house and ate the catfish Kate fried up every day of the year."

"Then how'd the house get to Orange?"

"Thirty or forty years ago a fellow bought it, cut the building in half, jacked up one side at a time, and loaded the pieces on a barge there at Sabine Pass. Then he brought them slap up the Intracoastal canal to Orange. They came in right there alongside Front Street, there by the old railroad tracks. My daddy watched them unload the barge with a couple of cherry pickers. He used to tell how they almost demolished the thing, right then and there." Bobbie Jean gestured as if smoothing out a wrinkled tablecloth.

"And he put the two halves back together?"

Bobbie Jean nodded. "But talk is, ole Kate didn't like the new location. Folks have seen her there, short, redheaded, wearing a long white gauze-kind of dress. Now from what I hear, the real live Kate never wore anything so frivolous as white gauze, but anyway, they say she's protecting the place or something."

"From what?"

Bobbie Jean shrugged. "Personally, I don't believe she means any harm. If she did, she'd have done something long ago. My guess is she's just looking after her place. But man, if she could talk she could tell some tales. She's a legend in these parts, not only fought off a plague of yellow fever, but she also stood up to the union army."

Goosebumps large as boulders rumbled down Sid's arms. Damn, and she'd let Annie talk her into moving into the house.

"Anything else I should know? About the ghost, I mean?"

"Not that I can think of, but if you see her again, let me know."

"Sounds like Kate was quite a woman," Sid said, standing to leave. "I don't mean to be rude, but I'm still skeptical as to whether I saw her ghost or not. But thanks for your time." They shook hands and Sid headed for the door, then stopped and turned back to Bobbie Jean. "While I'm here—do you know anything about shell mounds in this area?" It was probably meaningless to the case, but she better check it out, just in case Jack Agnes had heard correctly.

"Shell mounds? Oh, you're talking about those piles left behind by the aboriginal groups. Yeah, a small tribe was still here when the early settlers arrived, but they're all gone now. The library probably has information on them." Bobbie Jean paused, rubbed her forehead in thought, and then pointed her index finger at Sid. "You know, there's a local guy who's an expert on the group. Fellow named Ian Meade. He teaches over at Lamar University at Orange. Nice fellow. I've heard him say the tribe dates back more than 10,000 years. Called themselves Ishak-Atakapa, which means *the people who eat flesh*." Bobbie Jean shivered. "Cannibals."

Eight

Annie looked up as Sid walked in the door of the Third Eye. "Sid, this is Ella Bluett. She's been waiting for you. I offered to call you on your cell phone but she wanted to just wait. I checked your calendar and told her you're free the next hour or so."

Good for you, Auntie. Make her think she lucked out and I can squeeze her in. Sid knew what her calendar looked like—blank.

They walked into Sid's office and sat. Sid couldn't help but notice Ella's simply-styled, mousy brown hair and prim demeanor.

"Pardon me for intruding, but I wanted to meet you. I heard that you'd moved to town to take over your brother's business. I didn't know him, but I'm sorry for your loss."

Sid nodded graciously, not wanting to revisit the subject of her brother's death. "Your name sounds familiar, Ms. Bluett, but I don't remember meeting you before."

"It's Mrs., really, but just call me Ella. And no, we haven't met. But you used to be married to a Baptist preacher, right?"

Sid did a double-take. Boy, gossip did get around in a small town. Only a couple of people knew about her past, and she'd intentionally kept it that way. "That's a subject I'd really rather not talk about if you don't mind."

"I'm sorry. Certainly I respect your privacy. I just thought I'd be neighborly and come meet you since we have something in common. My husband pastors a local church."

Oh yes, the one with the flashing blue cross. And meet, my eye, target her, was more like it. Sid raised her guard higher. One of Sam's expectations had been that she seek out newcomers before they found another congregation to attend. Now, her body bristled in anticipation of the invite.

But the woman didn't issue one. She just sat—hollow eyed—staring at Sid, begging, it seemed. She wasn't unattractive, but her understated outfit—Goodwill-dressy—fit the role of submissive wife. Sid remembered her first 'preacher's-wife' suit. She and Sam had been married less than a year when Sam accepted the call of his first pastorate. At seventeen, she didn't dress like a preacher's wife, so he took her shopping and picked out a boxy two-piece suit and hat that made her look forty years old. She still had the picture of herself in that outfit; a small hat perched on her head, hands clasped in front, smiling primly at the camera. She'd looked ludicrous—a kid playing grownup.

Sid stirred and looked at Ella, who still sat twisting her hands in her lap. "Ms. Bluett, is there something you need? Something I can do for you?" The polite thing, Sid knew, was to use the woman's married title since she had introduced herself that way, but Sid had erased the word from her vocabulary. Should the English language ever create married titles for both genders, she might reconsider, but for now, she had no use for the patriarchal custom.

"I've—I've got to talk to someone who can help me figure out what to do about…"

Sid interrupted her mid sentence. "Excuse me. I'm really not into church stuff these days, perhaps there's someone else you might talk to?" Guilt eased in around Sid's words, for she knew Ella's choices were limited, to non-existent. Isolation was one of the most difficult parts of the job. Sid needed to check out this Bluett guy, since Jack Agnes had also mentioned him, but she wasn't getting involved in Ella's problems.

"I walk every day." The woman kept talking as if Sid had hadn't spoken. "I love the walking trails on Meeks Drive. That's where I met him, walking his dog in the park."

"Met who?" Sid bit her tongue on the last word.

"Ian Meade."

Oh boy, the woman at the museum had just mentioned the same guy.

"I knew he was a ladies man. I tried to say no, but he just moved closer, claiming me it seemed. I don't know what he saw in me." The red on Ella's cheeks crept down her neck.

This conversation led down a road of no return. "Are you sure I'm the person you want to tell this to? I'm not a therapist or a lawyer, you know."

"But you're a woman—and a divorced preacher's wife. I thought maybe you...." Ella stared at Sid, questions behind her eyes. "You were a minister's wife, weren't you? A friend told me you were."

Sid blinked. Would she ever get rid of the title? At times she still felt like she wore a sign around her neck.

"You know what will happen if this gets out—my husband will lose his job."

Sid's heart softened like a dryer sheet had been tossed into her chest. "Not necessarily. Mine didn't. He had too many people ready to polish his halo. You know what one woman called me? *Sam's Delilah.*" Bitter laughter rippled out her throat.

Ella laughed, too, and her laughter sounded just as acidic. "I'm sorry that happened to you. I feel guilty, but I think only because I've been taught I'm supposed to. I can't feel sorry for what I've done. Ian touched me in ways I never imagined. I'm not just talking about sex," she flushed again, "but everything. I feel alive for the first time in my life, beautiful, desirable, intelligent—like I matter."

The woman's words scraped across Sid's heart like a tongue depressor shaving the scab off a sore wound. She stiffened her back. "Ella, I truly am sorry, but I don't think I'm the one to help you with this."

"I just need someone to talk to, that's all. Someone who understands."

"It's too soon. I have too much healing to do myself, before I can help someone else." Sid stood, ending the conversation.

Ella stared blankly for a few moments, then she stood and walked to the door, head down, shoulders slumped.

What a shitty thing to do, Sid told herself as Ella shuffled out.

As soon as Ella walked out the front, nosy Annie headed into Sid's office. "Ms. Bluett looked terrible when she left, worse than when she got here. What'd you do to her, Siddie?"

Sid only shrugged.

"Well, I come to tell you I'm leaving, and driving home for the weekend to pick up some more of my pretties. You okay by yourself?"

"I'll try to be. Have a good time." Sid suppressed the smile lurking behind her words.

After Annie left, Ella's visit got Sid to thinking about Sam and why she'd left him. It hadn't been for reasons like Ella's.

She'd just flat been drained by the overbearing evangelical fundamentalism given in doses meant to induce conformity by guilt, worn-down-to-the-nub compliance—well, she'd been worn down all right.

👁 👁 👁

On the way home that evening Sid felt generous and stopped off and bought steaks for both she and Slider, and the makings for a salad, plus a second stop for the french fries. With Annie gone, she welcomed the luxury of time by herself—she'd had so little of it.

After taking Slider for his potty break, Sid changed into baggy jeans and sweat shirt, slid her sock-feet into her favorite Birks, and opened a bottle of red wine. Sam had never let her drink alcohol before, swearing it led to damnation. So now she picked out a large crystal glass from Annie's china cabinet and filled it three-quarters to the top.

With Slider at her heels, she headed back to the kitchen. Standing in the middle of the room sipping her wine, she began wondering how many women had washed dishes in the old porcelain sink, or washed their hands in a stream of warm soapy water, drying them on a flour sack-towel. She stepped over to the cabinet to fetch a knife for the vegetables, but when she pulled on a handle, instead of opening a drawer, an old flour bin plopped open. The musty smell whisked Sid back to earlier generations—to Kate—who lived in the house in the 1800s, baking breads and cakes, dipping into the flour bin and coming up with her hands full of the comforting white powder.

While Sid seasoned the steaks, her mind went from Kate to breakfast and Ben. He and the woman at the museum had both called the house haunted.

But she didn't believe in ghosts. "You believe in ghosts, dog?"

Slider's eyes stayed glued to the steaks.

Sam had always accused her of having too colorful an imagination. Maybe on that one thing he'd been correct.

The meat sizzled when she plopped it into the hot skillet.

While the beef grilled she made a salad, and then the two of them ate, Sid at the table and Slider from his bowl nearby.

Startled when the telephone rang, she snatched up the receiver.

"Sid? This is Marv Bledsoe. You okay talking to me?"

She heard a smile behind his words. "Good evening Marv. You recovered?"

"From our meeting the other day? Yes, thank you—other than embarrassed as hell. I'm scared you'll think I'm a real scum bag."

"Not at all. Just wish I'd knocked first."

"No problem, a hundred years from now we'll never even remember. Say, the reason I called is to see if I could change that bad first-impression. Tomorrow afternoon I thought I'd drive out to Sabine Pass to their annual crawfish boil. Why don't you go with me?"

In typical southeast Texas parlance, Marv had combined the first three words of the sentence into one, making them sound more like y-oncha, and it took Sid a minute to realize she'd been issued an invitation. "Okay," she answered, hesitant to what she might be getting herself into. "But what's a crawfish boil?"

"Cajun excuse for a wing ding party. Big crowds of local folk get together. It's beer-drinking, Cajun and Zydeco music, dancing, and big pots of boiled crawfish."

👁   👁   👁

The next afternoon Marv arrived right on time in his shiny red Dodge Ram pickup. He took off his western hat and gave a deep bow when Sid opened the front door with Slider at her side. She stepped out and turned to lock the door. "You behave, Slider, don't get into anything while we're gone."

The dog looked up at her, whining.

"He can come, too, if you like. You might need a leash."

"You sure?"

"Absolutely. Lots of folks bring their dogs."

Sid went back inside and collected the leash while Marv and Slider headed out to the truck. By the time Sid reached them, Slider pranced around in the truck bed, tail wagging, his eyes sparkling with excitement.

Marv held her door, closed it, and then jogged around the front of the truck to the driver's side and climbed in.

"How'm I doing?" He asked, grinning. "Would my mama be proud of my behavior now?"

"She'd be quite proud." Sid laughed, and felt herself relax. This was going to be a fun day.

They drove through Bridge City where small, one-story businesses squatted along both sides of Texas Avenue. On the edge of town they passed Sparkle Paradise, a dilapidated nightclub with the metal walls almost falling in, and then past saltwater marsh hovering along both sides of the highway. Despite the cooler weather, small groups of folk stood at waters edge alongside ice chests and folding chairs. Each of them held a net in one hand, and a string in the other, the end of which dangled down into the water.

"What are they doing?" Sid asked, staring out the passenger window. "It doesn't look like they're fishing, I don't see any poles."

"Crabbing." Marv explained, one arm atop the steering wheel, and the other resting on his leg. "You take a piece of raw meat, like a chicken neck or a piece of fat bacon, tie it to a string and drop it in the water. You can see the crab come up and snatch the meat with its claws. Then, all you have to do is stick your net in, catch the little bugger, and lift 'im out." Marv alternately looked at the crabbers, the highway, and her. "It might sound easy, but you have to be fast. We'll go crabbing some day if you'd like to try."

"Sounds like fun. Then I guess you cook them, huh?"

"Sure do—add 'em to seafood gumbo—mm, mm." He patted the slight paunch that hung over a large, silver belt buckle.

Soon they'd reached the pinnacle of a high bridge, and Sid realized this was the route she and Ben had taken the night they went on their first date. Now, in daylight she watched tiny tugboats negotiate huge barges into place, or ease them further down the Neches River. Nearby, plumes of smoke emanated from smoke stacks of chemical plants while flames from waste-gas flickered skyward.

Down the other side, they passed Esther's, the rustic-looking Cajun seafood restaurant sitting almost underneath the tall bridge. A twinge of regret made Sid think of Ben, but then she pushed him to the back of her mind.

The highway led through miles of oil refineries and chemically-induced fog banks, and finally to the small coastal town of Sabine Pass.

Marv turned off on a rough-paved road surrounded by tall grasses and water-filled ditches. "That's Sabine Lake over there on your left, and if you look across it—way over to the Louisiana side—see—that lighthouse there—" he pointed. "It was built before the Civil War."

"Interesting." She liked that he took pride in the area's history.

"Sabine Pass has quite a history," he went on. "It's where Dick Dowling and his men fought and won what's now called the Battle of Sabine Pass. Historians say if it weren't for that victory, the Union would have won the war much earlier."

"I wonder how many lives might have been saved had Dowling lost that battle."

"Good question, but probably not one you want to voice in these parts."

"No, probably not."

"We're not far, now, it's just up there where you see all those cars and trucks along the road."

Marv parked, hustled around to open Sid's door, whistling for Slider to join them. As the three headed on foot across a large open field toward the crowd, Marv grabbed her hand in his. It startled Sid at first. Except for that brief time with Ben, no man other than Sam had held her hand in years. She felt a little guilty but didn't pull her hand away.

As they approached the throng, Sid noticed a five-man band perched atop a flat-bed trailer blaring out Cajun music. Dressed in a western shirt, blue jeans, and beat-tapping cowboy boots, one man played an accordion like nobody's business, making Sid's heart dance.

Nearby, folks had thrown down sheets of plywood and called it a dance floor; the make-shift contraption was filled with laughing couples scooting in boots and tennis shoes to the infectious music.

Over to the side, men tended gigantic aluminum pots perched atop large propane burners. The hot-lidded containers steamed out a spicy-fish aroma.

A group of children—and dogs—played Tag You're It. Slider whined to join them, tugged on the leash, but Sid held tight. "No, boy, you stay here."

"Let's head over there," Marv said, taking her by the elbow. He led them towards a tent where folding chairs and tables were set up, the tables covered with long rolls of white paper.

Sid scanned the crowd sitting and eating, and did a double-take when she saw Ella Bluett at one of the tables; she reminded Sid of a butterfly fresh out of its cocoon—nowhere close to the same woman who'd come asking for help. Now she wore a body-fitting, red, sleeveless top, cleavage showing, and hip-hugging blue jeans that revealed a great figure. Her mussed hair, flushed cheeks and sparkling eyes revealed a woman in love, or at least in lust. She and the tall, robust-looking guy beside her, obviously not the preacher, laughed and touched their foreheads together in the intimate gesture of lovers.

A 'coke flat,' the cut-off bottom of a cardboard box, lay on the table in front of them, piled high with boiled potatoes, onions, corn on the cob, and scalded-red crawfish. Juice ran off their elbows as they broke the tails off the distinctive-smelling crawfish, sucked yellow fatty-looking stuff out of the heads, and then dumped the spent shells in a large bucket on the table.

Sid stopped a few feet away, hoping Ella hadn't seen her. But Ella looked up, and when she recognized Sid, her face turned as white as the butcher paper spread across the table. Mumbling something to the man at her side, they both stole a glance at Sid, then he took Ella by the elbow, and they hustled off into the crowd.

Sid looked for them throughout the afternoon, wanting to reassure Ella she'd keep her secret, but she never saw them again.

However, impressed by Marv's attentiveness, Sid pushed Ella's problems out of her mind and relaxed, didn't guard every word or move—like she'd done the last thirty years. Marv wasn't a man she saw herself with over the long haul, but what the hell. It felt good to have a man interested in showing her pleasure.

Dusk had fallen by the time they got back to Annie's house.

Sid unlocked the door and let Slider inside while she and Marv stood on the wide, wraparound front porch, both of them awkwardly silent.

"Want to come in for a nightcap?" Sid finally asked.

"I thought you'd never ask." He smiled and gently ran his hand down Sid's arm as she opened the door.

Jittery, she headed straight to the wine cabinet, poured two glasses of wine, and joined him on the sofa.

"So, how long were you married to that preacher?" Marv asked, taking a sip of wine.

"Over thirty years."

"I guess you haven't had a lot of experience with other men, then, huh?"

Sid snorted. "I guess you could say that."

He set his glass on the table and turned toward her, quick heat in his eyes.

A glimpse of the redhead on Marv's lap flashed through her mind, but she shoved the girl aside. What the hell—consenting adults and all that jazz.

Marv traced her jaw line with his finger. "You're a beautiful woman, you know."

A vision of her fifty-year-old body coalesced into the young thing on his lap, and she suppressed a giggle.

He ran his finger along her jaw to her chin, down her throat, and between her breasts then inched closer, covering her mouth with his soft lips while fumbling with the bottom of her sweater. Part of her responded, but the other part assessed his actions, wondering if she really wanted to do this. But his musk cologne overtook her assessment when his warm hand slipped underneath her sweater and touched her moist skin. She shouldn't. Really, she shouldn't—but it had been so long.

Something shifted in the corner. Probably just Slider—or the ghost. Oh hell, if it was the ghost, at this moment Sid didn't really care.

"Ahem."

Sid's eyes jerked towards the sound, and there stood her ex-husband leaning against the kitchen door, a sandwich in one hand and a glass of milk in the other. A lock of hair curled against his forehead.

"Sam? Where the hell did you come from, and how the hell did you get in here?" She jumped up, snatching down her sweater and tossing Marv backwards against the sofa.

Slider crouched alongside Sid, a deep growl resonating at the back of his throat.

"The back door was unlocked." Sam's bitter-tinged voice spat the words at her. "Figured you'd be home soon, so I just waited." He looked from Sid to Marv, then back to Sid. "So *this* is why you left me? So you can go whoring around? I didn't think you'd stoop this low. Where'd you meet him, at some dance hall—some honky-tonk?"

Out of the corner of her eye she saw Marv take a step toward Sam, his hands balled into fists. Slider inched closer to Sam, hackles up.

"Slider, no," she said, and grabbed Marv's forearm. "It's okay, you two, this is my ex-husband, Reverend Samuel Smart."

Marv stopped mid-stride, and Slider dropped to his belly with an humph.

"We're not going to do this Sam, not now, not here." Her stomach in a knot, she strode out the front door to the porch, Sam on her heels. The other two stayed where they were. She didn't blame them.

Outside, the porch light cast weird shadows across Sam's face, but did nothing to hide the grief lines lingering behind his eyes.

"Why are you here, Sam? What do you want?"

"I just wanted to ask you a question."

"What question?"

"Can you tell me in one sentence what happened to our marriage?"

"One sentence? You want the reason for the break-up of a

thirty-year marriage summarized in one sentence?" Her voice sounded brittle, like icicles broken off and crunched underfoot.

Sam looked at her, helpless, confused as all get-out, like they'd never talked about the subject. Like every gut-wrenching thing she'd ever said to him had been spoken in a dead language, and then evaporated in the wind.

"Okay, I'll try again. I'm not sure I can do this in one sentence, but here goes." Sid grasped for the right words to wrap around fluid feelings, but the words came slowly, separated by double-spacing. "I love you Sam. I always will. But I can't live with you, because you need to feel superior to me, to everyone. I can't live like that. I'm not inferior, but your denomination treats me like I am. You can't live outside your denomination, and I can't live in it."

She sucked in a deep breath and expelled it. "Besides, I'm about questions. You're about answers. I've spent a lifetime with your answers, but they don't fit me anymore, and you can't accept that."

He stood in the warm humid night, a vacant look behind his eyes.

"I'm sorry, Sam. I love you but… " Sid walked inside and eased the door shut. She'd caused enough pain, no need to inflict more by slamming the door in his face.

Marv leaned forward on the sofa, arms across his thighs, his hands hanging toward the floor. "What the hell was that all about?"

"Old stuff. Let's call it a night, okay? I'm exhausted."

"Sure."

She led him to the door. "Thanks for a fun day."

He planted a kiss on her forehead. "Sure. Sleep well."

Nine

After both men were gone Sid trudged upstairs, forcing one heavy foot after the other. The sadness in her chest reminded her of the proverbial big blue elephant that had stood in the middle of their living room for years. The same elephant they'd all walked around, Chad and Christine included, pretending it wasn't there. Neither of them acknowledged the emotional guilt heaped upon them by Sam, and by a belief system so steeped in dogma that her spirit had starved near to death.

She headed down the long hall and into her bedroom, stripped off her clothes, and crawled in bed. She tried to zone out, to will the world—and everyone in it—away. But she didn't cry, for there were no tears left.

She shouldn't let Sam get to her like that. It wasn't any of his business what she did now. But maybe she still felt like it was, for being married to *God* for over thirty years had really screwed up her soul. Hell, she'd always had difficulty telling Sam how she felt. Probably because she knew she wasted her breath.

As she eased into sleep, her last thoughts were of hope. Hope for her life without Sam, hope that she would sleep through the night dreamless, without a nighttime visitor floating around on the ceiling.

Her wish came true. The visitor didn't float around the ceiling. The crinoline-clothed woman sat on the foot of Sid's bed, a Bible in one hand, and a ring of keys in the other.

You're dreaming, Sid told herself, wake up and the woman will disappear. But when she heard herself gasp, realization whooshed inside her chest like gasoline thrown on a blaze. She wasn't asleep, and she wasn't dreaming. "Who are you? What do you want?" she demanded, sitting straight up.

But no one answered back, for the woman was gone.

Restless anxiety forced Sid out of bed. She stomped down the darkened stairs to the kitchen, hoping the noise kept the ghost away.

While the coffee dripped, she sat and stared at the clock on the microwave as it clicked from 2:06 to 2:07…chiding herself for reacting like a kid afraid of ghosts.

Coffee in hand, she booted up the computer and checked her email. She answered the ones from Chad and Christine, ignored the rest. Chad wanted to know how she was handling living with Aunt Annie. Christine had a new guy in her life and this one was Mr. Right—maybe. He played the tuba and taught high school band.

Positive so far. At least this one had a job.

👁   👁   👁

When Sid awoke the next morning she forced herself to get up and dress for church; she wanted to see this Rev. Humble Bluett in action. Jack Agnes, the murdered couple's neighbor, indicated the preacher was connected to Abe and Cherrie's murder, but Sid had her doubts. Didn't sound like anything a preacher would do—not any she'd ever known. Master manipulator, maybe, but gruesome murderer? She couldn't see it.

After preparing her usual, she sat at the table nibbling on the blackened toast and sipping a cup of reheated coffee from the pot she'd made earlier, dreading the day's planned activity. Twice she'd gone to a worship service since leaving Sam. Not Sam's church, not even the same denomination, but still she'd fled during the first song. Dropped her hymnal in the rack and ran, tears streaming down her face. Today, she was breaking the promise she'd made to herself then, that the next time she went to church it would be a Hindu temple, where she wouldn't recognize the songs—or the gods.

Fact of the matter was, there wasn't a better way to check out the preacher than to see him in action. She'd put her name on absolutely nothing, and if anyone asked if she was a first time visitor she'd tell them no. The thought of her name on a list of prospects made her sick to her stomach.

👁   👁   👁

Rev. Humble Bluett did not remind Sid of her ex-husband, nor was he humble. Instead, his charisma filled the sanctuary, caressing and cajoling people into hypnotic states. She watched the congregation as he spoke, every face focused his way, looking as if he talked to them alone.

Sid didn't see Ella in the crowd.

Instead of listening to the reverend's words, Sid focused on the man's persuasiveness with the crowd; how the timbre of his voice seemed to pull them along, gentle—but at the same time demanding, stern but loving—authoritarian. It wasn't what he said, but how he said it, that wooed them along like mice following the flute player.

Politicians, all.

Throughout the sermon Sid fought the urge to march down to the front, turn around to the congregation, and say think, people—think for yourselves.

She had to admit, however, even with her own blind spot, she found it difficult to imagine this man murdering the Collins couple. Manipulative and controlling as hell, but not a murderer.

And yet—Jack Agnes had certainly implicated the man at some level.

After what seemed an eternity, the service ended and the congregation filed out of the sanctuary. Reverend Bluett stood in the front vestibule shaking hands with his parishioners, greeting men and women alike with sparkling white teeth and a wide, Ben Affleck grin. He squatted down for the small children, shook their hands, spoke directly to them. Sid had to admit, it worked; she hadn't seen an empty pew in the building.

At last, the line dwindled to half-a-dozen blue-haired ladies—groupies vying for attention from Pastor. Over the years, hundreds of the like had awaited their time with Sam.

Sid sucked in her breath and joined the line, smiling as the 'blue hairs' greeted her, wishing for a moment that she could regain her own blind obedience; life had been so much simpler then. Debilitating, but simpler.

Now, she had nothing left but a husk of a belief.

The line moved forward and it was Sid's turn. She stepped toward the tall, good-looking Rev. Bluett. He looked her straight in the eye and grabbed her hand, blue eyes twinkling, charm in fast forward. A tiny scar at the edge of his mouth marred an otherwise perfect complexion.

"First time visitor, ma'am? Glad to have you. I hope you'll come again."

Sid nodded like a robot, livid with herself for doing so.

"If there's anything I can do for you, just give me a call."

"As a matter of fact, there is. May I come by your office to talk?"

"Why of course, anytime."

"Tomorrow?"

"How about around two? I think I'm free then."

"I'll be there." Her hand felt hot when she pulled it away from his.

Outside, she made her way through departing cars, families tucked in and on the way to Sunday dinner. Their pasted smiles had already melted back into frowns of confrontation that they'd put on hold as they arrived.

Sid punched the clicker and unlocked her car door, but before she could get inside, she saw Ella, red-faced, rushing towards her, the jacket of her powder blue suit flapping in the breeze.

"How dare you betray me," she hissed, glaring at Sid.

"What? I didn't betray you Ella. I wouldn't do that. I looked for you during the service, and thought maybe you weren't here today."

"I'll just bet you did." Ella clenched her jaw so tight a small bulge showed on each side of her face. She swiped at tears threatening to run down her cheeks, then shook her head in defiance. She grabbed Sid's hand, still on the door handle, and squeezed. "You came here to tell him, didn't you—about seeing me yesterday?"

"What? No, no, I didn't."

"Yes, you did. Why else would you come?"

She thought of saying because she wanted to attend church, but even the thought tasted bitter on her tongue. Instead, she explained, "On a matter that has nothing to do with you, believe me."

"You saw me yesterday with Ian, I know you did." Ella stuck her face in Sid's.

The mixture of Ella's coffee breath and cologned clothes charged Sid's senses, taking her right back to her days of Sunday School and church socials. An ache, like a tightened vise, squeezed Sid's chest, an ache for Ella, for herself, for every woman in denial of herself. "I don't judge you, sweetheart. I won't divulge that information to your husband. I promise. I'm sorry how I treated you in my office. I wish there was something I could do, but..."

"Ella? Good girl, you've met our first time visitor." The Reverend walked up before either of them noticed. The two women exchanged a brief glance of fear. Sid gave a quick squeeze to Ella's arm as she jerked it away, stumbling backwards.

"Yes, good day to you Ms. Smart. Come again." Ella turned her back to Sid. Reverend Bluett gripped his wife's arm, and they walked off.

It was like watching herself and Sam.

👁   👁   👁

Right on time, the next afternoon Sid strode up the sidewalk to the church, relieved the blue cross wasn't flashing. She knocked on the door marked Pastor's Study, and waited. Off in the distance a storm brewed. Dark clouds roiled toward her as the door swung open. "Good afternoon Mrs. Smart. How are you this glorious day?" As Reverend Bluett spoke, a loud clap of thunder sounded just over them, Sid jumped.

"Fine thanks, Reverend." Sid offered him her hand. "But I prefer Ms., please."

"And everyone just calls me Brother Blue." The reverend swung the door wide and propped it open as if he didn't trust Sid's behavior. Sam always did that when he met alone with a woman. He'd said it was to protect his reputation, but Sid always wondered if it had more to do with trusting himself. True, female parishioners often fell in love with their pastors, thinking him the perfect man. If they only knew.

Brother Blue closed the Bible on his desk and slid it aside.

"Do you know the lord, Mrs. Smart?" He straightened his tie with one hand while motioning Sid to the chair in front of his desk.

If she hadn't shaved the hairs that grew low on the back of her neck that morning, his question would have raised them.

"Do you know Jesus as your personal savior?" He asked the same thing a different way, as if she hadn't understood him the first time.

Okay, time to move the conversation her way. "Mr. Bluett, did you know Abe and Cherrie Collins?"

He squared his shoulders and sat up straighter. "They were faithful members of my congregation, yes. Sad, sad situation. I'm sure glad the police know who did it—God rest Ned's soul. It's terrible to commit suicide, but in this case, maybe it's for the best."

"I'm a private eye, Mr. Bluett. Dempsey Durwood hired me to find their killer. He's convinced his son didn't do it. Someone suggested I talk with you, thought you might know something about the murders."

"Why would anyone think that?"

She wasn't sure if the divine expression on his face was innocence or affect.

"The police claim Ned murdered them." Blue fingered the edge of his Bible. "Why are you getting in the middle of this? Mr. Durwood doesn't have any money. Why not just let the matter rest?"

The phone rang and he rushed to answer it. She listened to his platitudes for a minute. "Yes, but you just have to trust Jesus to take care of this for you, Mrs. Burch," and then "But you've got a lot to be thankful for. Yes, I know it's difficult, but..."

Sid stood and browsed his library row by row. Books of theology, sermons, Bibles of various translations, and Bible commentaries lined the shelves.

One book lay open and looked out of character with the rest. She flipped up the front cover. "*The Last American Mound Builders: Ishak-Atakapa*," she whispered.

"Are you looking for something inspirational, Mrs. Smart?"

She swung around as the reverend loomed behind her. She smiled sweetly. "Call me Sid, please. Just killing time. I'm sorry—I didn't hear your call end. I see you're interested in shell mounds."

The preacher stood speechless, eyes fixated on the book in Sid's hand.

"What are they, and why are you interested?" Sid held up the open book.

"I wouldn't call it an interest in them."

"What would you call it?"

"I'd call it leave well enough alone." Blue strode over to her, gently took the book from her hand, but then snapped it closed. "People make all this big deal about the mounds. They're just trash heaps left behind by pagan savages."

"Who makes the deal big?"

"Archaeologists, local historians. They act like it's some kind of holy shrine or something. They just need to leave them alone. All that stuff about them being here maybe some 15,000 years goes against the teachings of the Bible and Creation." Blue ducked his head and tugged on his shirt collar. "Why do you ask?"

"Just a fascination with ancient cultures, I guess. And the topic of shell mounds and flat-head Indians keeps coming up."

"Who's talking about them?" The Reverend walked back to his chair, tucked the book in a drawer and sat.

"According to Jack Agnes—Abe and Cherrie Collins."

"Humph." The reverend swung sideways in his chair and placed the ankle of one leg across the knee of the other. He picked up a pen from a cup on his desk and tapped the end of it on a shiny, black shoe. "Now, I'm sorry, Mrs. Smart, but I've got things to do. Unless you have something else to talk about."

"What's more important than murder, Reverend?" She refused the friendly title of Brother Blue.

"The most important thing, Mrs. Smart, is that you've asked Jesus into your heart and He's forgiven your sins and saved your soul."

"Then I guess we're done. Thank you Reverend." She walked out the door and closed it behind her.

Just as she pulled out of the church parking lot, the blue neon cross flickered on.

Ten

Sid took the long way home, needing time to think about her conversation with the preacher, about shell mounds, and about what Jack Agnes had told her. By the time she pulled into the driveway next to Annie's Olds, the overcast day had grown even darker. But not too dark to notice a white van parked in the shadows of a large oak tree across the street. Darkness hid the license plate, and she'd never been good at identifying vehicles, but it looked like the one she'd seen in the church parking lot when she'd talked to the reverend.

She switched off the motor and sat motionless, staring in her rearview mirror at the dimly lit van, certain someone sat behind the wheel.

Deciding caution was her best course of action, she wrapped her hand around the cold, hard Glock in her handbag, sucked in a deep breath, and exited the Xterra.

Soon as she did, the van driver started the motor and sped away. It sure looked like the preacher's vehicle, but then again, who'd ever heard of a preacher stalking someone.

Between Slider's snoring and Sid's tossing and turning all night, by the time she reached the Third Eye the next morning, she'd made up her mind. Regardless of Ella's relationship with Professor Ian Meade, Sid had to talk to the man. Since it seemed he was the local expert on shell mounds, and since everyone she talked to mentioned the Paleolithic remains, she had to find out more about them.

A quick check of the phone book, and Sid scribbled down Meade's home address. She'd just grabbed her bag and keys as Annie walked in the front door sporting a giant yellow hibiscus pinned behind her ear, and an unbuttoned Hawaiian print blouse over a lemon-colored tee-shirt.

She took one look at Sid and her face fell. "Oh, Siddie, you must've forgot that I told you to dress Hawaiian today."

Sid stepped over and kissed Annie on the cheek. "I guess I didn't hear you, sweetheart, but maybe next time, huh? I was just heading out, I'll be back later," she called over her shoulder as she strode toward the door. She didn't own anything that looked Hawaiian, and wouldn't have worn it if she had, but no need to go into all that now.

"You have your cell phone, huh?" Annie called after her.

Sid waved it in the air. No need to tell Annie to call—if need be, she would.

👁   👁   👁

Annie humphed at Sid's back, knowing her niece considered her a mite senile. Well, maybe she was, but her brother would never forgive her, even from the grave, if she let anything happen to his daughter.

Sid had just driven off when the phone rang. Expecting it to be her niece with further instructions, Annie snatched up the receiver. Instead, it was the hometown busybody, Maggie Peveto.

"Annie? 'Sthat you? Frank told me you'd moved to Orange and was workin' in Sid's private detective office. What in the world do you think you're doing, child? You gone crazy or something?"

Annoyance ruffled across Annie's back. Leave it to Maggie to mettle in her business. "She worries me Maggie. Why else would I be here." She stuffed down the truth—that Siddie's new profession drew her in like flies on sweetmeat. "She needs me to look out for her. Cover her back, so to speak."

"Annie this is Maggie you're talking to, not Sidra. I know better." Maggie's voice boomed out of the receiver, already held at arm's length.

"Why don't you wear your damn hearing aide, Maggie? You're busting my ear drums."

They'd been friends forever—from diapers to Depends. Might as well be sisters, couldn't be any closer. It surprised Annie that Maggie hadn't called earlier.

"Leave that girl do her job. You're as possessive as that preacher-husband she ran away from. You want her to run away from you, too?"

"Aw Maggie, you know I don't, but it's so excitin'. I told you about the last murder we solved. I just want to be a part of it."

"Annie, *she* solved the murder not you, give her a little space. Let her spread her wings, fly away if she has too. This ain't about you."

Shit fire and save matches! Annie wanted to hang up on Maggie—just slam the receiver down and let it pop in her ears. Deaf old fool—she wouldn't hear it anyway. Annie fumed as she listened to Maggie go on and on about letting Siddie live her life without Annie's interference.

"What makes you think I'm interfering?"

Maggie's laughter boomed loud as thunder across the airway, enough so Annie had to pull the receiver further away from her ear.

"Yeah, right Missy. You meddling old fool, you wouldn't interfere in anyone's life now, would you? And I've got some prime land down in Florida to sell you. Pay no mind to the 'gators. It's just a little swampy, but not too much, at least it won't be when the rainy season's over." Maggie cackled.

Maggie knew Annie, as well as Annie knew Maggie; both were meddlesome fools—had been all their lives. "When you got something better to talk about, you call me." Annie slung the phone down.

👁   👁   👁

Sid pulled up to the curb of Ian Meade's house, a pale yellow cottage trimmed in white. A thick carpet of St. Augustine grass covered the front yard. A flower bed of yellow roses ran the length of the sidewalk. Nearby, a massive oak tree fringed with Spanish moss guarded the front door.

A good-looking man walked across the yard toward a car parked beside the house.

"Ian Meade?" She opened her car door, slipped out and strode up the driveway toward him.

His finger must have pushed the car remote on his bright green Miata convertible, for the headlights flashed and she heard the door unlock as he turned toward her. "Yes?"

"Sidra Smart." She stuck out her hand and shook his. "Got a couple of minutes?"

"Uh, I'm running late for work."

A fire engine hurtled down the street, siren wailing. She waited until it passed before she continued.

"I apologize. I won't keep you but a couple of minutes. I wanted to talk with you about the Collins murders and Ned Durwood."

"I'm afraid I can't help you. I don't know anything about it except what I read in the newspaper. Now, if you'll excuse me." Opening the car door, he crawled inside.

"Mr. Meade, I know you saw me at the crawfish boil the other day."

"So what?"

His hands clutched the steering wheel, turned white.

"I heard you were interested in the area's shell mounds. That's what I wanted to talk with you about."

Ian puffed out his cheeks, exhaled. "What do you want to know?"

"Why are so many people interested in the mounds?"

"I don't know why anyone else is interested. I'm fascinated by archaeology, the culture. Why other folk may be interested I haven't a clue. But I do get the idea there are some in the town who'd rather I not go out there. I guess it's the tales of buried treasure."

The wind picked up, leaves skittered across the driveway. Sid pulled her jacket tighter and shifted her weight.

"Buried treasure?" She regressed to make-believe, childhood, playing with a bunch of kids. A chuckle slipped out. "I thought that was just a child's fantasy."

He crawled out of the car, all legs and broad shoulders. Up this close, she smelled his cologne, mad at herself when her knees wobbled. No wonder the man attracted Ella.

Closing the car door, he leaned against it, crossing his arms over his chest. "Hardly the imaginings of a child. The story goes—Jean Lafitte brought chests of Napoleon's wealth here. The chests had been loaded onboard Lafitte's ship in anticipation of Napoleon fleeing France, but when the agreed upon time came and went and no Napoleon, Lafitte and his men took off with the chests. No one knows what Lafitte did with them, but stories abound that he buried them out in the shell mounds."

The wind whipped his thick, dark hair against his face and for an instant, Sid saw a pirate standing on the bow of a ship unloading a treasure chest.

"Now, if you'll excuse me, I really have to get to class. I have students waiting." He crawled into the vehicle again, and waved as he drove off.

Still in disbelief about the buried treasure, she wondered who and why someone wanted to keep Ian away from the shell mounds. She walked to her car, puzzling over the conversation with Meade, when her cell phone rang. She didn't recognize the number on the caller I.D., surprised it wasn't Annie.

"Siddie," Annie cried, anxiety in her voice, "you need to come back to your office, or what's left of it."

"What do you mean—what's left of it?"

"Fire trucks are here—"

Sid flipped the cell phone closed and raced toward The Third Eye.

After she'd parked as close to the building as possible, she saw Annie had been correct, there was indeed little left. Soot darkened the gigantic eye sign dangling from the front of the building. The walls were scorched, the roof caved in, and water ran down the sidewalk and into the drain at the curb.

Annie sat on the bumper of an ambulance, an oxygen mask over her nose and mouth. Chesterfield lay in her arms, his head tucked inside her elbow. Sid switched off the motor, opened the car door and sprinted toward them.

When Annie saw Sid, she pulled the mask off and looked up at her. Tracks ran down her face where soot and smoke residue had been washed away by tears. Sid's friend, Police Chief Quade Burns, the man who had helped her solve her first case, now stood beside Annie, his arm around her shoulders.

"Quade—Annie, what the hell happened?"

"Oh my God, Siddie, someone burned down our business."

The paramedic took the mask out of Annie's hand and helped her stand. "Your cat okay?" the paramedic asked, and pulled Chesterfield's face out of the crook of Annie's arm and checked his breathing. "You're both good to go." She turned and began to pack her gear.

Quade took Sid by the elbow, leading her aside. He ran his hands through his close-cropped sandy-colored hair and offered, "I don't like the looks of this, Sid. Evidently someone has it in for you. The Fire Marshal hasn't ruled yet, but we both think it was a hot cocktail."

"A Molotov? Wow." She stood with her hands on her hips. "Guess I hit a nerve somewhere."

"Sheriff Bonin tells me he ran into you at the Collins place. Breaking and entering, he told me." A smile slipped across Quade's face, but he extinguished it. "I had to cover for you, Sid. But be careful. I can't always do that. Now, tell me what's going on."

The Fire Marshal interrupted them. "Are you Ms. Smart?"

Sid nodded.

"We haven't ruled conclusively, but it sure looks like someone intentionally burned you down. Your aunt," he motioned toward Annie, "heard the window break in your office right before the explosion. She had the good sense to grab the pet and run out the front door. Would you walk around to the back with us?"

Sid followed Quade and the fire marshal as they sloshed through puddles of water and debris littering the alley.

"On quick observation, and your aunt's description, it looks like the bottle went in through this window. I'm guessing it is—was—the window to your private office, right?"

Sid nodded.

"Best I can figure, whoever did it sneaked down the alley, broke the window and tossed the bottle inside." The fire investigator reenacted the actions he described. "The windows in these buildings are pretty thick, so I doubt the bottle itself would have broken the glass, especially since there's not much room back here to make a strong throw. Probably used a rock, or a brick or something." He paused, his eyes fixed on debris, then stepped across the alley, leaned down and came up holding a soggy baseball cap. "Hmm, looky here." He brushed across the cap with his gloved hand. Embroidered words were still readable, *Houston Astros*.

Eleven

Sid had agreed to meet Quade at the police station after taking Annie home, getting her in and out of the tub, and bedding her down to recover from the shock.

Out of town when they'd held their open house a couple of weeks ago, Sid hadn't as yet been inside the new Orange Police Department. Now she wheeled into a parking space at the rear of the multi-storied red brick building and went inside. After getting directions to Quade's office she walked down the long hallway, located his office, and went in.

"Jack Agnes wears a cap like that." Sid walked in and perched on the edge of a chair across from Quade, who sat staring down at the baseball cap.

"Jack Agnes? Isn't he the one who lives next door to the Collins place?"

"One and the same. I went to see him about the murder."

"The same day the sheriff caught you breaking and entering?"

Sid cringed and smiled. "Since you insist on putting it that way, yes, I suppose it was."

"I'll send my detectives out to talk to him. But what would he have against you?"

"Too nosy maybe? Do you actually believe Ned Durwood killed the Collins? That was a gruesome act, and from what I've learned about Ned, he doesn't fit the profile."

"Bonin tells me he's reached dead ends on any other lead.

Ned left fingerprints—not much else to go on. Meanwhile, we've got to find out who burned down your office. We'll work with the fire department and see if we can get that tied down." Quade tucked the baseball cap back into a plastic bag and tossed it in an evidence box. "What do you think? Is this fire going to put you out of business? You got insurance?"

"Warren had insurance, yes, but how much, I don't know. Hadn't gotten into that detail yet. Him dying and me inheriting the Third Eye all happened so fast I haven't gone through the safe deposit box at the bank yet. That's my next stop."

Quade leaned back in his chair. Stretching his arms over his head he banged his hands into a framed black and white picture of the famed Spindletop Oil Well. Startled, he looked around, straightened the picture, and then put his feet on his desk and his hands behind his head. "I don't know what to tell you about the Collins murder. If you find anything you'd like unofficial help on, let me know, but the case is Bonin's, and as far as he's concerned, the case is closed. I don't know if your investigation on those murders has led someone to burn your building to the ground, or not, but I'll call you should we find anything."

Sid left Quade's office, strode through the lobby, her mind a million miles away, when she bumped into Ben.

"Sid, my god, I was looking for you. What happened? I just drove by The Third Eye, or what's left of the place. The fire chief thought you'd come here." Lines in his face betrayed feelings Sid wanted to ignore.

"Come have lunch with me." He took her elbow and led her to his car, doggedly, without waiting for a response. It seemed odd, she realized, that every time she and Ben were together, they were eating.

They stopped at the Old Orange Café, just a couple blocks away, and he eased her into a booth in the back. "I feel like such a jerk," he reached his hand across the table and took hers in his. "I know the timing is off, but right at this moment, the only thing I want to do is to take your clothes off and kiss every inch of your body."

"Whoa." She laughed. "Do you have any idea how many inches that is? I doubt you have that much time." Looking him in the eye she tried to explain. "Ben, I don't know where I am with all this right now. You can't just bounce in and out of my life on a whim. I'd rather change the subject from us, to me. The only thing on my mind at the moment is what I'm going to do next. Whether that's rebuilding, getting the hell out of dodge, or drowning myself in the river."

They ordered a sandwich, discussed her options for the business and by the time they finished eating she'd agreed to spend the afternoon with him.

Okay, so she wasn't as resistant to the effect he cast over her as she wished—tried to be.

Leaving her car at the cafe, she rode with him down Green Avenue, but when he turned right at Sixteenth Street, instead of left, she put her hand on his arm. "Where are we going? You turned the wrong way."

"What? No—oh, I've moved since you were last at my place. God, has it been that long? I sold the place, too big, too many memories of Irene and the past. I had to let it go. I bought a new house out toward Little Cypress."

Ben passed the traffic light at Echo Road and turned into a cul-de-sac at the first right. The homes looked freshly completed, sporting brand new landscape and manicured lawns. None of that 'lived-in' look about the subdivision. Fresh, clean of memories, both good and bad, except perhaps those memories resident in the hearts of the new owners.

Ben pulled into his driveway and turned off the ignition. Sid sat, apprehension tugging on the inside of her gut. Ben got out and led her up a freshly poured sidewalk yet to be stained with the area's omnipresent mildew.

Inside, new mission-style furniture filled the great room— the focal point of the house. The ceilings were tall, with exposed beams. The back wall of windows overlooked pine, sycamore, and sweet gum trees. Twin deep-brown leather recliners sat in front of a flat-screen television, a table and lamp between them. A matching sofa perched in front of a fireplace.

Ben took her bag and jacket. "Why don't you go out on the patio, I'll get us something to drink and join you." He talked as he slipped off his own jacket and tie, and rolled up his shirt sleeves.

Damn, if he headed over right now and yanked off her clothes, all she'd do was help him with the buttons. But he turned and strode into the kitchen, and she stepped outside. The breeze had died down, and the welcoming sunshine warmed her upturned face.

Soon, Ben, carrying a tray, opened the door to the patio. "Lemon vodka martini for the lady." He handed her a glass, laid the tray down, picked up his drink and sipped. "So, how's your ghost?"

"My what? Oh, my ghost. She's been absent the last few nights." Sid waved her hand. "Probably just my imagination. Mother always believed I had a vivid one. But tell me," Sid ran one finger around the moist rim of the martini glass, glancing up at Ben through her eyelashes. "How's your daughter?"

He sipped his drink, stared at the glass, swallowed, and sat the glass on the table. "I always thought I was a hard-ass, handle any crook or murderer, stare them down till they melted. Daughters don't play fair all the time, do they?"

👁   👁   👁

A couple hours later, Ben dropped her off at the café where Sid collected her car and drove home. During the afternoon, she'd decided to talk with Annie about using the large room off the side of the main house for The Third Eye office until she decided whether to rebuild. The private entrance could be set up as the entryway to her office. The only nagging doubt—beside the even-closer proximity to her aunt—was, under the circumstance, was it safe? But she had already spent part of Dempsey's advance catching up on her bills. She sure couldn't repay him; she had nothing with which to do so. All she could do was go forward.

Annie had been a quick fix. The old gal was tough, dug her heels in just like Sid. "Someone burning down our business like that pisses me off royally. Hell yeah, you can use the room. It takes more than that to scare me off." Annie got up from her easy chair and paced as she talked. Red hair, white at the roots, stuck up in back, parted off from leaning her head against the chair since she'd come home from the fire.

Maybe Sid sold the woman short. Had spunk, she'd give her that.

The next morning, after walking Slider and feeding him yogurt-covered dog food, Sid called the insurance agency and reported the fire. After that, she called the old man who'd painted and hung the sign originally, and asked him to collect and repaint the sign, with the eye as big and as blue as ever, and keeping the words *Intuitive Investigations*.

After she drove to the thrift store and hauled back a couple of desks, chairs, and file cabinet, she realized that the Third Eye's new location made it feel more like hers than Warren's. Good things come from bad, she'd heard, and this was the good, but, of course, following that theory around to meet the other end meant bad things came from good as well. For now, she'd had all the bad she wanted to think about.

"Looks great Siddie," Annie called from the doorway. "Where do I sit? That my desk over there?"

"It is. What do you think?"

"Nice. But you don't have your private office. Now you have to share with me. I'll tell you what, when you need privacy, you clear your throat or scratch your head, and I'll go to the other part of the house for a while." Annie walked into the room. "You know, this is going to work just fine. I can answer the phones and cook our dinner at the same time. How about some of your Aunt Annie's famous chicken and dumplings for dinner tonight?"

At this rate, not only would Sid have to buy office furniture, but also a new wardrobe. "Sounds great, Annie. What time, six maybe? I need to go out for awhile, but I can be back by then." A new respect for Annie swelled inside Sid. The woman had handled the fire pretty darn well for someone her age—and emotional maturity.

Since the fire-bombing of her office had made yesterday's evening news, Sid figured she better bring Dempsey up-to-date. She drove out to his place and found him puttering in the yard. "Mr. Durwood, hi," she stuck her head out of the car and waved.

"Sid, how you doing, gal? Heard your place got torched; hope you're okay. Think it had to do with your investigating the Collins's murder?"

"Possibly. Mind if we sit?" She got out and they walked over to a couple of lawn chairs and brushed off the dust. A whoosh of air escaped Dempsey's chest as he flopped into the chair.

"Gettin' old sure ain't for sissies," he laughed at his non-original joke. "What you got goin' on?"

"I wanted to let you know I've set up office at my aunt's house on Pine Street," she handed him one of her freshly printed business cards. The logo she'd chosen was a big blue eye. Gaudy as hell. She loved it.

He chuckled, looking at the card. "I like it. Gives a certain class to the business—not high, you understand."

"It's funny how that damn eye has grown on me. At first I thought it looked hideous, but now..."

She went on to report all the people she'd talked with, and of the Astros cap at the scene of the fire. The only thing she withheld was what she'd learned from Ella Bluett about her affair with Ian Meade, which didn't have anything to do with the murders anyway.

"Tell me more about your son Ned. I don't feel like I know him well."

Whiz ambled across the yard, slurped water out of a bowl beside the house, then flopped under a sycamore tree. Flies buzzed around his head, he twitched his ears in mild irritation.

"Ned was my only child. Never gave me a lick of trouble. Kept to his self. Quiet, didn't talk much. Never was interested in dating girls, although they liked him a lot. They'd go do things together, but just as friends, don't you know."

He looked away, and Sid gave him a minute to collect himself.

"You okay?"

He nodded. "I'm okay." He sniffed and wiped his nose on his shirt sleeve.

"I keep hearing about shell mounds along the shores of the swamp," Sid continued, keeping an eye on the old man. "Ever hear him talk about them?"

"No'm, can't say I did. I know some of his yard art statues had to do with some of the critters living out in the swamp, so's he'd go out there and do drawings of 'em, alligators, them giant turtles, nutria, that sort of thing. But I never remember him talking about shell mounds. Now I know that preacher—Bluett? He was a visiting Ned a lot. Don't have no idea what that were about. Trying to save his soul I reckon."

The old man looked weary and ready for a nap. He accepted Sid's offer to help him inside and together they negotiated the steps up the front porch. After settling him in with a blanket around his knees and a hot drink in his hands she excused herself and turned to leave.

There sat the photo of the woman who haunted her dreams. No wonder the ghost at Annie's house looked familiar. It was the same woman in the picture. "Mr. Durwood, may I ask who this woman is in the picture?"

A smile played across his lips. "That's my great-great Aunt Kate. *Scrappy Kate,* folks called her. She and her first husband moved over from Georgia to Sabine Pass in the early 1800s."

After Sid left the old man she looked at the clock on the dash. Five thirty. She'd promised Annie she'd be home by six. She headed that direction. Sure enough, when she opened the front door, odors of southern cooking wafted throughout the house.

Slider lay in wait, and made a beeline to her as soon as she stepped into the house.

"Hey sweetheart," she said, rubbing the top of his head.

"Oh good Siddie, you're home just in time for supper. Come wash up and we'll eat." Annie stood in the doorway to the kitchen, wiping her hands on a dishtowel.

"You look tired, sweetie. Need some help?"

"Set the table?"

"Sure." She and Slider followed Annie into the kitchen where Slider parked himself by his bowl. Sid washed her hands, and then pulled two plates out of the cabinet while Annie dished up the food.

Chesterfield walked in about then, spied Slider, and both animals raised their hackles at the other, hissing and growling.

"All right, you two, settle down or you're both outta here." Sid warned, carrying the plates, silverware, and napkins to the table.

Chesterfield strolled over to Annie, purred, and rubbed against her leg.

"That goes for you, too, cat." Sid said, irritated at both the critters. "Don't think you're gonna get favoritism by buttering her up."

Annie shot a look at Sid, who shrugged. "I mean it, we all four have to get along here."

Slider grunted and stretched out on his belly. The cat stalked out of the room.

"Making any progress on the case?" Annie asked as she joined Sid at the table.

"Before we get to that," Sid lifted her glass of sweetened ice tea at Annie, "let me express my thanks for the food. It looks, and smells, delicious, sweetheart, thanks for all your work."

Annie blushed, her chest expanding. "Most folks make pasty-white dumplings, I like my broth nice and brown, gives 'em a pretty color."

Sid stuffed a forkful of dumplings into her mouth and ate

the tender morsels before answering. "Now, back to your question about progress on the case; I feel like I'm spinning my wheels. These are delicious, by the way." She pointed her fork at her plate. "I know Jack Agnes is related in some way. Maybe he killed them—certainly had opportunity, living right next door. He could've set up Ned. Perhaps he saw Ned get killed by the train and used that as his out."

"Possibly."

"But what about motive? That was a heinous murder. Strong feelings set that off. Between all the people I've met so far, though, if Ned didn't do it, Jack Agnes seems the most likely."

After they both finished eating, Sid insisted Annie go upstairs and watch her favorite program, wrestling, while Sid cleaned the kitchen.

👁   👁   👁

The alarm clock woke Sid from a deep sleep. She threw back the covers and staggered down the hall to the bathroom, leaving Slider still asleep in the easy chair, all four legs in the air, snoring. After a quick, hot shower she flicked her short hair dry with a towel, snuggled into a white terry robe, and headed downstairs, eager for her first cup of coffee.

Some days that first cup seemed the best reason to crawl out of bed. Sam, Christine, and Chad were all three morning people. Long ago she'd learned to steal herself against the onslaught of noise and chatter before her brain woke up. After several disastrous attempts at early morning humor, when she'd pissed off Sam, she'd finally learned to just keep her mouth shut until the first cup of coffee evaporated her head fog. Two cups and a little quiet gave her access to rational thought and understandable speech patterns.

Sid shuffled through the swinging door, but was soon disappointed to see she'd forgotten to prepare the pot the night before. Making quick work of the chore, the pungent aroma filled her senses. Soon as the dripping slowed, Sid poured a cup, added sweetener and slurped down the hot liquid. Then, after a quick refill, she strolled through the house until sunshine beckoned her out the front door. A soft nip in the air felt good against her damp skin. She inhaled the early spring morning, and admired the Redbud trees, already in full bloom.

She collected the newspaper off the sidewalk, headed back inside and tossed it on the kitchen counter. "Might as well take out the trash and get that chore over with." She sat her cup down and yanked the white bag out of the can. Opening the back door, she again stepped out into the cool morning air.

But without warning, her world made a sudden nose dive and spun off its axis. Up switched places with down, and left screwed around with right. She felt herself tumbling head first across the small porch, and then down the steps, grabbing air on the way down.

Everything went black.

She tried to breathe, but couldn't. Something covered her nose and mouth. Instant panic pounded her chest. Fighting whatever covered her face, she lifted her head and opened her eyes to whiteness. The trash bag she'd been carrying lay on the ground in front of her. She flipped over onto her butt and looked back at the porch. What the hell had she tripped over?

"Jack?" He lay there—Jack Agnes did—sprawled across the porch, obviously dead. Thick blood still oozed out of a slit in his throat.

Time slowed and stopped as she scrambled on hands and knees toward the porch, her robe untied, wide open. She tripped, flattened out on the steps with an oomph, and again rose on hands and knees. She knew he was dead, but she had to get to Jack Agnes, as if being near the man would resurrect him from the dead.

Once she reached him, she hesitated, cringed, and stuck her fingers on his carotid artery.

Nothing.

Blank eyes stared up at the blue sky.

She glanced across the backyard and saw Jack's truck in the driveway. The same one he'd worked on when she'd visited him. He'd come here, evidently to tell her something, or maybe even to kill her. Someone must have followed him, slit his throat right here on her porch, and she'd heard nothing. My God, she and Annie had slept right through a murder.

Twelve

Quade walked into the kitchen where Sid and Annie sat at the table, hands wrapped around coffee cups. "The coroner agrees with you, Sid, it happened right here on your porch. Of course we still have to run tests, autopsy, that sort of thing."

Sid gave a weak smile and looked at Annie, who sat white-faced, hands still clinching the untouched coffee.

Quade placed a hand on Sid's shoulder and squeezed. "You okay, kid?"

"Yeah, I guess I am, just startled more than anything—and puzzled." She ran her fingers through her hair until it stood in short spikes.

"You have any idea why Jack Agnes would come to your house?"

"Absolutely none." Scraping her chair across the aged hardwood floor, Sid stood, strode across the kitchen and looked out the window to the backyard where police detectives stretched crime scene tape around her own backyard. "I'm positive that was his baseball cap in the alley behind the Third Eye. So I was thinking he'd been the one that burned it down. But if he did, why'd someone kill him on my doorstep?" For the first time since she'd stumbled over Jack's body, she realized she still wore her bathrobe, and nothing else. She turned her back and tightened her belt.

Chesterfield waltzed in demanding his breakfast as if nothing superseded his mealtime. Without a word, Annie picked him up and headed to the pantry. But halfway there, she turned back to Sid. "Siddie, you know how I've always prided myself in not being a hysterical broad, but first the fire, and now this dead body on my porch. I was thinking—you and me could be next." Stroking the cat's fur, she continued. "Honey, I'm sorry, but I think I'll go back to the farm—just for a few days, you understand. Give myself time to get over all this. But I hate to leave you here by yourself..."

Sid went over and put her arms around Annie's shoulders. "You go ahead. I have things to do here, I'll be okay."

Ben walked in just as Annie headed upstairs to dress and pack a bag. "Hey, Quade, thanks for calling me buddy, what's going on?"

Sid piped up before Quade could reply. "Another dead body, that's what's going on—and on my doorstep." She headed into the living room, and the men followed. "Now I'm really confused. I thought maybe Jack Agnes had killed Abe and Cherrie Collins, but if he did, he wasn't alone, else why would someone kill him?"

A police detective entered, whispered something in Quade's ear. He nodded, and the detective left. Out the front window Sid saw EMS pull off, sirens silent.

👁   👁   👁

After everyone had left Sid found Slider prone on the front porch, looking as lost as he had when she'd found him in the ice storm. "Come on inside, buddy. What a patient boy you've been. Let's go get you some breakfast." With Slider following along behind, she went back into the kitchen and dug out some leftovers, warmed them in the microwave and filled the dog bowl for Slider, who went to work on the food.

While Sid prepared breakfast for herself, recent events barreled through her thoughts. Four now dead—two murdered in their beds, one accidental death—maybe—her office burned to the ground, and now Jack Agnes. If she'd ever wondered about

Ned's guilt, she didn't now. Even if he had killed Abe and Cherrie Collins, someone else was involved in something. What had she missed? She went upstairs, changed into street clothes, and as she drove off, dialed her Cajun-speaking, rotgut drinking mentor, George Léger.

"It's your nickel, start talking."

"Hey, George, it must've been a while since you called from a pay phone. Nickel won't buy you nothing."

"Sid, honey, too good to hear from you, sha. I was just fixing to call you—had something to jaw about. I been outta town a few days, and when I got back in last night, I read in the papers 'bout The Third Eye done burn down to the ground don't you know. Heard arson. What the hell's going on?"

When he finally took a breath, she laughed. She loved his Cajun accent. Sometimes she had difficulty understanding him, but she knew he'd move out of it when he got down to business. "What's going on is this woman seriously needs to talk. Where are you?"

"I'm moving as we talk, Sha. Just tell me where you done be."

"Actually just leaving my house." She looked at the upcoming street sign. "I'm on John and…"

"Had breakfast? I'm as hungry as an alligator on a vegan diet. Want to meet me over at Gary's Coffee Shop on I-10? That's where I was a headed."

Not food again. At this rate she'd soon be big as that hungry alligator.

But she agreed to meet him there anyway.

Stepping inside the coffee shop she spied George at the back of the dining room, his back to her. Just the sight of him and her muscles relaxed. She had a while longer to work under his supervision, and she was in no hurry for that to pass. Something about the tall, big-bellied Cajun made her feel more confident.

She slipped up behind him and kissed him on the top of his thinning pate, "Good morning, you." She eased into the other side of the booth, feeling better already.

The waitress saw her come in and walked over. "Can I git you somethin', honey?"

"Just coffee." Sid drug her eyes off the woman's bosom to the nametag pinned atop them. "Rebel—is that your name, or your behavior?"

"It's both, sweetie, but it's my mama's fault. She picked out the name. All I done is live up to it." She tapped Sid on the shoulder and guffawed before heading to the kitchen.

"You're a sight for sore eyes, Mr. Léger."

"You're not so bad yourself, Sha. Catch me up on what's going on?"

"You know Dempsey Durwood?"

George nodded. "Yeah, the old man that lives out on the river bank."

"He hired me to clear his son's name in the Collins' murders. Shortly after that was when someone burned the Third Eye to the ground. In the ruins we found an Astros baseball cap just like the one Jack Agnes wore. He's the man that lived next door to the Collins. So I thought maybe he'd set fire to the *Eye*, but this morning he shows up on my doorstep with his throat cut. I don't know what to make of this mess."

The waitress brought George's food. He salt-and-peppered his eggs, uncapped the Louisiana Red Hot and splashed it over the eggs. "Wow, that is a mess huh?" He slathered butter and Mayhaw jelly on his biscuit.

When George got down to business, he slipped out of the language of his ancestors and into the language of business. "Well, where are you based since the fire? Need to work out of my office? We're tight, but we'll sure squeeze you in."

"Thanks, I've converted a room at Annie's into an office. She was okay with it until this. Now, she's pretty shaken up. She went home for a couple of days." Sid held her cup up to the waitress for a refill. "She'll be back, though. She's a tough bird. But until then, I'll just forward the calls to my cell phone."

"What's your next move?"

She shrugged again. "I have no earthly idea."

Something about the way George never told her what to do, but just sort of nudged her along, letting her screw up all by herself felt comforting, inspiring even, confidence building. She liked it.

"How're you handling all this? Still have your firearm?" George leaned forward, concern in his eyes.

Sid pulled up her handbag and snapped it open. Inside, between checkbook, wallet, car keys, and sundry, laid the black Glock glistening in the overhead light.

"Good, keep it with you at all times."

"I'm good for now. Got any ideas what I should do next?"

George finished his breakfast and when the waitress came he handed her his sopped clean plate. "Them eggs was cooked just right, I ain't used to that. For a Cajun, my wife ain't such a good cook. You've heard of blackened catfish? That ain't nothing new to me, I been eating blackened eggs for over thirty years."

The waitress laughed and laid her hand on his shoulder. "Now George, I know that ain't so. Your wife's a good cook. You better be careful spreading those kinds of tales about her, she's gonna get you." She laid their bills on the table and carried away the empty dishes.

George scrutinized his tab and pulled out a ten-dollar bill. "There, that covers both ours. Now, Sha, tell me how you're really doing. Not the business stuff, you're getting that down better'n you think."

"I'm okay. Know who I am a lot more than I did, but…"

"Well, as I always say Sha," George reached across the table and covered her hands with his, waiting until she looked him in the eye. "It's hard learning who you are, but it's a hell of a lot harder learning what to do with what you learn."

Sid chuckled and leaned back, her hands slipping from underneath his.

"Say, what's going on with you and Ben? The two of you still a hot item?"

Sid shook her head. "It's cooled off some. I guess I should say he's cooled off. I think he has family problems."

George's eyebrows reached toward the top of his forehead. "I figured so. He looks like hell. That daughter of his has never gotten over the death of her momma. You want my opinion? She thinks as long as he's a widower she can go around pretending Momma's not dead. Either that or she wants all his inheritance when he dies. Sometimes I bank on the latter."

"It's okay. I'd rather not talk about it anymore. I'm going on with my life." She wasn't sure if she'd convinced George any more than she'd convinced herself.

"So what you gonna do now?"

"Thinking about taking a trip out to the shell mounds. They keep popping up in conversation. Ever been out there?"

"Many a year ago, I did," George said, standing. "If you're going sloshing through the swamp, you'd better come by my house and pick up a pair of hip boots. You might even want to take a spade. Tell you what, follow me home, and I'll get 'em for you."

They each got into their own vehicles and headed out. She had no idea where George lived, nor had she ever met his wife, but now she recognized they headed to Bridge City.

He turned at the Shell Station, and soon she saw well-kept frame houses on large, tree-filled lots. Dark green elephant ears grew rampant in a drainage ditch between the road and the houses. He swung left onto Meadow and, after a couple blocks, turned into the driveway of a ranch-style house with a sprawling front porch. Two white rocking chairs sat motionless in the still air.

"Get down and come in." George beckoned with his hand as he exited the truck. Leading her through the garage, he opened a door and stepped into the house. Just as he did, he reached up and clanged a brass bell that hung just inside the doorway.

"Martha, we're coming in," he yelled.

A short, squat woman came from the kitchen wiping her hands on an apron. George leaned down and smacked Martha on the mouth as she swiped a loose strand of coal black hair off her forehead. An aura of pride glowed around the man. "This is my bride. Martha, honey, this is Sidra Smart—Warren Chadwick's sister and the newest private eye in town."

The two women shook hands. "'Je content"— the woman mumbled automatically, then laughed, covering her mouth with her hand. "Excuse my French, I just got off the phone with Mama, and that's all she speaks. Nice to meet you, Ma'am. George has talked about you so much, I feel like I know you already. Come on in and sit a spell. I'll put on a fresh pot of coffee."

"Thanks, no. I just came to pick up a couple of things George is loaning me. Maybe next time. But whatever you're cooking sure smells good."

Martha looked back at the kitchen. "Oh, just a little Catfish Couvillion. No big deal. You come some time, I cook it for you."

"That's a deal."

"Sid's gonna borrow my hip boots to wade out in the swamp," George announced. "That is if I can find the keys to the store room."

"That husband of mine can't find nothing but bad guys." Martha stepped around them and collected a ring of keys off a brass key rack near the bell. "Come on, Ms Smart, I'll take you to 'em. I know right where them boots are at." She winked at Sid. "Don't know how he finds his office, much less a missing person."

"Now, now, Martha, you don't have to go into all of that." He poked Sid with his elbow.

Martha led them through the den, out a patio door, and across a wide expanse of grass to a storage shed near the back cyclone fence.

At the shed, George took the keys from Martha. "Here, baby, let me do that." He opened the lock, dangled it through the hinge bolted to the door, and stepped inside. Rummaging through piles of junk, mumbling about needing to clean the place up someday, he pulled out a huge pair of black hip boots.

"Don't you think my pair here would fit her better?" Martha held up a smaller pair.

"No, no, these'll be fine." He turned the boots upside down and shook out the legs. "Critters have a tendency to hide in these things. I remember one time I stuck my foot down into 'em and found a whole family of bullfrogs." George chuckled. "Boy, talk about getting them things off fast..."

When nothing fell out of the boots, he handed them to Sid.

Leery anyway, she sat on a nearby box and stuck her legs down into the blackness and then stood, adjusting the outfit. The top of the hip boots, which she knew should stop mid chest, came up almost to her chin. She looked down at eighteen inches, or more, of boot leg lying on the floor. Her own legs looked either club-footed or broken.

Martha started first, and then George and Sid. Paralyzed with laughter, all they could do was hold their bellies and stomp the floor. When Sid felt a dribble between her legs, she laughed even harder, thinking that soon they'd need waders to get out of the storeroom.

"What'd I tell ya?" Martha roared when she caught her breath. "George you don't know jack-shit." She handed the other pair to Sid. "Here, try these."

👁   👁   👁

Locating the toothless old man with the flat-bottomed boat wasn't as difficult as Sid had expected. For when she pulled into Blue Bird Fish Camp there he sat with his fish traps. She got out of the car, opened the trunk, collected the spade and hip waders, and headed his way.

As Sid approached, the bent-over man held onto the dock rail and eased to his feet. A red-gummed grin spread across his face. "I know you. You the same woman what went out with me when we seen *le feu follet* out yonder in the swamp. I never forgets who I's with when feu follet shows up." He shook his head. "Hadn't seen that dancing light since then t'either."

Sid hoped she never saw the dreaded phenomenon again. She had sat huddled in the back of the boat, eyes glued to the flame-like phosphorescence as it danced just above land. The old man had rowed over, climbed out, and driven his pocketknife in the ground to *break the spell* of the Cajun will-o'-the-wisp.

"Did you come back the next day to get your knife?"

"Yes'm, 'fraid not to. Don't want no black magic going bad, you know."

"Did you find the knife?"

"Really wanna know?" His eyes looked like two dark slits slashed into wrinkled cowhide.

She nodded.

"Had blood on it all right. Somebody ya know die?"

"As a matter of fact, yes."

"It mighta been you self, if'n I hadn't stuck that knife in the ground."

Superstition or not, Sid shuddered remembering how close she'd come.

"You want to go back out yonder to Andrine's house?"

Pirogue Pat crammed the first four words of the question into one. Yonah—like Jonah with a Y. *Yonah go back out yonder to Andrine's house?*

The colloquialism made Sid smile. "Not this time. Can you take me out to the shell mounds?"

A shadow crossed a face already darkened by too much sun. "What ya got doin' with shell mounds, ma'am? If'n ya don't mind me askin'."

"Not real sure. Folks have mentioned the shell mounds. I guess I'd just like to see them for myself."

He plopped a sweat-stained, felt hat on his head and took her hand while she climbed into the flat-bottomed boat.

Fish-stench filled her nostrils; she tasted it in the back of her throat.

The old man climbed in, slipped the loop of rope from the dock, and stuck the paddle down into the murky water. He recited local history while he paddled. "This swamp's been here since time began. Took them flat-head Indians over fifteen thousand years to build up these mounds. Took the early settlers seventy-five to demolish most of 'em. Some are left, but not many. If'n you look, you can still find tools left behind, stone ax heads, the like."

Fifteen thousand years ago—about the same length of time she'd been a preacher's wife. "Tell me more about the mounds, what are they?"

"Piles of shells, like oyster, crab and clams. Most folk lived near the water, but the old folk and them women what were with child, they lived further inland, away from varmints and diseases they'd get from the swamp. Men fished, and crabbed, and dug oysters. When they was done eating, they dumped all the shells in piles. I hear tell giant sloth and saber-tooth tigers roamed the area." He raised his arm and moved it, trance-like, over the waters, "even mastodons."

He grew quiet, turned and looked at Sid, his eyes as black as the water. With reverence, he nodded toward brush-covered mounds bordering the marshy swamp and lowered his voice. "When it came time to bury their dead, they buried them right here in the middens. The shamans and chiefs lived on top—like priests living next door to the church."

He removed his hat and crossed himself again.

"But wouldn't the mosquitoes have eaten them alive?" Sid asked, swatting one against her arm. She wiped off the squashed bug along with a splatter of her own blood.

"Smeared they skin with oil they got from alligator glands. Kept the mosquitoes away, but I hear tell made 'em smell to high heaven. A few of 'em still lived here when the early settlers came. Might be a little cross-breeding leftover—but I don't rightly know. Early settlers knocked the mounds down so as to build houses for their slaves. When they did, they uncovered bones that poofed into dust soon as the air hit 'em. Slave trading was plenty heavy around here, you know. Lots of misery and suffering passed through this here place."

He turned and looked at Sid. "Can't you *feel* it? Don't it make your bones ache?"

Until he asked, she hadn't realized that her bones did indeed hurt—the ache of horror enacted on one human by another, trapped by humidity and oppression, past and present. What would it take to clear the aura of abuse? Certainly not oil refineries zapping the earth's resources.

"I hear tell in the 1700s Jean Lafitte's men built shacks just up the river near Deweyville and stored the slaves they'd stolen from plantations in Barbados. Brought 'em in on pirate ships and left 'em there till they could find a buyer who'd ship 'em east."

Near Sid, a snake slithered up the trunk of a water tupelo tree. Something slithered inside her as well.

"Jim Bowie?" The old man half-turned again, and cut his eyes toward Sid. "He was a slave trader, too. Bought 'em off of Jean Lafitte, ferried them overland, or upriver, to the sugar plantations in Louisiana. Yep, he bought and sold human souls with the worst of them. Humph—some hero if'n you ask me."

A fog moved in as if in sympathy with Sid's mood, saddened now, from the stories. Her clothes clung to her skin, hair plastered against her head.

The past lay as heavy on them as did the fog.

They moved deeper into the swamp, around a bend, through a narrow stretch where cypress trees brushed the tops of their heads as they paddled underneath. Just as her back cramped from the bent over posture, the passage way opened up and she straightened just in time to see an alligator slide into the water and head off behind them. Mosquitoes buzzed.

After several more minutes, they eased alongside a shell midden that sat higher than the others. He slung a rope around a cypress knee, stepped out into the half-solid marsh and reached for her hand. "This one here is the main one. It's the last of the big'uns. No telling what's buried 'neath all these shells."

Thankful she'd borrowed Martha's hip waders, she stepped out into the bog and climbed atop the mound, kicking at odd pieces of fallen branch and rusted tin cans that had floated up during high tide.

An old Dr Pepper bottle lay on its side, half buried in the muck. The logo of 10, 2 and 4—like hours on a clock—prescribed the perfect time to consume the drink. Her civilization, too, left behind its most prized trash.

She inched along, fearful she'd fall into a pit of alligators and swamp monsters, wondering why in the hell she'd come—she had no idea what to look for.

"Ya okay missy?"

When she looked over at Pirogue Pat to wave, her foot caught on something and she tripped. Recovering before she hit the soggy mess she glanced down at the sole of an old shoe, abandoned by some hunter, probably.

Whatever secrets Jack Agnes thought this place held, the swamp still held them. Nothing she saw made any sense to her. "Let's go home," she called, "I'm done here."

If she never came here again, that would be too soon.

Thirteen

By the time Sid crawled into her own bed that night, Slider was already asleep in his chair. He'd assumed his normal position on his back, with all four legs up in the air.

Sid lay staring at the ceiling, comforted somewhat by the dog's snoring, but hyper-vigilant in case the figure from *the other-world* visited again. Irrational fear wedged itself between rational thought and emotion. She shuddered, and pulled the bedcovers tighter. But between the spaces of her thoughts, she felt her body relax, let go.

In the midst of slave traders and pirate treasure, hurricanes and hotels, a loud banging startled her awake to a raging thunderstorm. The ceiling fan had stopped, the room felt muggy. She switched on the lamp—nothing. From the streetlight outside the window, she could make out Slider, still as she'd left him, except now his mouth looked stretched into the smile of a lover.

"That dog can sleep through anything." She threw back the covers wondering why she'd ever thought he'd make a good watchdog. She pushed her feet into slippers while grabbing her flashlight from the nightstand, and then headed into the hall.

The sound was louder there.

Bang, bang.

It didn't sound like gunshots, but what else made such a noise? Hairs on her arm stood on end but she wasn't sure if it was from her earlier fear, or from the storm-charged air.

The noise grew less as she headed downstairs, but increased

as she went back up, and louder still as she ventured further down the dark hallway toward the back of the house. She cringed with every creak of the hardwood floors as she tiptoed toward the attic door, shunting the flashlight ahead of her. She didn't relish going up in the old attic in the dead of night, and in the midst of a storm, but if she didn't find out what made the noise she'd never get back to sleep.

Of course the noise might find her.

She yanked on the swollen attic door, but it refused to budge.

Annie had such a phobia of attics and basements, Sid was certain she'd never been up, and evidently no one else had either. Blood pounded in her ears as she stuck the flashlight under her arm and tugged. At last, the doorframe relinquished its hold.

Shunting the light ahead of her, she climbed the creaking steps. The banging grew louder the higher she went.

But when she stepped out into the large, musty room and flashed the light towards the noise, she saw it. Shutters, loosened by the wind, banged against the window.

She headed across the wide expanse, weaving around piles of junk.

"Dammit," she swore, stubbing her toe on a table leg.

She hobbled to the window, banged, pushed, and pried until the peeling paint released its hold. Soon as she got the sash up, cold rain whipped her face, and took her breath away. Swiping wet hair off her face, she plunged her upper body out into the storm.

After several futile attempts, she got the shutters latched back in place and closed the window. Shivery, she brushed off her arms and face and pulled her soaked nightshirt away from her body.

Her flashlight reclaimed from the floor, she headed back towards the stairs, but halfway across the room, stubbed the same damn toe on the same damn table leg. Throbbing pain radiated up her foot. "Idiot." She dropped the flashlight and hopped around the room on one foot, dodging odd pieces of dusty furniture and other accouterments of a bygone era. The flashlight rolled under a table and its light slashed across the floor. Frustrated as hell, she flopped on an old trunk, cringing, rocking, and holding her angry toe. When the initial pain subsided, she glanced around the room, and then down at the trunk beneath her. Wide metal strips banded the curved top. She'd seen these in movies—something from another century.

Curiosity gradually pushed aside the lessening pain in her toe. She scrambled under the table for the flashlight and without stopping to think, tucked her damp nightshirt between her thighs and tugged on the trunk lid. Rusty hinges squeaked open.

Inside lay paraphernalia from the past: an old pocketknife, a hand mirror with its silver long gone, and hand-carved knitting needles. A yellowed receipt made out to Kate's Catfish Hotel lay in a tray on the right. At the bottom of the page the date was scrawled in small, tight figures. 1853.

1853? Someone actually held this piece of paper and wrote this date over a hundred and fifty years ago.

Rummaging through someone else's treasures she found a stack of daguerreotype-photos. The early method of photographing had always fascinated her. The picture of one woman stood out among the rest. Short, freckle-faced, probably red-headed, although difficult to tell in the sienna-colored photo. A younger version, it seemed, of the woman in the photo at Dempsey Durwood's—and—Sid swallowed hard—the one haunting her dreams.

"Kate?" Sid whispered as if trying to summon the woman from the past. "That's impossible." She laid the picture aside and scratched to the bottom. The thought of a snake hiding from the rain crossed her mind, but she could no more brake her curiosity than she could stop her breath.

She lifted out a small wooden box emblazoned with a family crest. "The chest," she whispered. The same chest the ghost held in Sid's dream—nightmare. She tickled her fingers across the cracked wood, her throat dry with anticipation—dread, waiting for courage.

The lid opened with ease. Something—perhaps a book—lay wrapped in several layers of crinoline. She pealed back the cloth, opened the cracked, leather-bound book and read.

December 12, 1852

Sabine Pass is the most miserable and at the same time the most exciting place to live. We finished building out the hotel with much help from our neighbors. I have dreamed of this day. Finally I can feel like I am at home.

Sid put her quivering hand over her heart. History lived in the palm of her hands, a record of a woman, of a house, of a time.

Arthur gave me this journal for my birthday. The binding is so supple I swear my rough hands almost cry from the softness. I waited until today to write in it.

The day is now spent. Folk have all gone home. My poor feet feel like I have been standing on them ever since we moved here. But the place is finished. It took us the best part of a year—start to done.

I must be honest and say that when first we arrived here along the Sabine River I wondered why in God's name Arthur brought us here. The swampland looks the most god-forsaken spot in all the earth. After leaving my beautiful Georgia for this marshy bog of mosquito infested lowland, I did weep. The heat and humidity so wets my garments I can almost wring them out while they still cover my body. But Arthur says this is the future. He says the coastal area will bring in ships, commerce, and families. All I see are slave traders transporting men and women and children in the most wretched of conditions. Thank God not many people here own slaves although we do have an auction block in the middle of the community. I think there are not many more than 20 slaves in the whole town. D. R. Wingate owns 13 of them who help him run his sawmill.

But now I have my hotel. We built it on the edge of the Pass, at the north end of the wharves. Fish are plentiful in the surrounding waters. Even during drought we can catch freshwater fish. I surmise folk around here are tired of sowbelly and ham hocks, and that is why they like my cooking. In the drought season our water gets salty, brackish, which brings in the saltwater catfish. Folks around here call them gafftops. Lands a Goshen, I had to fry up a big mess of them before we ever finished the restaurant. People came from all over. I reckon they smelled the fish a cooking.

With the wharf at the front of the house, we cast nets right here and catch redfish, mullet, croakers, and flounder. The steamboat captains can dock right here and get their vittles.

Arthur and I call the place the Catfish Hotel, since bed and fish seem to be what most folk want and need. The house is big, two-story, modern-looking. It has tall white columns on the front porch, like the houses I saw in Georgia as we traveled down to Texas. The place will sleep up to twenty-four people, that is, when folk double up. Before we even got the place finished people moved in. I guess I can't blame them. Living quarters come in short supply around here. What with the storms coming so sudden and tearing down what little is here.

Further down the page, Sid read an undated entry.

Looks like I'll be running the place mostly by myself since Arthur got hired off as engineer on the mail packet T.J. Smith. But I will have help. Many women around here look for work. With the baby coming, and me laid up for a while, the help and comfort of the other women will be nice. Sarah and Peggy both said they would assist me. Do not know what I would do without the help and friendship of those two women in this ungodly paradise.

We are all glad hurricane season is about over. A couple of storms came in this summer that nearly wiped the place out. Arthur had to replace some of the boards on the hotel where the wind blew them off. The next morning we went out to the front porch and there were alligators 15-17 ft long sunning on each step of our front porch.

But then the mosquitoes came, some of them almost as big as blood-sucking bats. Doing laundry out in the backyard is a battle, the mosquitoes against my strong will to get my clothes clean. The men laugh and say, "Kate, you are so little, those dang mosquitoes are going to plumb carry you away." I tell them no, my clothes are so heavy from the dank air, that they hold me down to the ground as if my skirts had lead weights sewn in the hem.

I am happy here, but I could not stay if we had not brought Janie with us. We buried her up the rise behind the house under the lone cypress tree. My arms still feel empty from the loss, but at least we did not leave her behind. Maybe the baby coming will bring some comfort to me. Lord, I'm tired.

Tears dripped off the end of Sid's chin and splattered onto the page, the moisture spreading into uneven edges. She closed the book and laid it in her lap, pulling her own damp nightshirt away from her body. The feeling of having been inside another woman's soul touched Sid as no other. Insatiate, she wanted to carry the book downstairs and sleep with it under her pillow but she couldn't. It belonged here, as it was. She rewrapped the journal as if it were sacred text, put it back inside the trunk and crept downstairs to bed.

Kate seemed real to Sid now, regardless of whether she had gone around the loony bin, seen floating crinoline, or what. She'd never believed in ghosts, and still didn't, but she dare not ignore the presence of something, even if it was just in her head. She'd read how imagination can create reality, perceived reality, at least. That's what it was. She'd gotten so hooked into the history of the place her mind had created a reality.

Fourteen

Ella Bluett tore the page out of the high school annual, stunned that she had never noticed it before. Boys, arm in arm, fishing poles nearby, big smiles across their faces. She'd recognized Blue standing next to a boy whose face had been scratched out with an ink pen. When had that happened?

The others, she suspected, were Marv Bledsoe-the church's lawyer, Abe Collins, and some guy she didn't recognize.

Ella walked to the telephone and dialed.

"Sid? This is Ella Bluett, I know you don't want to talk to me, and I understand that—what with your background and all—but I need to talk to you. Something weird is going on. I can't figure out what's happening." She tried to keep the fear out her voice, but the effort only resulted in a squeak. Sid agreed. 2:00 p.m.

That gave Ella an hour to get packed.

She pulled a suitcase down from the closet shelf. She didn't know how he'd found out about her and Ian. She could go talk to Ian, but right now Sidra Smart seemed the best bet.

People at the church would not believe her. When they looked at Blue, all they saw was perfection, godliness. They hadn't seen the deterioration like she had, the driven look, the compulsion, the anger. Maybe she'd be safe if she could just get away and hide. Sid might have some suggestions. An hour to go—if she made it out the door.

👁   👁   👁

Blue battled the demon inside him. It had taunted him since childhood when all he'd wanted was to become an alcoholic—the only way he knew how to escape the guilt of this unholy drive.

What was it about the brew that taunted him, tantalized him, and drove him mad with desire? He'd found that the only way to keep the monster at bay was to refuse even a drop. He'd used God, he knew he had, but if he hadn't, he'd be a raving maniac. The alcohol or guilt would have destroyed him, body and soul.

Every time he went into the pulpit he wished for a shot of something to steel his nerves. Something—anything—to give him the courage to stand in front of all those hypocrites. He knew some of them indulged in the sinful liquid themselves then acted so innocent, as if they, too, resisted the devil.

But the temptation to drink had just gotten harder to fight—now that he knew Ian Meade had been fucking his wife.

Blue guessed it didn't matter anyway; he'd only used her as a receptacle of his demons, for solace to cleanse his mind and body, but when honesty rose to the top Blue had to admit, he'd used her for cover.

What would his congregation think if it got out that his wife was unhappy with him? Would they suspect?

The blame belonged on Cherrie Collins. If she hadn't found out about he and Abe and threatened to call the deacons…

Before he or Abe could stop Cherrie she'd swung the knife at Abe then turned on Blue. He had to defend himself. God understood. Even now Blue could smell the stench of blood all over him. Blue had panicked that day until he realized Cherrie and Abe were his sacrifices, like Jesus had been God's. He'd often wondered what kind of God sacrificed his own son. Now he knew. One like Blue—pushed into a corner.

He tore open the brown bag and held the bottle between his hands. The coolness of the glass, the sparkle of the amber-colored liquid, begged him to partake of its pleasures. Resistance faded when the mouth of the bottle touched his lips and the pungent aroma wafted into his nostrils. He tilted the bottle up and waited for the first bite, then, choking, spewed the liquid sin across the room.

His thoughts switched to Ned getting killed by the train the same day of the incident and then getting blamed for Abe and Cherrie Collins's death. Poor bastard. Perfect example of imperfect timing—for Ned—worked out perfect for Blue.

He turned the bottle up again and swigged.

👁 👁 👁

When Blue walked into the bedroom, his eyes icy slashes across his face, Ella knew she'd run out of time. She backed up until his long thin fingers grabbed her shirt and tore it open.

"So I'm not enough for you, huh? You have to go whoring around with someone else—Meade, of all people," he spat. His breath reeked of alcohol. She'd never known him to drink. He preached against it with too much conviction for the truth to have been otherwise. Years ago, however, he'd told her his goal as a teenager had been to become an alcoholic. She'd never asked why; now she was sorry she hadn't. He'd gone on to say that goal changed the day he asked Jesus to come into his life and save his soul. Since then, he hadn't tasted a drop.

The madman, released from his shackles, pushed her across the room and down on the bed, snatching, tearing off her slacks and underwear, clawing the insides of her thighs with his fingernails as he shoved her legs apart.

"No, Blue, no, don't," she cried, knowing all along he was too far gone to even hear her, much less stop the attack.

"I'll show you a *real* man," he said through clenched teeth as he sat up and unzipped his pants and rammed himself against her, pumping hard, fast.

But all she felt was the pressure of his body against hers.

Enraged by his inability to get an erection, he rammed harder, endless, jarring.

When he paused, she squinted her eyes open enough to see what he was doing, wary of his next onslaught. He'd grabbed the phone from the nightstand and dialed a number. "Don't utter a sound," he warned.

Who had he called? Were they listening? Dare she scream? Ella forced herself to lie still and endure, waiting for a chance to run, hoping he'd finish soon, while tears ran down the sides of her face and pooled in her ears. Somewhere off in the distance she heard the doorbell ring once or twice, then whoever it was must have given up and left.

He laid the receiver on the nightstand and returned to grinding against her until at last he reached orgasm. After ejaculation, he hung up the phone. His sickening laughter echoed off the walls.

👁   👁   👁

Three thirty and no sign of Ella, Sid should have known she was being taken a fool. Her head felt stuffed with antimatter from her night of carousing in the attic. She laid her arms on the desk and rested her head on them.

Her thoughts ran to Ben. Marv crowded in as well, but Marv wasn't even a contender for her feelings. Besides, she hadn't ruled him out of the murder of Abe and Cherrie Collins. Maybe he'd even been the one that slit the throat of Jack Agnes on her back porch. Why she'd think that way, she wasn't sure, except perhaps his vagueness with the whole thing.

The door clicked open and Sid looked up. But it wasn't Ella. Ian Meade strode in. His deep voice resonated across the room.

"Ms Smart? I'm Ian Meade, we talked the other day?"

"Sure, Ian, have a seat."

He shook his head. "I'm looking for Ella Bluett. I know she came to see you before and wondered if she'd been by today? I've looked everywhere else."

Sid stood, walked around her desk. "No. She called and made an appointment for two o'clock, but never showed."

"Oh." His voice grew tight, stilted. "Then I'm worried. She's not answering her cell phone or her door, despite the fact that I heard music playing inside her house. I'm heading out of town to speak at a conference. I left a message on her cell phone, but she hasn't called me back. That's not like her. I have an uneasy feeling. Something's wrong." He paced the room, smoothing down unruffled hair. Then: "she told you about us didn't she?"

"I knew you were having an affair, yes."

"You can call it that, but I'm in love with Ella, and I can't find her." Panic crept in his voice. He let his outstretched arms fall to his sides.

"Maybe you're over-reacting, Ian." She remembered the fear in Ella's voice earlier that morning. Something had definitely scared her. "I'll check it out. Give me your number and I'll call you if I hear from her."

Fifteen

From below, Ella heard a CD player belting out *Onward Christian Soldiers* as her superior, holier-than-thou husband forced her into a skirt and blouse then grabbed her arm and dragged her down the hall. As they started down the stairs, she banged into a framed photograph on the wall; it hit the carpeted rung and tumbled in front of them, then shattered at the bottom. When they reached the first floor their shoes pulverized the glass shards into the floor, heightening Ella's fear even more. Blue was a fanatic about those oak floors.

"Blue, stop. What're you doing?" she screamed, as Blue dragged her through the kitchen. "Let me go, don't do this." She grabbed at the table, a chair; she snatched at a drawer handle and broke a fingernail to the quick.

Blue kept going.

When he shoved her into the garage, Oprah's words echoed in her head: "Don't ever let yourself be transported to another location."

Then again, Blue wouldn't kill her. He was her husband, her *preacher*-husband for God's sake.

"Stop, she screamed again, half believing he would, terrified he wouldn't.

But Blue didn't stop. Instead, he shoved her behind the front seat of the van, held her on the floor with his knees while he retrieved a rope from under the seat, and then bound her wrists together.

Ella stared, disbelieving, sobbing, snot dribbling into her mouth. She licked her top lip and watched as Blue looped the rope around seat brackets bolted to the floor. When he finished, he glared at her as he slid backwards out of the van. His eyes raged with the flames of hell.

He climbed into the driver seat, revved the engine, and drove off.

Ella lost track of time. Horns blew; wheels screeched. Sharp turns slung her back and forth. A rotten-egg smell filled her nose and throat. Was it her own fear, or was it refinery wastes from chemical plants?

Lie quiet, she told herself, and he'll come to his senses, take her home, all sins forgiven. Wasn't that what he preached? Forgiveness? Seventy times seven?

The vehicle turned onto what felt like a gravel road and with every grating mile her body bounced a half-beat off the van's jolts. Just when she thought her teeth were jarred loose, the van screeched to a stop, making gravel ping against the underside of her prison.

The driver's door opened and closed, footsteps crunched around the vehicle, and Blue opened the side door. When she heard his heavy, raspy breath she knew he'd not calmed down. Quite the contrary. Something drove her husband, something ugly, something she'd never seen before.

He crawled atop the passenger seat and bent his head down toward the floor. The bald spot on the top of his head, the spot he so carefully covered from the world—from her—now shone in all its glory. The freedom to stare at it felt odd, almost unforgivable. Almost.

After loosening the rope he yanked her out of the van, with her kicking and screaming and snatching at anything to hold onto. When her feet hit the ground, her legs, numb from the long, scrunched-up ride on the floor, buckled under her. She hit the gravel roadbed on her hands and knees, driving tiny bits of shell into her bare skin.

Realization of the dire situation hit her full force, the panic exploding her insides. She tried crawling away, but as soon as she did, waves of nausea ripped through her gut. She stopped and retched up her insides, watching the vomit splatter on the ground, on her hands, on the bottom of her skirt.

"Get up," Blue leaned over and yelled into her ear. He jerked her to her feet and spun her around.

The Sabine Lighthouse loomed in the distance, its buttressed base looking like a missile ready for launch. If only it was a space ship—with her in it. She'd never understood Blue's fight against the structure's restoration, but one thing she did know. It sat on the Louisiana side of Johnson's Bayou. Blue had kidnapped her and taken her across the state line. That was a felony, even for a husband.

Without a word, Blue sloshed them through tall weeds, up to their ankles in marsh water. A bullfrog jumped away and right into the mouth of a crane. An alligator darted into a cluster of narrow-leaved cattails. Still he marched, not saying a word.

"Say something, Blue," Ella cried. "Talk to me. We can work this out, I know we can." She pawed at his arm, sniveling like a kid headed to the woodshed.

When they reached the lighthouse, a large wooden plank lay across brackets on either side of the door. Blue saw it, too, and swore, shoving her to the ground. "Don't move," he ordered through clenched teeth.

Ice-cold marsh water seeped through her clothes. Ella shivered, pulled her knees up and hugged them to her chest. She watched his movements, feeling dragged to her own execution, whimpering—wanting to run, die, anything but watch her husband destroy her. But she obeyed him—again.

He shoved on the plank until it thudded to the ground, and then pulled on the door. It squeaked open on rusty hinges. Grabbing under her armpits he dragged her across the raised concrete threshold, scraping the skin off the backs of her legs and knocking off her shoes.

After he'd dumped her on a concrete floor amid piles of boards, bricks, sawhorses and nails, Ella lay in a huddled mass, her arms over her head, expecting the blows to start again.

Time stretched into forever as he stood nearby, his breath loud, raspy. She knew he stared at her because she felt his eyes boring into her cringing, sniveling, pathetic soul. Just do it—get it over with.

But instead of killing her, he stormed out and slammed the door. The plank screeched as he slid it back across the brackets.

Then nothing.

Ella crawled to her feet, the concrete floor cold and damp against her bare soles, surprised she still lived. Oddly the dead quiet felt comforting, safe. Blue was gone. She hoped.

Being careful of her bare feet she stepped through clutter around the large round room. Small puddles of water on the floor reflected tiny shafts of light from a vent and a window high above. The place smelled of dust, mildew, stale air—but she breathed it in anyway, the first safe breath she'd taken that day.

In the dim light a rotting foam-rubber mattress lay under a dangling spiral stairway. Ella dragged the mattress away from the stairs and, despite its filth and smell of decay, she crawled onto it and closed her eyes.

She'd seen Blue close to the edge before, but never like this. Where had he gotten the liquor? Had he bought it himself? He wouldn't want anyone to have seen him in a liquor store.

In time, the pressure of a full bladder forced her up. She rummaged through trash until she found a rusty bucket. After she'd relieved herself, she blotted her bottom with the edge of her skirt until the stinging subsided, and then returned to the mattress.

Blue had been distracted lately, but even in her wildest dreams, she never imagined he'd slip this far. Was he coming back? Somehow she didn't think she'd seen the last of him. Not with what she'd seen in his eyes.

👁   👁   👁

On the drive back to the parsonage Blue's demons came at him like swine charging over a cliff. He'd fought the stampede so long—all his life—but they seemed closer today. For years he'd purged his guilt by screwing his wife. Her looks mattered not. All he wanted was her regenerating chamber, hoping for his own rebirth and cleansing of his soul. Every time he'd driven into her he'd poured out bitterness, the culmination of rejection—of himself.

He'd gone into the ministry hoping to kill his demons. No, he guessed, not to kill them, but to exorcise them. Martin Luther lashed his back with a whip to subdue his evil spirits, but Blue's demons were different. No amount of lashing would drive them out. God knows he had tried.

He'd hoped marriage would purge his guilt. Wash away all thoughts of the sin. He'd given his heart and life to God. Even gone into the ministry to prove his refusal to let them live.

True, they'd gone underground for awhile, but like anything submerged, they'd just grown bigger. If it hadn't been for Abe, he would have won. But seeing him all the time at church had been too much to resist.

There were such things as false gods. He'd studied about them in seminary. They disguised themselves as good to tempt a man. He'd been tempted—oh God how he'd been tempted.

Then again, God was bigger than this monster. Bigger than Ella. If he could just let go and let God take over his life, he'd be free of this *thing*. He had tried. But he must not've tried hard enough, because the serpent still tempted. In the darkest of night, it tempted. Lying awake, while Ella slept, the demons drove God out and let Satan into the deepest part of his soul.

His passion for men.

He'd kept it at bay for so long the effort wearied him. But God understood. After all, God was a man—a He. Blue was a man too. With God's blessing, he had the authority to claim his property. The Bible even says so. He flipped the pages to 1 Corinthians 11:9, and read, "...for indeed, man was not created for the woman's sake, but woman for the man's sake."

He smiled; he had his text for Bible study next Wednesday night. He could pull this off. No one would know. When the time came, he'd convince them of his innocence.

Of his right.

👁   👁   👁

Sid had found it difficult to concentrate on the murders of Abe and Cherrie Collins—the paying job—but she comforted herself with the fact that Ned Durwood wasn't sitting in jail falsely accused, even though death was not a better alternative.

But she still hadn't located the preacher's wife, and her gut told her she must. She'd called Quade again, tried to submit a missing person's report, but he'd called the church. The secretary reported Ella had gone out of town to visit relatives. She didn't know where, only that Ella's parents needed her help, and Brother Blue would be at church on Sunday.

So would Sid.

Now, she slipped into the back row while the congregation stood and sang *Just As I Am*. She stood, but she didn't sing. She couldn't. Since she'd divorced Sam, she found it impossible to sing a hymn without hot tears clogging her throat. Once-meaningful words now seared as if they were red-hot pokers pushed deep into her heart. She used to sing them in celebration. Now she didn't sing them at all—she guessed for the same reason—but why did hearing them hurt so much?

At length, the hymn ended and the congregation sat. The Most Reverend Humble Bluett stepped to the pulpit and began his sermon on the importance of making God first in your life, and of the evils of alcohol and homosexuality. He claimed the power of God to remake a man, to change a man's very nature from one of sin, to one of righteousness.

Sid had no intention of making herself a spectacle, but in the midst of the sermon, she found herself standing and staring straight at the man.

Taken aback, Blue stopped talking mid-sentence and in those static moments, the congregation followed his line of sight straight to her.

Sid, *the perfect pastor's wife* who never drew attention to herself within her husband's congregation, was now the center of attention in Blue's.

Murmurs, questions, flitted around the room, eyes bouncing from Sid to Blue as if they played a tennis match.

A burly man in a dark blue suit stood and started toward Sid, but before he reached her, she stepped into the aisle, raised her chin, and walked out the door into fresh air.

Damn, she knew he had Ella, but where? And how did she prove it? No one would believe her but Meade. Stomping to her car, she looped her Blue Tooth over her ear and dialed Ian's number.

He answered on the first ring—his voice tight, pinched. For the first time, doubt over Ian eased into Sid's thoughts and coated them like a light layer of dust on fine furniture. Did he know something about Ella's disappearance that he'd not told Sid? Did his interest in shell mounds have anything to do with Abe and Cherrie Collins's murders? At this point Sid couldn't rule out anyone or anything.

"Ian, Sid. Have you heard anything from Ella?"

"Hey Sid, I was just about to call you. No, not a word, but I had a strange message on my answering machine when I got back into town a few minutes ago. I'd tried to check my voice mail while I was gone, but couldn't get it to work. It's—"

"Get to the point, Ian." Sid didn't try to smooth away the irritation in her voice. "What was the message?"

"It was muffled, disguised. At first I thought it was just a prank call, but the more I think about it, the more I wonder. It sounded like a man, well, having—sex—you know."

"What about your caller ID? Can't you tell where the call came from?"

"That's the thing. The caller ID just read Private Call."

Dead air hung between them until Sid spoke. "I'm clueless who it might have been. Maybe it was a wrong number or something. Maybe Quade is right; maybe Ella's gone off to visit family." Sid's words didn't match the lead weight in her chest. "I went to church this morning hoping Ella would be there, or he would say something about her. He didn't. But damn he's good at what he does. The whole congregation sits there mesmerized, hanging onto his every word. He seems more inspired than ever. Energized or something. I don't know what it is."

"I just don't see it." Ian sucked through his teeth. "After what Ella told me, maybe I'm too biased against the guy."

"Like what? What'd she tell you?"

"He's a phony. It's all an act. Ella describes how at times she's awakened in the middle of the night with him lying next to her cursing out loud. One morning after such an event, she got the courage to ask him if he'd been dreaming. But no, he was awake—he knew he'd cursed. She asked him why. He'd simply replied because he felt like it. Weird, huh?"

Sid said goodbye to Ian and they promised to call the other should they hear from Ella.

Times like this were when Sid really missed her former landlady, Sophia. She hadn't lived in the old woman's upstairs apartment long, but enough to develop a respect for her wisdom. She had a way of grounding Sid, and helping her see the big picture. The sight of Sophia, sprawled unconscious among her prized roses, still pinged at Sid's heart.

On impulse, Sid turned under the freeway, drove the short distance to Meeks Drive, and headed toward the Sabine House, where Sophia now lived. Tall pines on both sides of the road created a tunnel of shade as Sid turned into the driveway at the assisted living center.

An attendant invited Sid in and ushered her down the hall to Sophia's room. "Don't be surprised if Sophia doesn't recognize you," the pleasant young woman warned. "The stroke left her able to talk some, but her words might not make sense. It's good you came, though. She needs visitors." She smiled and left Sid at Sophia's door.

Sid knocked and peeked in. "Sophia? It's Sid. May I come in, honey?"

The wizened woman sat hunched in a rocking chair, a shell of the woman Sid had known. Her beautiful white mane lay plastered against her head. Once-wise, sparkling eyes were now dull and red-rimmed. She lifted her head toward Sid's voice.

"I'm sorry I haven't been by sooner, sweetie. How are you?"

Saliva filled the droopy corner of Sophia's mouth. Sid grabbed a tissue from the box on the table and dabbed it off, tossed the tissue in a nearby trash basket.

Sid talked about her aunt and the house on Pine Street, her office burning down and the relocation of the Third Eye. Eventually she ran out of conversation and just sat, her heart bleeding at the woman's deterioration.

Sophia stared at the floor.

"Its okay, Sophia, you don't have to talk. I just wanted to tell you I miss you."

Tears welled in the corner of the old woman's eyes. "K-K-a..."

"No, sweetheart, it's Sid." Sid's heart thumped faster.

"No, no, say, Aun—Ka—waitin'—for—me." The sentence was disjointed; the words were mumbled half-syllables, but clear enough to make the hair rise on Sid's arms. She leaned closer to the crone who still struggled to speak.

"No, 's oay—Ka say—I can—cross. Sh—helpin' you now."

👁   👁   👁

Kate visited Sid that night. She called the apparition Kate now. It didn't matter. No one would believe she saw a ghost anyway, except maybe Sophia. Hell, Sid didn't believe it herself. Maybe she was going crazy, but she swore the woman flitted through the room, staring at Sid while she lay wide-awake. Or was she? In dreams, sometimes, a person felt like they were awake. And if it were a ghost, wouldn't Slider sense the energy in the room, instead of sleeping through it?

Sid collected her flashlight and slipped out of the bedroom, careful not to awaken Slider. At least she didn't have to worry about disturbing Annie, who was still at the farm. That's all she needed, Annie believing she was crazy, too.

At the top of the stairs, Sid flipped on the small light bulb and inched over to the chest.

The air wasn't as musty as it had been. A quiet stillness blanketed the room. Quiet, not only from a lack of sound, but from a silence so full she felt like some type of transmutation melded her into someone else, into Kate.

She really was going crazy.

The diary lay where she'd left it, wrapped in its cocoon of crinoline. She opened the book and flipped through the pages, transported backward, to the 1800s.

September 6, 1862

Yellow Jack came ashore by one of the blockade-runners sometime in July. The dreaded fever is now epidemic. Folks are dropping like flies. This time it is bad. Really bad. We have lost close to a hundred people by now and still many more are near death. Today we lost our precious adopted daughter Alberta from the virulent fever. She was twelve years old. We had hoped she was immune, since she was a just a baby during the epidemic in Mobile, over ten years ago—the same epidemic that took their parents. I can still see her and Josie playing Annie Over *out near the swing. Breaks my heart to see—*

A long blank space was left at the bottom of the page, as if grief had overtaken the writer and she'd simply stopped. Sid turned the page, her own heart feeling the pain of the other.

September 15, 1862

Still the yellow jack kills. Our settlement has gone from over 3,000 souls, to just under 300. Most of the residents fled at the first outbreak, and I fear they carried the yellow fever with them. We have lost near forty Confederate soldiers to the disease, and only a handful of us left to tend them. My dear friends Sarah Vosburg, and Peggy Watson, stayed behind with me to nurse those who couldn't leave. Sarah was the first one to recognize the disease. Since all three of us are immune, we turned the Catfish Hotel into a hospital, doing what we can to alleviate suffering. It is the least we can do for these boys fighting a terrible war here on the home front. Only about thirty soldiers are left on their feet from two military companies, and their main job is to bury the dead.

Another wide space, and then...

September 30, 1862

The pestilence still rages. Now, the Union squadron invades the Pass. With only sixteen defenders fit for duty, they evacuated Fort Sabine. The Blue Coats have destroyed the fort and its barracks, but for the most part they have left us in town alone. No one wants to come close to the fever. Union soldiers captured our steamer the Dan and were harassing all points along the coast. So during a heavy fog our soldiers bound about 40 pine knot torches together, put them in a whale boat, along with a wash pot of live coals surrounded with bricks to blaze their torches, rowed out and set fire to the Dan. Lifted all our spirits.

Sid sat a moment while the energy of the past spiraled around her.

October 15, 1862

As if we did not have enough to contend with caring for the sick and dying, three Yankee gunboats fired a few shells at the town today, and a shore party burned the Confederate barracks and stable. Then, three or four dozen Yanks came ashore toting a howitzer they stole off the Dan and took my horse and cart to carry it to use against our boys. Folks say my red hair matches my ire. Well, today it sure as hell did. When I saw them Yanks out front I was perfectly enraged, picked up my skirts and ran out into the yard, my husband fast after me. Shook my fist at them I did, and told them I hope the Rebels kill every blasted one of you. I'd do it myself if I had twenty-five able-bodied men to fight with me. You come in here and do this to my town when my men are all laid up with the fever? Shame on you.

God forgive me, I used blackguard language in the severe tongue-lashing I gave those Yanks. If Mama'd been there she would have taken me to the woodshed for sure. I don't know if the men felt ashamed or whether they were just polite, but they returned my horse and cart, and told my husband, if you don't keep your damn wife's mouth shut we will come back and hang you. Then they demanded I apologize or they would come back and burn my hotel down. I guess I should have kept my mouth shut, but I yelled at them, I'll see you in the lower regions of hell first, and you may burn it down if you damn well choose.

Despite their advice, Captain Dorman never attempted to quiet my acidic tongue. He never was one to take up lost causes.

The next entry was short, unfinished, as if written in a big hurry.

October 22, 1862

The Union soldiers returned today, and burned down a quarter of the town. But they didn't touch the Catfish Hotel. I laughed…

The next entry was undated, as if its author felt driven to record critical events.

I heard today that the T.J. Smith, repaired from the explosion that killed my dear departed first husband Arthur, was confiscated by the Rebels when its owner H. C. Smith defected to the Bluecoats. His defection so angered me that tomorrow I plan to sue Captain Smith to collect Art's wages never paid to me after his death.

Images of her Kate holding off the Union Army with only her tongue as a weapon brought a smile to Sid's lips. After a few minutes, she closed the diary and returned it to its rightful place. Fascinating history, but why did Sid feel it had something to do with her and the Third Eye, now burned to the ground? And what about Ella?

Maybe the place was more than a structure.

Sixteen

The next morning, Sid took Slider for his usual *potty walk* and when they returned he gobbled down his usual yogurt-coated dog food. Just as Sid poured herself a bowl of shredded wheat, minus the yogurt, she heard someone on the back porch, and then, "Siddie, I'm home."

For once, the fingers-down-a-chalkboard voice of her aunt didn't seem nearly as bad as Sid remembered. "Hey. You're back." Sid held Annie at arms length, gave her the once over. Annie wore black spandex pants, stretched out at the knees by what looked like tennis balls, a purple knit top that stopped below her hips, black dangly earrings, and deep purple lipstick. "You're a sight for sore eyes."

"I'm back where I belong." Annie plopped Chesterfield on the floor.

Slider backed into the corner.

"I felt like such a wuss running out on you like that. I don't know why a dead man on my doorstep upset me." Annie laughed. "It's not like I don't see one every day."

Sid looked her square in the eye. "You sure you're okay, and that you can handle this?"

"Of course I'm sure," Annie said, puffing up her chest. She poured herself a cup of coffee and headed to the table. "Come on, sit and eat your breakfast, I ate already." She patted Sid's chair. "You eating okay? Did you pay the bills? We don't want them to be late now, do we?"

Sid opened her mouth, hesitated and then shut it.

"Tell me what's happening?" Annie scooted Sid's bowl closer to her niece.

While Sid ate, she brought Annie up to date.

But Annie seemed more interested in Sid's love life than she did the case. "What about that Ben fellow, he been around?"

Sid ignored the question. She stood and dumped her empty bowl in the sink, picked up Annie's bag and led her out of the room with, "Come on, let's get you unpacked."

Upstairs, Sid perched on the bed as Annie rattled off the latest news from the farm while unpacking her suitcase and hanging the outlandish-looking clothes in the closet.

Half-listening to the prattle, Sid battled with whether or not to tell her aunt about the ghost. After all, it was Annie's house. Finally, she gathered her courage and confessed she'd seen a ghost, but stopped just short of the diary—why, she wasn't sure. After all, the diary's presence couldn't be disputed, the ghost's could.

"Horse feathers." Annie blew Sid's story off with a hand wave. "Now I don't mean to laugh at you, but there ain't no such thing as ghosts. You know better than that."

"Yeah, that's what I keep telling myself." Annie's response shut down any further revelations from Sid.

They spent the day getting the new office organized, making trips to the office supply store, going over the financial situation, and discussing advertising opportunities. Sid didn't bring up the subject of ghosts again, but her mind kept wandering to the diary upstairs, and for some weird reason, kept feeling its author looking over her shoulder.

That night Sid crawled in between the covers and lay wide awake watching the moon creep higher in the sky. Ghost or no, it felt good to have another living, breathing person in the house. She reviewed the clues to the murders of Abe and Cherrie Collins like chess pieces moved around on a board, with no idea who was innocent or guilty. Marv still flitted in the back of her mind. He knew more than he had let on. And what about Ella?

Hell, Sid didn't even know if the woman was missing or not. Admonishing herself for worrying about Ella, who wasn't even listed as a missing person, let alone her case, Sid realized she'd slid back into trying to save the whole world. Her job, the one she got paid for, was to clear Ned's name of the deaths of Abe and Cherrie Collins.

Sid flipped over and adjusted the covers.

Jack Agnes was now dead—on her doorstep, nonetheless—but what was his tie to the murders? And why was he coming to see her that night? It must have been late, or rather early; she'd been up until the wee hours, and his blood was still fresh when she'd found him.

The pillows thumped and the covers adjusted once again, Sid flipped to her other side, switched on the lamp, looked up a number and dialed Ella's cell phone.

Nothing.

Stop it Sid. Leave Ella alone. Focus on Ned. After all, Ella was probably just off visiting family, as the reverend had said.

The one person she hadn't categorized yet was Sheriff Bonin. Good-looking son of a… It irritated the hell out of her that her knees felt weak when he came around. But why was he so quick to close the case on Ned? Was he that convinced? If so, what did he know that Sid didn't?

Seventeen

The next morning, without a clue what to do next, Sid again busied herself in her makeshift office. She called the insurance adjuster who promised, one more time, that he'd be by to check on the burned-out building and get her an estimate on the claim.

Just to touch base, but with nothing new to report, she called Dempsey Durwood.

Then, unable to resist the urge any longer, she again dialed Ella's cell phone. No answer.

At mid-morning, the phone rang, and it was Ben calling to ask her out for dinner. Relieved to at least have something on her schedule, she accepted, but this time built a shield around her heart.

The rest of the day passed as boring and uneventful as the first.

That evening, Ben showed up right on time as usual, and she greeted him at the door, dressed and ready. The last thing she wanted to do was leave him alone with Annie for any length of time. But before Sid could get Ben out the front door, Annie stuck her head out of the kitchen. "Hi, Ben, it's about time you showed them charmin' charmin' eyes around here, young man."

Sid cringed.

Ben smiled. "I love this old place Annie. You've fixed it up right nice, hey, Slider," he stopped and patted the dogs head. "No one would guess it had lain empty for years. It has a lot of history, you know." Sid shook her head at Ben, but he continued. A hint of a smile played around the corners of his mouth. "Rumor around town is that the place is haunted, and has been for years. I'm sure Sid told you."

"Haunted, shmaunted." Annie waved her hand. "That's just kids making up stories."

Sid nudged Ben in the ribs.

"Sure, kid stuff." He squeezed Sid's hand. "Nothing to it—besides, you and I don't believe in such things do we?"

Sid did. She'd *seen* Kate.

They drove to Tuffy's in Mauriceville. When they were seated, their server delivered a basket of yeasty, fresh-baked hot rolls and a small ramekin piled high with honey-butter. Sid wouldn't dare tell Annie how good the rolls were.

Over dessert, Sid broached the topic that had been on her mind all afternoon. "What do you know about Sheriff Bonin?"

"Bonin?" Ben's brow furled. "Why?"

Sid shrugged.

"He's okay, I guess. Always runs unopposed. I keep trying to talk Quade into running against him, but so far, I haven't been successful."

"Humph." Sid licked blackberry cobbler off her spoon. "I don't know. I just keep feeling like he's taking the easy way out with the Collins couple's murder."

"But, Sid, Ned's fingerprints were on the murder weapon, his footprints were in the house. What more do you want?"

"Motive. What possible reason would Ned have had to brutally murder a couple who wanted to hire him to create a piece of art for their front yard?"

"No telling. Maybe they argued over the price, and Ned just lost his head, I don't know."

"I can't buy that."

"Well, good luck, but I think you've taken on an unsolvable case. Don't feel bad, we all do that. We can't win 'em all."

Irritation crept up Sid's backbone. He tried to sound encouraging, but Sid felt like an idiot for taking the case.

They finished dinner and walked outside. The humid, southeast Texas air swallowed them up like a lizard gulping down a fly.

Without even asking, Ben drove to his house. After parking in the driveway, he hurried around and opened Sid's car door, saying, "No more talk of business tonight, okay?" He offered her his hand out, and then circled her waist with his arm as they walked up the sidewalk.

Inside, he poured two glasses of champagne, dimmed the lights, and then sat beside her on the sofa.

Champagne was a drink she'd learned to reserve for special occasions due to its influence on her resistance, or lack thereof. She took slow, deliberate sips.

When he leaned over and kissed her ear, she smelled his earthiness, his pheromones in overdrive.

"God you look good." He walked his fingers down her arm.

Tired of resisting, she didn't.

👁 👁 👁

Ella heard the crackle of footsteps over dead branches just before a bright light slashed into the room, and there stood Blue silhouetted in the entrance. He pushed the door shut behind him and disappeared in the darkness, but she could feel him moving toward her.

She heard the rattle of glass against metal, the strike of a match, and then a small flame flickered inside a kerosene lamp Blue had set on the floor.

For one brief moment Ella thought the nightmare was over, that he'd had his kicks and felt repentant. But when he knelt beside her and she looked into his eyes, she knew she was mistaken.

He grabbed her chin and squeezed it between his fingers. "Miss me?" His alcohol breath churned her empty stomach.

"Blue, don't do this," she begged. "You don't want to hurt me. You're just upset, angry. I'm sorry. I won't ever do that again."

"Do what again?" He shoved his face into hers. "What did

you do? Tell me. Say it."

"Unfaithful—I was unfaithful to..."

Before she could finish he'd slammed her down hard. "I want to see tits again, *my* tits," he yelled, straddling her. He snatched at her blouse and ripped it open.

She writhed and thrashed in a desperate attempt to escape him. "Blue, don't. Please don't, not this way."

Infuriated with his flaccid member, he rubbed it in his hand until it hardened enough to jam inside her. But as soon as he did, it went limp again. He repeated the action over and over, growing more agitated with each attempt. Finally, he snatched his jacket off the floor, pulled out a bottle of water and tossed it at her. "Make it last," he ordered, picked up the lantern, and slammed the door behind him.

Outside, the wooden plank squealed in place.

👁   👁   👁

Sid parked in front of the charred remains of The Third Eye. If she ever got this thing settled with the insurance company, she'd have to decide whether to rebuild a new office or stay at Annie's. She mused as to what the business represented to her, perhaps even to others. Funny that Warren had chosen a double-entendre for the business name. He always had been rather mystical.

Her religious world hadn't allowed for such things. Now, she guessed there really might be something to the metaphysical world she'd been taught to shun.

She backed out, circled around and drove to George Léger's office, a yellow prefab building squatting beneath palm trees. She felt relieved when she saw his car parked out front.

"George, I'm stumped on the murders of Abe and Cherrie Collins." Sid threw her hands up in the air. "I don't know where to go from here. I've farted around here and there, but still have no clue what happened that day. I'm even ashamed to go back and see Mr. Durwood, Ned's father. I'm not sure I'll even have a business if I can't figure out this mess. And what's worse, I have this sinking feeling Ella Bluett is missing, although her husband swears she's not. Call me crazy, but at times I even wonder if he might have killed the Collins."

George dunked his doughnut into his coffee and bit off the soggy piece, dripping crumbs and coffee down his shirt. He grabbed a napkin and blotted. "How do you figure?" He dumped the napkin on the table and looked up at her. "By the way, did you get out to the shell mounds?"

Sid nodded. "Absolutely nothing. Oh, that reminds me, I've got your waders in my SUV. Help me remember to give them to you before I leave."

"Sure. No hurry. So how do you tie the preacher in to all of this?"

"Abe and Cherrie Collins were members of Blue's church. Ella's disappearance, Jack Agnes's death on my porch—it all seems too coincidental." Sid bit the bottom of her lip. "Maybe it's my own bias. Maybe I just don't like the Reverend Blue. Something about him seems unreal, dishonest. I can't put my finger on it."

"You know he was born and raised here." George leaned back in his chair and patted his full belly. "Most preachers don't come back to their hometown to pastor. I was surprised when he moved back here with his wife and got this church going. Started meeting in people's homes, had Bible Study, that sort of thing. Before long, he had enough money to put up a building. Have you met that holy-woman secretary of his? Now she's a tight-ass if I ever saw one." George held his stomach and laughed.

"Who did he hang out with when he was a kid?"

"Far as I recollect, he hung out with this one group of boys who'd been friends for years. Until one day, one of 'em up and disappeared. Family lived down on Scott Street."

"Where's Scott Street?"

"Down yonder off of Border—right before you get to the Cove. House sits on the right between two empty lots, or did, unless someone's built there lately. It's been a hundred years since I been down that way."

"And he just up and disappeared? What happened?"

"Dangedest thing. One day he was here, going about his business like any other kid, and then the next day he was gone. No trace. After a couple of years the police just stopped looking."

"Hmm." Not wanting to get sidetracked off the Collins murders again, Sid asked no more questions about the missing teenager. Instead, she gulped her last swallow of coffee and invited George outside.

They transferred the waders and spade from Sid's car to his truck then George put his arm around her shoulder and pulled her in tightly. "What 'cha thinking about kiddo?"

"About Ella and Blue, and if they tie into Abe and Cherrie Collins' murders."

"Then I guess I didn't help you none." He laughed and gave her a final hug. "Sorry, sha. But just be patient with yourself. It's all gonna come together. You just wait and see. Keep asking those questions and following them leads—a tried and true process that'll get you there every time."

By the time Sid got back to her office, the phone was ringing off the hook. She snatched it up and greeted the caller without checking the caller ID.

"Mom?"

"Chad. Hi, Sweetheart. What a neat surprise. Everything okay?" She always asked that first, settling any discomfort that arose when either of her children called unexpectedly. The curse of motherhood, she supposed.

"I'm fine, Mom."

Just hearing her son's voice made her smile. A forensic archeology graduate student at the University of Texas, he always sounded like fun and adventure hid just below the surface of his words.

"Having a blast," he added.

"Great." Chad seldom called just to chat. He had at first, but after a couple years of college life he grew involved in his own world of friends. She missed his chatty calls.

"How's the Third Eye business? You're not taking anymore cases like that first one are you?"

"I'm fine, honey, staying busy." She ignored the second question. "You got my email that I'd moved in with Aunt Annie, huh?"

"That was a big surprise." Chad laughed.

"To me, too, but it seemed reasonable at the time. So far, everything's working out okay."

"We were wondering…"

Okay, here it comes, Sid thought.

"…a bunch of us guys were sitting around here talking about coming over there for the weekend to go frog-gigging."

"Frog-gigging? I would ask what that is, but I'm afraid I know. How do I figure into this hunt?"

"We were wondering if Aunt Annie's house was big enough that we could bed down with y'all. We'd bring our bed rolls." Male voices in the background almost drowned out Chad's voice.

"How many guys are you talking about? Sounds like a dozen or more."

"Just four of us. These guys are just acting like fools." He muffled the phone and yelled, "Quiet down guys, I can't hear." Then back to her, "Sorry, Mom. What we're thinking is we'd drive over from Austin tomorrow, be there by noon, go gigging tomorrow night, and then drive back to Austin on Sunday. Some of us have exams on Monday."

As they talked, Annie came into the office with cups of steaming coffee. "Hang on a minute, Aunt Annie just walked in. Let me check with her." Sid lowered the receiver to her chest, looked up at Annie. "It's Chad. He and three friends want to come over tomorrow, go frog-gigging tomorrow night then go home on Sunday."

Annie grinned. "They want to crash here? We've got plenty of floor space in those empty bedrooms upstairs."

"That's the idea." Sid smiled, cringing.

"Tell 'em come on. It looks rainified though. They might should bring umbrellas, rain gear."

When Sid relayed the message and Chad passed it on, cheers rang out in the background. "Chad, do you know anything about gigging frogs?"

"I don't, but Aaron does. He's from Mermanteau, Louisiana. They went frogging as a kid. We'll get the gigs after we get there. Oh, and don't plan dinner for Saturday night. We're going to cook for you."

"You're going to cook?" Sid sputtered. "I didn't know you knew how."

"Hey, you're paying for an education aren't you? Besides, we're big fans of Alton Brown on the Food Network."

👁   👁   👁

Chad bounded up the steps two at the time. Just as he reached the porch, Sid swung open the screen door. "Hi, Sweetheart, you made it." After their traditional bear hugs, she held him at arms length, scrutinizing. "University life agrees with you, babe. Looks like you've put on a few pounds. You look fantastic. But what's with all this hair?" She yanked on his pony tail.

"I figured if I ever wanted to try long hair, graduate school was the best time to do it. What do you think?" He swung around his thick brown mane.

"You've got a beautiful head of hair, regardless of how you wear it." Sid delighted in bragging on her kids, and in Chad's enthusiasm. "Where are your friends?"

"They're unloading the car. Come on, I'll introduce you."

👁   👁   👁

That evening Sid and Annie sat around the large square table in the kitchen and watched as Chad, Aaron, Parker, and Kirk puttered around the kitchen, bantering back and forth, drinking dark beer. By the time the guys finished preparations, the table was loaded with Steak au Poivre, rice pilaf, broiled artichokes, and burned-peach ice cream for dessert.

Sid's chest felt tighter than her over-stuffed stomach as she watched Chad interact with his friends and the four of them relate to Annie, now putty in their hands.

Cleanup was a breeze with six people in the kitchen. By nine o'clock the guys had gathered their gigs, hip waders, headlights and mesh bags and tumbled out the door in a steady stream of energy.

Shortly thereafter, Annie retired to her bedroom, exhausted and giddy from all the testosterone-laden attention.

Sid went to bed near midnight and quickly fell asleep until her cell phone jangled on the bedside table.

"Mom?"

Her heart pounded. "Chad? Are you all okay?"

"We're fine, Mom, sorry to wake you. But I think you better get out here."

"Out where?"

"We're out on the Neches River…" The line crackled. At first she thought she'd lost the connection, but then, "…we just found a skeleton."

"What did you say?" Sid sat straight up in bed, brushed her hand through her hair.

"We were tramping through this brush looking for frogs. Kirk hadn't gotten one yet, and when he saw one, he got pretty aggressive—half-buried the poor critter. He scrambled after it, and when he did, he uncovered bones of a human hand."

"A hand?"

"Looks like the remains of a boy or a small woman. We haven't dug any further yet, but we don't think the bones are Atakapa Indian. They buried their dead in these middens, but first inspection, this one's not that old. Hopefully we can find teeth for dental identification. Figured we better get the authorities involved. You want to call them or shall we?" Chad's words ran a marathon out his mouth.

Chad—the consummate forensics archaeologist—"Tell me

exactly how to find you. I'll call Chief Burns, and meet you out there."

She grabbed a pen and paper from her bedside drawer and wrote down the directions, hung up and dialed Quade's house.

"Burns here." Quade's husky voice barked into the phone.

"Sorry to wake you, buddy. This is Sid. My son, Chad, is in town with some friends and they're out frog-gigging tonight. He just called on his cell phone. They dug up part of a skeleton out in the middle of the swamp, says its not old enough to be a part of the Indian culture."

👁   👁   👁

The sun cast its first orange glow across the muddy water as Quade's crew finished, and loaded paraphernalia back into their boats. Quade walked over to Sid, brushing swamp residue off his clothes. "We're about done here. God, this swamp will never be the same after all this traipsing across the mounds. Archaeologists are gonna shit their britches when they see what we've done." Regret softened his voice. "At least we had oversight from the students to help us minimize the damage."

Hours earlier, he had picked Sid up on his way out to the dock where the recovery team waited for them. Deep in the swamp, they'd found the four young men standing at water's edge signaling their location with headlamps.

The crew of four, counting Quade, had brought along a body bag for the recovery of the remains, shovels, rakes, latex gloves, and kerosene lanterns.

Quade had questioned the young men. How did you find it? Exactly where was the location? What have you touched? Did you see anything else?

Chad and his friends took turns answering the questions, proud of their forensics education. Big Kirk—with the buzz haircut—showed them an orange sock he'd found amidst the shell, leaves, and other trash in the burial site.

"Okay, let's wrap it up." Quade shook the student's hands.

"You did a fine job. Looks like we'll be in good hands after you graduate." He smiled at Chad. "Be sure your buddies leave their names and phone numbers with your mom here. I know we'll have more questions later." He turned to Sid. "Can you ride back to your house with Chad? That way I can go straight home, shower, eat, and then head to the coroner's office."

"Sure. I need to get home and work on myself, too." She pulled her damp jeans out from her body, and jiggled her foot to dislodge trash stuck on her shoe. "Plus, I need to get these guys something to eat before they head back to Austin."

Pride swelled her chest as Sid put her arms around the waists of Chad and Aaron as the five headed to the canoe.

Before Sid stepped into the boat, Quade called her over to the side. "When I get done at the coroner's, I'll give you a call." He stood with his hands on his hips, grinning. "I figure you're going to want to know more about who this is."

Sid's heart pounded. "Is that possible? Can I?"

"Come by and we'll talk. If this is who I think it is, I suspect we'll have an ID by then."

"You already know who it is?"

"From the looks of things, I think this may be a young boy who's been on the missing list for twenty years. Orange socks are dang easy to remember."

👁   👁   👁

Sid stepped under the steaming hot water and scrubbed the scent of swamp death off her skin. She stuck her face down into the soapy, sweet-smelling wash cloth and inhaled, hoping to rid the foul odor from her nostrils.

Just as she stepped out of the bathroom, a soft tap sounded on her bedroom door. "Mom, can I talk to you a minute?"

"Sure, son, just a sec." She gathered the belt around her robe and opened the door to Chad, dressed in blue jeans and burnt orange sweatshirt with a white logo of a Texas Longhorn, his hair still damp from his shower.

"There's something I wanted to talk with you about before we head back to school." Chad's lips stretched into a hesitant grin. "Something I should have told you earlier, but I was afraid you'd think I was crazy."

"Come in, sit down." Sid indicated the window seat, while she plopped on the bed. "I promise I won't think you're crazy, although I have some doubts about myself these days." She chuckled, but didn't explain herself to Chad.

She missed their talks. When Chad was thirteen, fourteen, he'd come in and lay across the cedar chest at the foot of her bed and chat about his life.

"I didn't tell you the whole story about why I called to come frog-gigging."

"Oh?"

"I didn't because I don't fully know why myself." Chad twisted in his chair. "I just—I saw something weird the other day—I don't know what it was—but—*it* wanted me to come here and dig in the swamp."

Sid's pulse thumped in her ears.

"I knew the guys would think I was crazy if I told them I'd seen a ghost or something, so I just made up the frog-gigging idea, and they latched onto that."

A nervous laugh slid into the room, but Sid wasn't sure if it had come from Chad or her.

He looked out the window then cut his eyes to the floor, and finally down to his fidgety hands. "You know how guys are, always interested in going somewhere and doing something—anything."

He stopped the nervous chatter and looked his mother in the eye. A discomfort filled the space between them.

She had to do it. She had to admit to her son that she, too, had seen a ghost. She sucked in a deep breath before she spoke. "Was your ghost a redhead, and did she wear a long, filmy dress?"

Chad blanched, his eyes, bugs on sticks.

👁   👁   👁

Sid walked into Quade's office, saw he was on the phone and started to walk out when he motioned her to a chair. Sympathy covered his demeanor as he talked, flipping through pages on a clipboard. "Skull fracture, uh huh…"

After Quade ended his phone conversation, Sid leaned forward. "I guess that means you've got an ID on the remains."

" 'fraid so. It's who I thought it was all right. Name was Caleb Hebert. Officials at the time figured either he ran away, or someone kidnapped him. Coroner made a quick, positive ID by the dental records on file. Blunt injury to the skull. We figure someone killed him then carried him out there. Good place to hide a body."

Sid sat with her mouth open. What overwhelming odds.

Eighteen

Blue flipped his Study Bible closed and shoved it across the kitchen table. Even though it was mid-morning, he still wore a bathrobe and a heavy stubble.

He'd tossed and turned all night, guilt eating him alive. Now what did he do? If only Ella hadn't gotten involved with another man—not just any man, but the man *he* wanted for himself. He'd never approached Ian Meade because something told him the guy was straight. Like Blue wished *he* was. He hated being different. He hated this attraction women had for him. They hung onto him like he was something sacred.

Truth was, he egged them on, used them as a cover of who he really was—a homo in the midst of homophobes.

The role of pastor insured he received equal treatment—no—more than equal.

Blue pushed his shoulders back, and for a minute, reveled in the superior feeling.

But the demons inside wouldn't let him alone.

Everything would have been okay if Cherrie hadn't come back to the house to get something she'd needed for her Sunday School class, and found him in bed with Abe. They'd tried talking her down but she'd been livid, threatened to go to the deacons. He'd told her they'd all be ruined if this got out, that they should all just get in their cars and go to church, act like nothing happened. But for once his persuasive powers over women held no control. Cherrie turned and stormed into the kitchen then returned with a butcher knife, catching both of them by surprise. One swing and Abe fell, a horrible sound gurgling in his throat. Then she had come after Blue too, but he'd grabbed the knife.

He hadn't meant to kill Cherrie, but he had to defend himself. He damned sure wasn't going to let her ruin everything he'd worked for. Not that he'd had much of a choice, as wild as she was.

Thankfully he'd maintained enough sanity to wipe his fingerprints off of the knife.

Blue shuddered, straightened his back and again flipped open his Bible. The book fell open at the Book of Numbers. He chewed on his fingernails as he scanned the page. That is until his eyes locked on the name of Caleb, Gods faithful servant.

Memories he'd buried years ago, crept around the edges of Blue's denial.

Like Cherrie, he hadn't meant to kill Caleb; he'd only shoved the boy, shocked by his own feelings when Caleb had leaned over and kissed him. He hadn't meant for Caleb to hit his head. He hadn't meant for Caleb to die. God knew he hadn't meant any of it.

He loved Caleb, Blue had known since he was three years old that he could spend the rest of his life with the boy. But he'd never admitted it, to Caleb or anyone else.

Images of himself, Abe, and Bonin shoveling shells into the grave tore through the shield Blue had erected around his heart.

Antsy, he flipped the pages again.

Yea, though I walk through the valley of the shadow of death, thou art with me. Thy rod and thy staff they comfort me.

Then—

If we confess our sins, He is faithful and just to forgive us our sins and to cleanse us from all unrighteousness.

Why didn't he feel forgiven?

But if we walk in the light as He is in the light, we have fellowship with one another, and the blood of Jesus Christ cleanses us from our sin.

His parishioners adored Blue, the community as well. Didn't that mean something?

A freight train barreled through his chest.

He'd thought his teen years were rough. Every ounce of energy went into convincing folks he wasn't who he knew he was. Hell, at spring break he'd even gone with college friends to San Francisco and harassed the faggots, just to prove he wasn't one of them. Whether to himself or to the world, he wasn't sure. But in the deepest part of himself, he'd been humiliated when his friends put down the homos, for he knew in his heart of hearts, he was one. Had he been conceived by Satan or something—to be born this way? People said it was a choice. Who in hell would choose this misery?

More from habit than hunger, Blue toasted a slice of bread, scrambled eggs, and then carried his plate into the living room and turned on the T.V.

Ellen De Generes danced, awkward, un-choreographed.

He poked at his food. Ella. He missed her. How could he get himself out of this mess? He hadn't wanted to hurt her. Truth be known, he didn't even blame her. Hell, if Ian had been gay he'd have beat Ella to him. He hated this urge, didn't understand why he couldn't change—couldn't be something he wasn't.

Ellen De Generes stopped dancing. The local news commentator came on with a special news bulletin. Lost in his own torment, Blue ignored the T.V. until he saw the newscaster standing in front of Caleb's childhood home.

He stopped, fork in mid-air.

"Early yesterday morning, the police uncovered the skeletal remains of a young boy, now identified as Caleb Hebert, a thirteen-year-old boy that disappeared over twenty years ago. The body, half-buried in shell mounds near the Neches River, was discovered by university students who were frog-gigging. Police have re-opened the cold case."

Blue's tray fell to the floor.

He sprinted to the kitchen and tossed the dishes, tray and all, in the sink. Upstairs, he pulled on jeans and t-shirt, and then charged to his van. He had to get to Ella.

👁   👁   👁

In the middle of the night Sid had awakened from a dream, convinced she'd entered another dimension. The scrappy woman had flitted in and out looking like a mixture between Sid, the picture of the red-headed spitfire in the attic, and the one on Dempsey's sideboard. An epidemic of some sort raged. Bugs as big as houses, rammed into people and knocked them dead. She was in a house—no, a hotel—but the hotel was a hospital, sick and dying everywhere. Tiny Kate—she guessed it was Kate—or was it Sid?—hustled around, breathless, tending to them all.

It took her a while to fall back to sleep, but she awoke again before daylight with the journal beckoning her upstairs. She threw back the covers, slipped on shoes and climbed the attic stairs to retrieve the leather-bound book. This time, giving up on her commitment to leave the book in the attic, she tiptoed downstairs, eased through the darkened house to the kitchen and flipped the light switch. After her eyes adjusted to the brightness, she pulled out the teakettle and made herself a cup of tea. Settling at the table, she ran her hands over the once-supple binding, took a deep breath, and opened the book.

November 3, 1859

Today, my precious husband joined our daughter Jamie and the angels in heaven. We buried Arthur McGill right down beside her, underneath the cypress tree. Yesterday, the boiler exploded on the 100-foot mail packet, the T.J. Smith. Killed him instantly. Arthur was the chief engineer of the steamer packing mail down the Neches River. He was proud of his job on the Smith and was well thought of by everyone far and wide. Henry Green, a correspondent of the Galveston Weekly News *wrote about Arthur's death aboard the T. J. Smith. He said Arthur made the packet run "like lightning with a thunderbolt after it." He also wrote that my Art was scientific in his line, very careful, and experienced. But, still, when the boiler exploded, Arthur died. Arthur this and Arthur that. I feel like if I keep saying his name he won't be dead. But he is. My Arthur is dead.*

Now, it's just the girls and me—alone—in this land of swamp and mosquitoes.

Kate's sadness penetrated Sid's senses, transported her back to that day standing beside a hole dug in the soggy ground. Next to her, Kate's cold, dead husband lay prone in a hastily built pine box. Men close the lid and lower it into the ground, cover it with shovels-full of wet, black, gumbo dirt. Red-headed Kate, so short she looks like a child herself, stands next to the grave, alone now with three small daughters to rear in a harsh, coastal frontier community.

Sid saw it all.

She flipped over a few pages, hoping for a brighter day. One short entry caught her eye.

June 1860

Today I wed widower, Captain John Dorman, master of the cotton steamer, the Doctor Massie. John was a friend of Arthur's. He is a good man and will be good help with the girls and the hotel. The war and the blockade-runners have kept my hotel and restaurant busier than I can handle by myself. Now, they set up a coastal artillery installation called Fort Griffin just about three hundred yards from here to help fight the war with the north.

Mesmerized by the woman, Sid flipped a few more pages and stopped again.

July 1861

Dutch Margaret marched into my dining room a few months ago, right in the middle of me serving my customers, and vilified me in some of the most blackguard language I have ever heard. Seems her man, Lem, did not come home for supper the night before. Seems he prefers Kate's catfish and doughnuts, to his own wife's cooking. I don't blame him. She cooks like an old goat. But I have never been accused of not saying what is on my mind and I let her have it right back. I thought that settled the matter. But without me knowing it, my dearest friends heard the attack and marched out into the street and caned the woman on the head with their parasols. Lord I wish I could have seen that. Dutch Margaret got so mad she went around telling everyone the caning caused her to lose the child in her womb. Hells bells, who ever heard of losing a baby from getting hit on the head with a parasol? That woman is insane. Now she is bringing a lawsuit, claiming the attack caused the miscarriage. H. C. Pedigo, Dutch Margaret's attorney, questioned the county residence of juror Will Collins. The trial had to be postponed until they could survey the county line and Mr. Collins' land boundary. Meanwhile the case was quashed. Now, three months later, Dutch Margaret births a healthy baby boy. I suppose if the case had gone to trial Dutch Margaret's baby would have been Exhibit A. I heard tell the woman is so embarrassed she plans to move out of the county. I say good riddance.

Sid chuckled under her breath, closed the book and tucked it under her arm. Back in her room, she crawled under the warm bedcovers, diary and all, and dreamed about wars fought between umbrellas, Cottonclads, and mosquitoes big enough to carry them all off.

Nineteen

"Hey lazybones," Annie announced in singsong fashion, slinging aside Sid's bedroom drapes. Her aunt had always personified the adage of early birds and worms, but how on earth could she possibly be so early-morning-cheery? Sunlight streamed through the windows like a spotlight glaring down on a police lineup.

Sid pushed the palms of her hands against her eyes, rolled over and groaned.

Meanwhile, Annie snatched up the remote control, punched on the television, and tossed the remote on the bed. "I thought you might like to see this tape delay broadcast from last Sunday. That preacher is saying something about his wife."

Half asleep, Sid swung her feet to the cold floor. The sharp click of Annie's heels on hardwood floors echoed down the stairs while Humble Bluett's voice crashed through the cobwebs in Sid's head. She blinked at the screen. The preacher stood at the pulpit explaining how his wife had gone out of town for a few days to visit her ailing parents.

By now, the dog was awake too. He'd schlepped over, leapt onto the bed, and curled next to her.

"Well, I guess the woman really is out of town, Slider. The man wouldn't lie to his congregation, would he?"

She switched off the television and flopped back on the bed, eager to reclaim sleep.

"Or would he?"

Her eyes popped open.

Why not? If he'd done something to Ella, wouldn't he try to deceive everyone?

She gave up on any more sleep, showered and dressed, and after taking Slider for his walk, they headed to the kitchen.

Annie stood at the table humming and kneading dough. "Fresh hot rolls," she explained as Sid entered the room.

Annie's apron, face, and hair were dusted with a fine layer of flour. Red lipstick bled into the age lines around her mouth. Her usual Tabu cologne competed with yeast for dominance of the kitchen.

Evidently Chesterfield didn't share Annie's mood. He circled her feet, scowling, his back arched high. He looked up at Sid with a do-something-about-this look on his face.

"What's up?" Sid asked. "You sure look busy, and you smell powerful. Are we having guests?"

"I am." Annie smiled like a school girl on her first date. "Husband's driving down this morning. He'll be here for supper. I think he'll sleep over." Annie always called Uncle Frank, Husband. Sid had thought his first name was Husband, and called him Uncle Husband, until she started junior high school.

"Hmm. Shall I vacate the premises?" Sid smiled over at Annie while she pulled a box of cereal from the pantry.

"You don't have to." Annie's words didn't match her tone. Images of her aunt and uncle in the throes of mad, passionate love were not something Sid wanted to dwell on—or be in the same house with.

Chesterfield didn't either, he violently swished his tail, marched across the room, pounced on the window ledge and caterwauled.

Annie ignored him.

His volume increased.

Sid cringed. "For Pete sake, she's not kicking *you* out of the house, cat. Hush."

Elevating her voice higher than that of the jilted lover's, Sid offered Annie, "What say I pack a bag? Got some research I can do at the library over in Liberty. I'll just hunker down there for the night and get an early start home in the morning. You can forward the calls to my cell phone."

Annie grinned.

Something was definitely up.

Sid ate breakfast and washed her dishes while a big, angry, yellow cat stomped—if cats can stomp—back and forth between Annie and Sid. She felt sorry for the animal, booted out of his number one slot for the first time in his life.

"Sorry, bub, you're on your own, can't help you." Sid reached down and scratched his head. Chesterfield looked up in disgust as she and Slider turned to leave the kitchen. She'd swear the dog had a big grin plastered across his face.

Annie was still humming.

In the doorway, the cat sprinted between Sid's legs, stopped, and took one last look at Annie before leading the other two upstairs. Head high, he strode into Sid's room with a disinterested air, pounced on the bed, and watched her pack a change of clothes and toiletries.

"It hurts, huh? Getting dumped for an older man? You gotta admit, sweetheart, you've had a long reign."

The cat howled.

Slider sounded like he snickered.

"You behave, Slider. Annie will let you outside to do your business and feed you. And Chessy, it'll be okay, Annie still loves you. Maybe she has room for two men in her life. Sounds like you and Husband better learn how to get along, don't you think?"

Chesterfield stretched out on his stomach, plopped one paw across his eyes and dropped his chin on the other foreleg.

She'd made up the ruse about the library to assuage Annie's guilt. Now that she'd committed to vacating the premises overnight, she wondered where to go and what she'd do until tomorrow morning.

Chesterfield and Slider followed her downstairs.

She put Slider in the backyard to chase squirrels and then

headed out the front door, bag in hand, the cat still at her heels. He stood on the porch, glaring at her, as she tossed her bag in the backseat of her car. "Sorry, buddy, you're on your own," she called out to one angry cat as she backed out the drive.

After stopping for gas, directionless, she drove through residential neighborhoods she hadn't seen before, concentrating on the street names, guessing that the small frame homes were built in the '50s-'60s, imagining who lived there, and what their lives were like.

With conscious thought up her rear end, she didn't notice a railroad crossing ahead, or the insistent train whistle in the background, until the sudden flash of red lights and bell-clanging jerked her to attention. She slammed on the brakes at the barrier just as the train barreled past. *God, Sid, pay attention.* She wiped beads of sweat from her upper lip as the train rumbled by.

After what seemed an eternity, she glanced down the tracks, sighed, and shoved the gear into park. "Take your time, I've got all day—and night."

She could go see Dempsey—or Ben. Sid drummed on the steering wheel.

The end of the train finally in sight, she eased the car in gear, ready to cross the tracks as soon as the gates lifted. Lost in the muddle of filling up her day, she'd paid no attention to the line of cars behind her until a driver blew his horn. Seemed everybody wanted her out of their way today.

The guy behind her blasted his horn again, reversed and swerved around before she could budge.

At first all she saw was the birdie flipped her way, but then she recognized the driver. The Reverend.

Where was he going in such an all-fired hurry? She thought about following him, but by the time the track was fully cleared, the van was nowhere in sight.

Wait a second. If Ella was out of town, and he was gone, that meant their house was empty.

Sid made a u-turn and headed to the parsonage that sat next

door to the church. She parked down the block and around the corner, just in case the reverend returned.

At the front door, she rang the bell, just to make sure. When no one came, she tried the doorknob. Locked.

Across the wide church parking lot, a lone car sat empty, she guessed it belonged to the preacher's secretary. Sid rounded the other side of the house and down the driveway to the backyard.

Her armpits felt wet. Was this how burglars felt before breaking into someone's house?

At the back, she stepped onto a leaf-strewn concrete patio, weaved around a white, acrylic-topped picnic table, and peeked through the kitchen window. Dirty dishes lay piled in the sink.

She tried the doorknob. It was locked too.

Hell, she'd done it before, she could do it again.

Open field lay behind both the house and the church next door. No one could see the backyard, or her—she hoped—unless they walked behind the buildings.

The window beside the backdoor was cracked open. Sid eased it up, pushed aside the dark green curtains and eased one leg over the window ledge, half-expecting Sheriff Bonin to be waiting for her on the other side.

The kitchen sat empty. Messy, but empty. A Bible lay open on the table.

If anyone would have told her a few years ago that she'd have the gall to break and enter a private home, much less a preacher's, she'd have called them nuts. Her pulse throbbed against her temples like drums of a marching army of Red Coats.

She wiped her armpits with her blouse as she tiptoed through the kitchen to a living room so quiet, it made her skin crawl. Books lay piled in stacks next to overstuffed earth-toned furniture.

With no idea what she was looking for, or how long the preacher would be gone, Sid did a quick check downstairs, stepped over a broken picture frame and headed upstairs.

The rooms looked devoid of life—guest room, sewing room,

bathroom—but when she entered the master bedroom, it carried a different feel. The bed was unmade, an empty whisky bottle lay tossed in the corner. A suitcase lay open on the floor, clothes tossed in at random. Ella's clothes. Sid recognized the powder blue suit Ella wore to church that first Sunday.

Stepping over the clutter, she made her way to the bathroom and nosed around in drawers and medicine cabinets. Make-up, two toothbrushes, combs hairbrushes. If Ella had left town, it didn't look like she had taken anything.

👁   👁   👁

Ella lay on the mattress listening for Blue's return, afraid he'd come back, afraid he wouldn't. Afraid they'd find her bones years later and people would wonder whose they were. She visualized them spread out on the mattress, covered by her skirt and blouse. Maybe the coroner would do a DNA study to identify them. She thought of the anguish her mom and dad would endure—if they were even alive by then.

When the board scraped across the brackets, she knew he was back. Had he come to kill her this time? He couldn't let her escape. Rape and kidnapping was not only a crime, but a sin, even if a wife had been unfaithful.

Oftentimes she'd ended up feeling raped anyway, violated. His disgust with the whole sex act always showed on his face after they'd made love. He'd been so upset when he'd found out about her and Ian—almost like he was angry because it was Ian she'd been with.

The door creaked open and Blue walked in. "You're still here, I see."

"Where'd you think I'd be?" she snapped back, surprised her fear was gone.

He lit the kerosene lamp again, walked over where she lay, and sat cross-legged on the floor, his head in his hands. His shoulders shook. He didn't make a sound, but she knew he cried.

"What is it? What's happened? Did the deacons fire you?"

He looked up, the light from the lantern reflected in his glassy-eyes. "The deacons? No. Why would you think that?"

She shrugged, with no answer to that question—or any other that raged in her head.

"I have to tell you something..." Blue choked, swallowed, then tried again to speak, his voice a mere whisper. "I should have told you this a long time ago, but I hadn't even admitted it to myself until just now. I was afraid if I said the words, they'd be true."

Ella held her breath, not sure she wanted to hear what was coming.

"I'm gay..." His words sounded like a cancer eating away his insides. "I've used the church, I've used you—hell, I've used God—as a cover up of who I am, but that's the truth. I'm a homosexual. I love men. I have sex with men. I don't want to, but I do." The last words were choked out between sobs.

Unable to say more, Blue rolled onto his stomach, crossed his arms and lay his head down. Sobs racked his body. Years of pent-up guilt, humiliation, honesty, and shame exploded—not for Ella—but for himself.

She waited for the right words, any words, but none came. Waiting for Blue, always waiting for Blue...

"Let me go," she demanded, finding her voice at last. "Take me home. We can work this out, I know we can." If she didn't get free now, he'd never let her go.

Blue raised his head, looked at her, his face contorted. "You don't understand. I can't let you go. It's too late—for you—for me—for Caleb."

"Caleb? Who's Caleb?"

⊚   ⊚   ⊚

Ben stood at the kitchen sink washing lunch dishes, his mind on Sid and how close he'd come to losing her on her last case. He should have protected her. How in the world had he not seen that coming? She wasn't a woman that belonged in law enforcement, crime, or detective work. He had to admit, she'd done a damn good job, even if she did come close to getting herself killed. All he really wanted to do was wrap her in his arms and make wild, unrestrained love.

The scalding water ran over his hands. "Ouch." He yanked them out and grabbed a dishtowel.

He feared his job as District Attorney only fueled her interest in the detective business. Maybe if he were out of her life, she would sell the Third Eye and leave town. He'd get over her as long as he knew she was safe.

But what drove him crazy was the thought of her safe, but with someone else.

He loved her hearty laugh, that unconscious chuckle from her belly. He'd never laughed with anyone like he had with her.

"The woman's damn addictive," he said, stacking the last dish in the cabinet.

Whoa, brother, better be careful, slow it down.

He'd felt bad telling Sid he stopped calling because of his daughter, but he'd known Sid would never buy the real reason—that he was scared shitless. True, his daughter had thrown a fit, but she'd get over that once she got acquainted with Sid.

Ben strolled to the living room, flopped on the sofa, and turned on the ballgame.

The small velvet box on the coffee table pulled his attention. He glanced at it for the umpteenth time that morning. What had possessed him to buy it yesterday?

He grabbed the box and flipped the lid open.

The damn ring had glistened at him in the store window, filling him with grandiose ideas. It was too soon—he knew it was—she'd turn him down.

The doorbell chimed, interrupting his thoughts. He snapped the lid shut and dropped the box in his pants pocket, depressed over his foolish plan. But his mood changed from hound dog to Christmas morning when he opened the door. "Sid, what a surprise." He knew he must look like a kid staring at a shiny red bicycle under the Christmas tree, but he didn't care. "You won't believe this, but I was just thinking about you."

"Am I interrupting anything? I seem to be interrupting everyone else today."

"No, not at all." He stepped aside and waved her in, his pulse pounding in his temples.

※ ※ ※

Sid hated that her heart fluttered every time she got close to the man.

"I just finished lunch. Have you eaten?" Ben swept his arm toward the kitchen.

"I'm not hungry." Sid spoke over her shoulder as she headed to the back of the house. "Need some help with cleanup?"

"Actually, what I need is—you."

Sid turned and stepped into Ben's open arms.

He caressed her back with one hand, cupped her chin in the other.

Eternity cologne, she thought. Damn, he smelled good.

His lips touched hers. "Would you do something for me?" he whispered.

"It depends."

"Would you take off your clothes?"

"What did you say?" Sid choked.

She felt his hands as they fumbled at her waist, slid her zipper open, and nudged down her slacks. She stepped out of her shoes, and then the pants, sorry she'd chosen her old standbys that morning. High-cut cotton whites instead of her one pair of red lace panties. Heat flushed her body, but she wasn't sure if it was passion or hot flashes.

Ben looked her in the eye, moved closer, backing her against the sofa table. The glass-top table felt cool against her hot, bare thighs. She shivered, wanting nothing more than to sink into him and stay forever.

"Marry me." He tucked a sprig of her hair behind her ear.

"What?" Sid came up off the table. She marched over to her

pants, yanked them on and fled to the kitchen.

Ben was right behind her. "I'm sorry Sid. I'd planned a romantic approach, but when I saw you standing at my front door, it just happened."

"God, Ben." No other words came. Sid flopped into a chair beside the breakfast table and put her head in her hands, squeezed her eyes tight.

The sound of Ben breathing, and a dripping faucet, melded into the drumbeat in her head. When she opened her eyes, she stared at a small black box in his hands, the lid flipped up.

"I-I don't know what to say."

"Say yes." His voice was thick, sultry.

"I'm not ready for marriage. I don't know if I'll ever be." God how she wanted to say yes; no man ever set her afire like Ben. But it wasn't just the physical attraction. She liked his intelligence. How he respected hers. She liked who *she* was with Ben—what he brought out in her—the freedom to be who, and what, she wanted to be. Marriage would change that.

"We don't have to get married right away. We can take our time. I don't know why I bought the ring. I just know that yesterday, when I saw it in the store window I knew it was yours."

Ben lifted the marquee-cut diamond ring out of the box and reached for her hand.

She let him slip it on her finger, unsure whether she would wear it tomorrow.

👁   👁   👁

Sid awoke the next morning in Ben's bed, his arm over her chest. She eased out from under him and headed to the bathroom. It took a minute before she remembered the ring. Then she stood in the middle of the room and stared at it, twinkling in the overhead lights. When she finished and came out of the bathroom, Ben lay propped on one arm watching her. He smiled and murmured, "You were so good last night, yesterday afternoon, hell, the whole day."

He snickered and sat up on the side of the bed. "I haven't done anything like that in a long time. I was already all hot and bothered, just thinking about you, then my doorbell rang and there you stood." He held out his hand. She walked over and clasped it, following his gaze down at himself. "I don't believe this. Who said an old fart can't fuck?"

They laughed and she tumbled on top of him, ignoring her ambivalence over the ring. Passion buzzed inside her, growing more insistent. Finally she realized it was her cell phone on the nightstand.

"Let me guess. Annie." Sid punched on the phone.

"Siddie? You okay? I feel so bad, running you off from your home yesterday. I've been worried sick about you."

Sid heard giggling in the background and wondered how much worrying Annie had done. "Is Uncle Frank still there?"

"What? Stop that—what's that you say? Oh, yes, he's still here, but he's leaving in a few minutes. He wanted to see you. Where are you and when are you coming home?"

Twenty

By the time Sid got home Frank was gone, and Annie was plumb giddy. Sid felt pretty giddy herself, or was it confusion cluttering her brain?

She held her left hand out to her aunt. "Look."

"Siddie! Ben?"

Sid nodded. "I didn't say yes—I'm not sure about this, but I let him talk me into at least wearing it."

"What do you mean, you're not sure? Of course you'll marry him."

"I don't know…" Sid called over her shoulder as she headed upstairs. While she unpacked the overnight bag and stuffed her dirty clothes in the hamper, she planned out how she could describe to Quade what she'd found at the preacher's house. Yesterday she'd gone to Ben's house to tell him, and then other things crowded the news out of her head.

But she must tell Quade how, although Ella wasn't there, all her possessions were, down to a toothbrush. If this didn't raise Quade's suspicions about the woman's whereabouts, then nothing would.

She found him at his desk, a hand clasped around a mug of coffee and a half-eaten omnipresent doughnut on the table in front of him. His eyes were locked on a computer monitor, scanning the previous day's traffic report.

Sid knocked on his door. "Morning, Chief. Got a minute?"

Quade swung around. "Hey, Sid, come in." He pushed a

chair toward her with one foot, turned to retrieve his coffee and doughnut. "Can I get you one?" He raised the doughnut up to her. "Big B—delicious as always—and absolutely nothing unhealthy in them."

Yielding to the temptation, Sid selected a golden-glazed orb, still warm from the fryer, and bit into the sweet, yeasty confection.

"What's on your mind? Making any progress on the Ned Durwood case?"

"That's what I wanted to talk to you about. I'm finding more questions than answers." Sid bit into the pastry again, and after swallowing a bite said, "Sometimes I wonder if I'm chasing rabbits—as my ex-husband used to say when he didn't stay on sermon topic. It seems like the more I dig, the more I uncover, but its nothing I can tie in with the Collins murders."

"That's standard. You start out on a case, thinking you know where you're heading, then, before you know it, you're off on some road you think leads to nowhere, but if you just keep driving, the path will lead you home."

"I have my own bias about preachers, so keep that in mind while I talk, okay?" She had revealed a little of her past to her friend, but very little. "What do you know about Humble Bluett?"

"Well, I know he's not a man I'd want mad at me." Quade dunked his doughnut into the coffee and lipped off a soggy mouthful.

"Why is that?"

"In constant need of strokes. Any time one of the other preachers in town gets a little recognition, he has to do one better. Recognition, always searching for recognition. If anybody ever questions anything he does, he goes on the defensive."

"Can he be pushed too far?"

Quade rubbed his chin. "He has a real issue with anger. I've seen him yell at other drivers who weren't driving like he thought they should—that sort of thing. Not a man that likes to be crossed. Why do you ask?"

Sid ran her hand through her hair, slumped in her chair, and sighed. "I don't know. Something about the man gives me the creeps. I don't trust him, and I don't think it's my own bias."

"I've been going through the old case on the Hebert boy." Quade shuffled through papers on his desk, "and I've learned that he, the preacher, Jack Agnes—the guy you found on your doorstep—Marv Bledsoe, and Abe Collins all used to hang out together when they were kids."

"Oh." Sid stopped and did a mental recall. "George told me these guys hung out together when they were kids until one of them disappeared. I must've been half-listening. I didn't make the connection to the Hebert boy, or to Blue."

"The interviews had been stuck in a separate box from the main investigation due to lack of space. When we moved to our new office, that box got reconnected with the other one. I've just been going through it."

Quade drained his cup and sat it on the table. "Wait 'til you hear they were all together that night before Caleb Hebert disappeared, and as far we know, the last ones to see the kid alive."

"Didn't the police interview them?"

"Sure. Their stories were all similar, almost too similar if you ask me. They all described how they had gone out to Sabine Pass the evening before. Bledsoe got pissed at 'em about something and rode back to town with someone else. Collins, Bluett, and Agnes all told how young Caleb fell and hit his head on a rock, but he seemed okay. Later, Abe Collins dropped off Jack Agnes, then Caleb. He and Blue fooled around town a while, then he drove Blue home and went home himself. The next day, Caleb was missing." Quade looked at his watch. "On my god, I didn't know it had gotten so late. I've got to go, Sid. My wife's got an appointment with the doctor, and I need to go with her."

"She okay?"

"If you can call being pregnant and near forty okay."

"Wow."

"She's a little nervous about it. I promised I'd go with her."

"Go, go. No problem, we'll pick up here later."

Sid followed Quade outside and climbed in her car. She guessed it was time to check out Caleb Hebert's old house.

She headed out Border Street. The area was rundown, grass and weeds everywhere. A few houses and a couple of businesses remained occupied, but for the most part, that side of town looked like it had drawn the shortest straw when it came to improvement projects. Sad, Sid thought, how a city changes over time. One day, she guessed, a revival would take place here. Folks would restore some of these old homes and breathe new life into the area.

She passed Evergreen Cemetery on the right. The ubiquitous cyclone fence surrounded the final resting place. She chuckled, remembering the riddle once asked her by a friend as they drove past a cemetery. "Do you know who's buried there?" The friend had asked. Immediate sympathy poured out, thinking perhaps a mother or father, or maybe a still-born baby. When she gave up, he'd said, "dead people." Sid had niggled him for his dark humor.

Scott Street indeed exited off of Border, turning into little more than a one-lane, but paved, roadway. Some of the houses looked forlorn, weary from neglect. Pride in upkeep came from a joy of life, she guessed, not when it was a cross to bear.

She stopped in front of an abandoned house with red and gray asbestos siding, the front yard covered with weeds. After parking alongside the ditch, she got out and rounded the house to the backyard. A dilapidated chicken coop sat behind a small, fenced area. She obliged a rusty tin can a kick, then stepped over a large dried-out bone, canine teeth marks on the ball joint.

A set of broken concrete steps led her up to the back door. She turned the knob, relieved and uneasy when it squeaked open. She shouldn't go in, she told herself, as she stepped into a large, square kitchen. The room smelled of memories—musty, closed off, protective, lest someone invade their space, thereby driving them into oblivion.

Sid swiped her index finger underneath her tingly nose and sniffed.

Faded yellow curtains dangled at the window by mere threads. The kitchen cabinets didn't fare much better. But the dirty porcelain sink spoke of Easter dinners, family get-togethers, of times good and bad, but of family, nonetheless.

The brick patterned linoleum crackled as she stepped through the kitchen into an empty dining room and then a living room. Caked-on wax coated hardwood floors, and piles of trash spilled out of crumbling cardboard boxes.

Layered with neglect, it seemed the heartbroken house awaited the return of someone who once loved it, perhaps the original owner, or the children of such.

Throughout the bedrooms, vandals had knocked holes in the walls. Large pieces of wallboard had been pulled loose from support beams exposing the gray backside of sheetrock. Piles of the stuff lay on the floor, crumbled and powdery. When Sid stepped through the broken bits of pressed gypsum, her foot slid sideways, and with nothing to break her fall, she hit the floor, hard.

After the first shock eased, she glanced around, feeling someone's presence—someone watching her fall like a big ape. She shook herself, muttering, "Silly, no one's here but you. Get over it."

But the feeling didn't leave, instead it crawled behind her eyes and itched.

She sat and waited for the return of a normal heartbeat, gathering her dignity, her equilibrium. She rubbed her eyes with the backs of her hands, the only part not coated in white powder, and then blinked.

As her vision cleared, she glanced around. A piece of broken sheetrock with something written on it, lay across from her.

Curious, she crawled through the chalky dust and picked up the broken piece of wallboard and read *Caleb + Blue,* and inscribed in the four quadrants of the plus sign, were the letters L-O-V-E.

Wow.

Sid flipped open the cover of her cell phone to call Quade, hoping he'd gotten back from the doctor visit. But before she could dial, the phone rang.

If she'd been caught trespassing again, she'd get charged this time for sure.

"Hello?" she said, hesitancy in her voice.

"Siddie? It's ya Aunt Annie, honey. I was just wondering what time you'd get home for supper? I wanted to cook us up something extra nice. I already made us a fresh-grated coconut layer cake with white icing. But I thought I might fix us a pan of crawfish cornbread. That's one of my favorites. When I take that to the potlucks at church, everyone raves over it."

No words formed in Sid's brain.

"So? What time do you think?" The voice carried its usual high-pitched note.

"Annie, I'm a mite busy at the moment, can I get back with you?"

"Oh, sure, baby, sure. Just call me when you get a chance. I'll be here."

Sid figured the woman would be.

After she disconnected from Annie, she tried to recall Quade's number, but it wouldn't form in her brain. She punched the caller ID, scrolled down until his number displayed, then punched dial.

"Quade, oh good, you're back. I think you might want to see this."

"Sid? What you got? I'm in a meeting at the moment." She heard pressure, frustration in his voice.

"Never mind then, just a clue to a thirty-year-old disappearance, but that's okay; I'll just tear it out and bring it to you."

"No you *don't*. I'll be right there."

She smiled, waiting.

"Oh, where the hell are you?"

By the time the detectives finished, Sid had a whole new theory in mind. She and Quade walked back to their cars, both deep in thought. "You think its possible Caleb's disappearance was a hate crime?" Sid asked, staring at the toe of her shoe as she stubbed it into the ground.

"Could've been."

"You going to question the preacher now? I'm convinced he has something to do with all this."

"Not yet. If it wasn't for him being a man of God, I'd jerk his ass in right now. Always did think the guy was a phony, but figured that was just my own bias." Quade looked down at Sid and grinned. "Yeah, you didn't know I had a bias similar to yours, did you? However, Blue's church and most of the community idolize him. He's up on a pedestal so tall I'll have a hard time even reaching him, much less getting him down. I could go ahead and bring him in for questioning, but his name written on sheetrock isn't exactly evidence. We're not even sure who wrote the words. Could've been a joke."

Sid looked up at the budding tree tops. "I still think the preacher's wife is missing."

Quade grimaced. "You keep saying that, but you haven't brought me any proof. What makes you think so?"

"I can't find her. When I asked the preacher about his wife, he shrugged me off, saying she'd gone out of town to visit relatives. Funny thing is, she didn't take anything with her, not even a toothbrush."

"How do you know that?"

"Breaking and entering."

"Damn it Sid." Quade banged his fist on the patrol car. "I told you to quit doing that. You're going to get yourself in a heap of trouble—trouble I can't get you out of."

"I've called her cell phone over and over, but she doesn't answer that, either."

"You're hopeless, Sid. I'll check into it. But I'd rather not alert the guy or his congregation, because if we're wrong, I'll have the devil to pay." He chuckled. "No pun intended."

◉ ◉ ◉

Sid's next stop was Marv Bledsoe's office. This time, an older woman sat at the front desk. She greeted Sid and ushered her into Marv's office with great aplomb.

"Good morning, Marv, I see you've found yourself a real secretary this time." Sid tried to make the statement with a somber expression, but failed.

"You like her, huh? Yeah, she's doing a much better job. I used to always go for the young, ditzy ones. But I've found out if I want the job done, I'd better change that pattern. The young girls I hired spent more time being social and sexy than they did getting the job done. Now, mind you, I don't have a problem with social and sexy, but there's a time and a place for everything."

"Couldn't agree more, and no, ditzy and intelligent doesn't usually describe the same person. A ditzy woman can be intelligent, but her behavior usually wins out."

"How the hell are you, Sid? Glad you came by. Been wanting to call you, but after the last time, I didn't know whether to or not. Everything okay?"

Sid waved off his question with a flash of her hand. "You remember the disappearance twenty years ago of a kid named Caleb Hebert?"

Marv's eyes opened wide. "Caleb?" He walked over to a small refrigerator and collected two bottles of water. "Yeah, a bunch of us boys used to hang out together." He handed her one of the bottles, shook his head and sucked through his teeth. "Heard they found him—never figured him dead, just run off somewhere."

The room grew quiet as both of them uncapped their bottles and drank, but Marv's eyes glazed over, like he'd gone somewhere else.

A clock on the wall ticked.

After the pause, Marv jumped back from wherever his memories had taken him. "Excuse my manners; let me get you a chair." He hustled over, picked up a pile of papers from a nearby armchair and dumped them on the floor. "Here, take this seat." As she did so, he leaned against the corner of the desk and crossed his legs at the ankles.

She still wasn't convinced of Marv's innocence, or how he played into all this. Maybe fishing with enough line, she'd catch something. "I'm looking for information about the old lighthouse out at Sabine Pass. Heard you and your buddies used to hang out there as kids, that you all were there the last night anyone saw the Hebert kid. What can you tell me about that night?"

"Yeah, we hung out there. One night a couple of the guys even scaled the tower and cut away copper roofing from the lantern room. We all took an oath never to tell, and heck, I'd even forgotten about it till now." A guilty smile spread across Marv's face. But was the guilt from recollection of a childhood prank, or from committing a murder?

"After Caleb disappeared, no one had the heart to go out there anymore. A couple of times, some of us wanted to, for old time sake, but Blue pitched a fit. Said we'd dishonor Caleb if we went out there without him. Eventually we grew up and went our separate ways."

"Tell me about Caleb."

"Caleb Hebert. I was sorry to hear they found his body. I'd always hoped he'd run away and had this fantastic life." Marv smiled again. "Caleb used to get teased a lot, other kids called him a sissy. He was small, more like a girl. Fine features, fastidious. Good heart. Blue brought him into our group. Said the kid needed a friend, even though we were older than he was. Blue always stood up for him. Wouldn't let the other kids pick on him."

Marv moved behind his desk and fiddled with a pen that had been lying on a desk pad, his eyes cast down. "The last I ever saw him was the night of the rival football game with the Port Arthur Yellow Jackets. After the game, a bunch of us went out to the lighthouse to hang out. I left early. My mom was already pissed at me for sassing her earlier that day, so I didn't want to get put on house arrest. The next morning I heard he'd disappeared." He tossed the pen on the desk, looked over at Sid. "That's about it. But why are you asking questions about Caleb's case? Aren't you working on Abe and Cherrie Collins's murder? This wouldn't have anything to do with that."

Sid stood. "Maybe. Maybe not. Just checking it out."

She left Marv's office convinced he had nothing to do with the murder, or else the man was a damned good actor—or both.

She looked at her watch. Seven o'clock and pitch dark. A storm brewed in the east, the early spring air hung warm and damp. Reluctant to talk to the preacher again, she guessed she didn't have much choice. Quade wasn't ready, and he'd probably kill her for doing so. Hopefully Blue didn't suspect she'd been in his home uninvited. She pulled out her phone and dialed.

"Reverend, this is Sid Smart," she said when Blue answered. "I know it's late, but I had a couple of things I wanted to talk to you about; thought I'd run by your house if that's okay with you?"

The line went silent, then, "About what?"

"You had a childhood friend named Caleb Hebert who disappeared when you were kids. I wanted to ask you a few questions about him."

He swore under his breath then, "Have you found out anything?"

"No, no I haven't. Thought you might shed some light."

Bells rang in the background. Sid wasn't sure if it was the doorbell or a ringing cell phone.

"Yeah, okay, come on by. Someone's at my door. I'll see you in a few minutes. I don't really like to talk about Caleb, but, come on." Sid heard a click and a dial tone.

👁   👁   👁

Blue hung up the phone and hurried across the living room. At the front door, he flipped on the porch light, looked through the peep hole, and opened the door.

"What do you want from me?" he asked. Then his eyes slid to the gun pointed directly at his head. "No—don't." he cried, stepping backward, his palms between him and the black gleam of metal.

In the wide empty entranceway the shot that echoed off the walls sounded like a Howitzer, and for Blue, it might as well have been. The slug hit him right between the eyes. He was dead before he hit the floor.

Not a good day for the preacher.

👁 👁 👁

The parsonage door stood open as Sid drove up and parked in the driveway. A slash of light from the entryway stretched across the porch and out onto the sidewalk. Uneasiness slid up her back as she got out and walked across the yard, surprised that the preacher left the door open for her. Was it a trap? She reached in her bag and wrapped her hand around the cold metal of her Glock.

But when she reached the open door and looked inside, the bottoms of a pair of shoes stared at her. The reverend lay crumpled on the floor, arms out to the side, eyes staring at the ceiling. In the center of his forehead, right between his eyes, a small hole oozed blood that ran down around his ears and spilled onto the floor.

"What the hell?" Backing out of the house, she snatched the gun from her bag and scanned the front yard and the church parking lot.

A sudden breeze came from no where and shivered through the tree tops.

She flipped open her phone and punched 911.

"What is your emergency?"

"I don't have one, but Reverend Humble Bluett certainly does; he's just been shot dead in his entryway. I'm Sidra Smart, and I'm standing here watching blood flow onto his hardwood floor."

"What is your address Ms Smart?"

"It's not mine, it's the reverend's." She gave the address, and despite their admonition, disconnected the call and eased back inside, her hand still on her gun. Double-O-Seven was a new feeling for her, and, except for the body on the floor, she'd have thought she played a game. If Blue had been playing a game, he'd just lost.

"Ella?" she called, walking over to the stairway. The broken glass she had stepped over earlier had been swept up.

Within a couple minutes, sirens wailed. Soon EMS drove up. Two women climbed out and strode in. The short one, *Karen*, wore a ball cap, her ponytail bouncing though the opening in the back. The other, a tall, hefty blonde walked alongside. Both of them carried black bags under their arms.

"I would ask where the victim is, but that's evident," the short one said. She bent over Blue, put her fingers on his throat, stuck a stethoscope in her ears and listened to his heart. After a minute she leaned back on her haunches and sighed. "No use in even giving CPR. He's gone. No way he could survive a shot like that. Ma'am, the first thing I have to do is ask you to come outside and wait until the police arrive to secure the house. Whoever shot the preacher may still be in the house." She took Sid's elbow and led her outside.

"My guess is, he didn't feel a thing." The taller of the two women—*Melanie,* her nametag read—shook her head. "I'll put a call into the coroner. No use in transporting him to the hospital. Might as well take him straight to the morgue. We'll just need a medical examiner to come declare him dead."

By then, a patrol car had pulled up. A lieutenant walked in, took one look, and turned to the radio on his shoulder. "Better tell the chief to get here. He'll want to see this."

In short order, the officer had secured the house and waited for the chief.

All the sirens and excitement brought the neighbors; a crowd built in the front yard.

"What'd you do, Sid? Shoot the guy?"

Sid spun around and saw Quade. Without a word she pulled out the gun she'd dropped in her bag and passed it to him. "Here, check it yourself. Hasn't been fired recently. Isn't even loaded."

He looked at her like he'd bitten into a sour lemon. "How the hell is it supposed to serve as a weapon if you don't keep the dang thing loaded?" He took the gun out of her hand, raised the barrel to his nose and smelled. "It's not this one, all right. Where'd you put the one you used?"

"Oh, hell, Quade, you know I didn't shoot the preacher. I'd called him and asked if I could come by to talk. He said I could. Said he didn't like to talk about Caleb Hebert, but to come on over. When I got here, I found him like this."

"No forced entry, Chief." The young lieutenant said as he walked over, hitching up his duty belt. "Killer probably used a 7.62 millimeter, from the looks of the wound. The guy opened the door to his own death. My guess is he knew the person. The door has a peep hole. More than likely he wouldn't have opened it without checking. No, he knew who it was all right. Probably just didn't see the gun until he faced it."

👁   👁   👁

The next morning, Sid sat across the desk from Quade and inspected the police report on Blue's murder. "Mind if I assist on this one?" Sid handed the report back to the chief. "Something tells me these cases are all tied together."

"That's what I'm thinking, too. Hell this is a small town. How many murders would you expect, given our size?" Quade rubbed the top of his head. "No, the timing isn't coincidental. Yeah, sure, you might as well. You're already in the middle of it anyway. I can put you on special assignment; that way I can keep an eye on you." He cut his eyes over at Sid, pulled his lips tight to suppress a grin. "I'm pretty shorthanded right now myself, so extra eyes will come in handy." He opened a file drawer, located a form and filled in a couple of blanks, then handed it to Sid to sign.

A booming voice sounded outside the office door.

"I called Sheriff Bonin to come over," Quade explained as he crossed the room. "We work together on these types of cases. Sounds like him."

A tingle ran down Sid when the sheriff stuck his cowboy-hat-head around the door. "Hey, Quade, what's up?"

"You've met Sid Smart."

"Sure."

No warmth in the greeting. One thing she hated, and that was the feeling of being looked through, discounted, and even more so, by a man as good-looking as Bonin.

"Wanted to let you know I'm bringing Sid in on these murders," Quade walked back behind his desk and sat. "She'll be working with us till we get this solved. She seems to think the discovery of the Hebert boy and the recent murders are all related some way."

"I hardly see how." Bonin looked at Sid for the first time since he'd stepped into the room. "What makes you think that?"

"Just a gut feeling, I guess. No hard evidence." Sid certainly wasn't going to tell him about the hints she'd received from Kate.

Bonin pulled his eyes off Sid and turned back to Quade. "What the hell does she know about this kind of thing? She'll mess this case up for sure. I already caught her breaking and entering. You need to tell her to just back off. You and me can handle anything that needs handling." Bonin sauntered over to a clay pot and spit into the dirt around the base of a croton. "I don't want her involved in this case."

Heat spread in Sid's chest; the hackles on her back stood at attention. She started to rise, but Quade stepped to Sid's chair, put his hand on her shoulder and applied pressure. "I understand where you're coming from, buddy. She ain't had much training, but she's been putting some long hours into this case. Plus, she got her feet wet on her first case—and solved it—putting her own life on the line."

Agitation oozed out of Bonin. He threw back his shoulders,

yanked on his gun belt, and paced the small room. "You're barking up the wrong tree. These murders can't be related, too many years in between. Besides, what do they have in common? The way I see it, Caleb's death has nothing to do with the murder of Abe Collins and his wife—the preacher, neither. Besides, everyone knows Ned Durwood killed the Collins." Bonin strode to the door, "But you do what you want." Dismissing himself with a wave of his hand, he left the room.

"Typical Boninian behavior," Quade laughed at the man's back as they watched him saunter down the hall.

Twenty-One

The evening sun spread wide swaths of oranges, pinks and yellows across the horizon by the time Sid headed back to her office. She had spent the day with Quade, trying to make sense out of recent events. As if things weren't tense enough, the mayor called Quade and applied more pressure. He wanted an arrest and he wanted it *now*.

"When the preacher gets murdered, that's a big damn deal…" Sid pounded on the steering wheel, "…especially when his wife is missing." The whole town had Ella tried, convicted and ready for hanging, and that was before news of her affair with Ian came out—then all hell broke loose. One of the deputies had reported that clusters of people had gathered in the church parking lot, plotting, it seemed, to burn Ella at the stake—more upset about the affair than the idea of murder. Sid wondered who had taken it upon themselves to tell the world about Ella's unfaithfulness. A fallen woman—a real *Mary Magdalene*— tried and found guilty of adultery, not of a mortal man, but of a *God*.

Sid glanced at the light-filled windows of Annie's house, knowing she wasn't ready to face her aunt's questions. So she parked in the driveway and headed around the house toward the business entrance to the Third Eye. A warm breeze skittered leaves across the sidewalk.

Inside, she dumped her handbag on her desk, kicked off her shoes and padded to the cabinet. After making a margarita on the rocks, she flopped on the brown leather sofa, tucked her feet underneath her, and sighed.

Had she been so blinded by her own prejudice against the preacher that she'd missed something about his wife? Where was the woman, and how did Ian Meade fit into the picture?

A soft knock startled Sid, and she spilled half the drink down the front of her slacks. "Damn it," she swore, swiping the liquid with a tissue. "Come in." She tossed the tissue in the trash basket as the door eased open and the visitor stuck her head around the door. "Mrs. Smart? Priscilla Preston. We talked on the phone one day when you called for an appointment with Pastor—God rest his soul."

Sid recognized the high-pitched voice of the preacher's secretary. The one George had described as the *holy woman*.

Priscilla walked in wearing a fur stole around her neck, offering fingertips as a handshake. At first, her facial expression had that let-me-show-you-how-holy-I-am look about it, but when she spied the drink in Sid's hand, a frown squinted across her eyes. "I wanted to come by and tell you what I just heard," she cooed, then, "I want that woman found and brought to justice as soon as possible."

Sid wanted to throw up.

She knew women like Priscilla; she saw right through their self-righteous butts. Lots of them had paraded through her life, outwardly humble, but inward, arrogant as all get out. An arrogance gained not only by their beliefs, but also by association with *Pastor*—and by affiliation—*the pastor's wife*. Women like Priscilla had thrown Sid's name around to the rest of the congregation as if she were their most trusted, intimate friend, in an attempt to make the others jealous.

Sid bit her tongue, but the rest of her shuddered. The force it took to smile used up another day of her life.

"Nice to meet you." Sid coerced the corners of her mouth to stretch just as wide as Priscilla's. "Do you know anything about the murder?"

"The murder? Heavens no. But I just heard Ella was being

unfaithful to Pastor and thought you ought to know."

"Did you take this information to Chief Burns?"

"No, but you're helping him with the case, aren't you?"

It seemed the woman kept herself pretty darn well informed.

"I came to you," she continued, "because I heard you were a preacher's wife yourself."

Sid turned to the cabinet and mixed another drink. "Operative word, *were*," she tossed the comment over her shoulder.

"Excuse me?"

"Divorced him." Sid turned to face Priscilla. "May I fix you a margarita?"

A slight hesitation and shake of the head left Sid unsure if Priscilla's *no* referred to the alcohol, or to the inconceivable concept of divorcing a preacher. Deciding the rejection was to both, she changed the subject. "Excuse my manners; would you like to sit?"

Priscilla took the chair opposite the desk and waited until Sid sat across from her before continuing. "I just don't know why Ella was unfaithful to Pastor," she mewed. "I've just been devastated. Why, I was talking to the Chairman of the Deacons…"

Sid cringed. Didn't the woman ever use anyone's name, instead of their title?

Priscilla's pouty mouth looked smaller than the diamond pendant peeping out from under the fur stole, which now lay tossed to one side of her shoulder. Titles continued skipping off the holy woman's tongue like tidbits of food scattered in the path of starving birds. "I thought I knew Pastor better than anyone," she said, adjusting a hairdo that couldn't move if it wanted to.

"Ms. Preston," Sid sat forward and rested her glass on the desk in dismissal, "I don't know how I can be of help. But thank you for coming."

Priscilla huffed with indignation, stood and stalked to the door in black stilettos, butt swinging wide. "You visited our church a couple of times," she said, turning back toward Sid and smoothing invisible wrinkles out of her skirt. "You are going to keep coming aren't you? You said you divorced a preacher and all, but we're a very forgiving congregation."

Sid's nausea didn't leave until the woman left the office.

Afterwards, Sid stood at the window and stared out at the darkness, irritated by Priscilla's sanctimonious offer of forgiveness. Startled when tree limbs brushed against the windowpane, she exhaled a breath of air she hadn't realized she'd held, and turned back into the room. "Choosing life doesn't require forgiveness, *Mrs.* Preston—not in my book."

But as she sat at her desk, truth hit her in the face. She didn't like Priscilla because the woman reminded her too much of the person Sid had been. The persona she'd assumed—been manipulated into assuming—as a preacher's wife. Hell, she'd been her own self-styled holy-woman.

So had Ella.

And the church members—the whole community—judged Ella guilty of murder. Ella hadn't killed her husband. She couldn't. No more than Sid could have killed Sam. Suicide maybe—but not murder.

No one even knew where Ella was, or whether she was safe. No one seemed to care but Sid and Ian. Perhaps now, Quade would start looking for her.

The weight in Sid's chest grew heavier. She sighed, finished the last of her drink then switched off the lights and walked through the house to the kitchen. Annie stood at the sink washing dishes, Chesterfield at her feet, Slider over in the corner chewing on a squeeze toy.

"Hey, Siddie, I gave up on you and ate already." Annie smiled in apology. "Want I should heat up the leftovers for you? Won't take but a minute."

"Sorry I'm late, sweetie," Sid walked over and kissed the top of Annie's head. "I had a late visitor, and now I've lost my appetite. Let's just save them for tomorrow night."

Annie insisted on brewing a pot of tea and making toast.

While she puttered at the stove, Sid cleared the kitchen table, pulled out a large sheet of poster board and felt tip marker, and began diagramming events that began with Ned's death.

She processed out loud, making notes on the paper as she talked. "This is getting more complicated every day. My head was already swimming, but now with Blue's murder, I can't...

One thing I still hang onto is that Ella didn't kill Blue, although my guess is she would have liked to. I had been moving into the idea that Blue killed the Collins', even Jack Agnes, but now, perhaps he killed none of them. Perhaps someone else did. Someone we don't even know. And maybe that someone is plotting whose next." She wrote Marv's name over to the side in big black letters.

Annie brought over the tea and buttered toast. Sid grunted thanks and bit into the bread while Annie leaned over Sid's shoulder and looked at the chart. "Anybody stand to make any money out of any of this?"

"That's always a good question. Not that I can see. At first, I thought the shell mounds held the secret, maybe some buried treasure. There are all kinds of stories about pirates and slave traders and blockade runners in the area. Who knows?" Sid drew a question mark above shell mounds. Had they all been interested in the mounds because of Caleb's body being buried there? "My guess is, Caleb's death is tied to these others, and whoever killed all them, has Ella. Why? I haven't the slightest..."

"Maybe whoever killed the preacher killed Ella, too? Don't you think that's likely?" Annie looked at Sid, wide-eyed with the thought.

"I won't let myself go there yet," Sid said, "not until I have to."

"Well, Jack Agnes showing up dead on our doorstep takes his name off the list." Annie pointed at Jack's name. Sid drew a line through it.

Annie stared at the outline. "Since Ella Bluett was sleeping with Ian Meade, I reckon he could have done it—killed Blue, but why would he kill Abe and Cherrie Collins, or Jack Agnes?"

"Huh. I'm missing something." Sid held her chin between her forefinger and thumb.

"Who else was involved? You said Marv hung out with the guys." Annie drew her finger from Blue to Abe Collins and then Jack Agnes. "Did he have anything else in common with them?"

"Maybe they knew something about Caleb's death. Maybe they were even involved in it. But Ella wasn't. She didn't even move here until after she married Blue. And why would these guys kill their best friend?" Sid glanced up at Annie, but in her mind, she saw Kate, the Bible, the key ring, the boy being pushed and hitting his head on a rock, the Sabine lighthouse.

"I told you about Kate, right?"

"The ghost? Yeah. What's a ghost got to do with this?"

"Hang on, let me show you something." Sid ran upstairs, collected the journal and returned to the kitchen. "I haven't shown you this. Look."

👁 👁 👁

The next morning, Sid drove straight to George's office, and unannounced, marched in to see him. "I need to process all this stuff with you, George, to see if you can help me make sense of it. Other than Quade and Ben, you're the only one I trust to not be involved in this thing. Five deaths all tying back in some way to Ned Durwood."

The tall Cajun leaned back in his chair, propped his feet up on his desk, and put his hands behind his head. "And good mornin' to you, too, sha," he said, grinning. "This case really gettin' to you, huh?"

"It sure is."

"Well sit and let's chew on it a while." He indicated the chair in front of his desk. "Looks like you've got a tiger by the tail. Okay, let's see... Well, what I do when I get stumped on a case is to go back and look for a common thread running through the whole dang thing. There's always something that ties the clues together, but it's easy to miss it if you're not careful."

"The only thread I see is the connection to Caleb Hebert." Sid straightened in her chair and crossed her legs.

"Yeah, remember I told you how they all hung out together."

"Yep. Best friends. Marv Bledsoe, too. Know any reason he might have interest in all this?"

"Bledsoe? Never figured him to be interested in anything but liquor and women."

Sid felt her cheeks blush. "I went to the crawfish festival at Sabine Pass with him a few weeks ago. He cleans up right nice."

George swung his feet to the floor, and his contagious chortle filled the room. "Get outta here, you did what? You dated Marv?"

"He can be a gentleman when he wants to, or maybe before he's had too much to drink." She didn't tell him about Sam walking in on them.

Nor had she discussed Kate's diary. But dang it, why did she feel such a connection with a ghost? What if Kate was the common thread? "You know the history of the old Dorman house Annie bought? I heard it was built in Sabine Pass in the early 1800s, then later cut in two and moved downstream to Orange on a barge."

"Know of it, that's all."

"Know who owned it last?"

"Man by the name of Clarence Clark. Volunteers over at the Orleck. You can probably catch him there. But what's that got to do with the price of eggs in China?"

"Nothing. I've just gotten interested in the place."

"You staying focused, Sid? What's that house got to do with the case?"

"Nothing. I'm just interested, that's all. Thought I'd find out a little more about it." She couldn't tell him she suspected a ghost from the past was giving her clues. Hell, he'd report her to the state licensing board.

"Clark you say, huh? I think I met him at the church the first day I visited the preacher. The two of them were talking—arguing—as I recall. I think I'll go pay him a visit."

George walked her to the door, his hand at the small of her back. She still cringed at the gesture. One of these days she had to say something.

👁   👁   👁

Sid found Mr. Clark giving a tour to a small group of school children in front of the Orleck, a WWII Gearing Class destroyer docked along the shore of the Sabine River, right near the heart of downtown Orange.

"The DD 886 steamed the world for over five decades," Clarence Clark spouted to the children with great aplomb. "She has so many stories inside her all the pages of history couldn't record it."

The children looked up at him, their eyes wide, mouths open.

"Like the Energizer Bunny," he continued, affection seeping through his voice, "she just kept on going. The last destroyer commissioned at the end of World War II, she saw active service for over 53 years."

Sid stood back and looked up at the gray vessel with 886 painted on its bow.

"Yes sir, she was built right here in Orange, Texas in the year 1945. I'll bet some of your great-grandpas helped build her." Clark chuckled, and added, "Probably even your great grandmas. In those days women worked at the shipyards, too, because most of the men were gone off fighting the war. Folks called them *Rosie the Riveter*. Well, A few years ago, a bunch of the men who had either built or served on the Orleck, wanted to bring her home where she belonged. Now she's a ship of memories. Folks around here are proud of the Orleck and the role she played in America's history."

Sid waited while the group toured the steel structure. When they finished and walked off, she smiled at their looks of awe.

"Mr. Clark? I'm Sidra Smart. You have a few minutes to talk?"

"What can I do for you, ma'am?" The man hiked up brown serge trousers, tucked his shoulders back, and walked toward her. "Time for the next tour is posted here on the sign. It's not for a couple hours."

"Maybe another time for the tour. I wanted to talk to you about some local history."

"We met before?" The man quizzed his eyebrows together as if the action aided recall.

"Over at the church. You were meeting with the reverend."

"Oh yeah, I was just leaving when you came in. That's something, him being murdered and all. Anyway, what can I do you for little lady?"

His editorial greeting sent a proverbial fingernail down Sid's spine. She was short, but she wasn't little, and at times, she certainly didn't want to be a lady and sit with her knees together. "I'm trying to find out information about the old Dorman place. My aunt bought the house. I live there with her. Heard it was built over in Sabine Pass in the early 1800s. That makes the place pretty old."

The two of them strolled over to a park bench and sat.

"I'm trying to learn some of the history of the house," Sid continued. "I hear you owned it last. What do you know about it when it was in Sabine Pass?"

"Not much. Sabine Pass is pretty much run down these days. They've got some ship sandblasting and repair operations, but not many folk live there anymore, just a few diehards scattered around the area. Hurricane Rita did a number on it." Clark scratched his head, glanced up at the destroyer, then back at Sid. "There's an abandoned lighthouse across the channel over on the Louisiana side. Kids used to row over and play in it. Or they'd drive over to Louisiana and walk through the marsh. We've tried to restore it, but Brother Blue's opposition made that impossible."

"Do you know why he was against it?"

"No, I never figured that out. I believe that's what we were talking about that day you came up. I was trying to convince him to stop fighting the restoration." Clarence waved his hand at the massive, gray Orleck. "Look here at this magnificent piece of the past. We gotta save history. It's important to our future."

"So has any restoration been done to the lighthouse?"

"Not that I know of. I don't go out there much anymore. Every time I do, I get mad at the preacher. Or did. God rest his soul."

Twenty-Two

Despite Sid's denial, her incessant intuition insisted that Marv had never been totally up-front with her about the Ned Durwood case. That bugged the hell out of her. So when he had called and invited her to meet him for dinner, she'd accepted, determined to clear the air with him—or her nagging inner voice.

Following his directions, she drove across the Rainbow Bridge, which still reminded Sid more of a boomerang than a rainbow—passed refineries belching out gray smog, and then exited to Larry's French Market and Cajun Restaurant.

As soon as she stepped in the door, her hope for quiet dinner conversation flew out the window. The hostess led her through the crowded dining room to the back, where Marv sat, unshaven, disheveled, drinking beer and listening to *Three-Legged-Dawg*, a small, but loud, band of middle-aged men in look-alike black T-shirts imprinted with white dog paws. They belted out ZZ Top's, *Jesus Just Left Chicago*—bound for New Orleans.

Maybe Jesus had left Orange, too.

They both ordered Crawfish Étouffée, and soon their server set steaming bowls of the spicy concoction in front of them. The contagious music eliminated any attempt at conversation. Sid ate, occasionally fanning her mouth with her hand as the Cajun seasoning did its job.

But Marv poked at his food, shifted in his chair.

When the song ended and the band took a break, he glanced up at Sid. "I hear the preacher was shot dead at his front door.

Know who killed him?"

Sid shook her head, surprised by the abrupt question. "No, do you?"

Marv shook his head. "Me? Hell no. But I hear his wife is missing."

"Yeah, I heard that too."

Marv laid down his fork and ran his fingers through his hair. "It's getting nasty, folks beginning to wonder. You think there's a link between the preacher's murder and the others?"

She shrugged. "What do you know about the preacher?"

Marv shrugged, raised an eyebrow.

"How about the preacher's wife?"

He lifted his glass of beer and sipped. "Talk around town is she was having an affair with a man named Ian Meade."

"Heard that too." No way in hell was she telling what she knew about that.

"I hear you've been visited by the resident ghost."

Marv's sudden switch of subjects caught Sid by surprise. Irritation crawled up her backside.

"I ran across your aunt the other day in Wal-Mart," he continued, "looking at a book on Southeast Texas ghosts. When I teased her about it, she told me what you said. We both laughed, but I know you're level-headed. Wouldn't make up something like that."

Patience, Sid, timing is everything. More bees with honey... Her hands twitched in her lap, itching to get around his neck. She refused to share Kate with a man she didn't trust. "Just a nightmare, that's all."

"Probably. I've never seen a ghost myself, even when I've been drunk." Marv laughed and pushed his half-eaten food aside. His smile disappeared. "But about the murders—you watch out, Sid. I'd hate to see you get wrapped around the axle."

What the hell was that—a warning—or a threat? She shivered.

Before recovering from that thought, the band roared into

The Devil Went Down to Georgia, and the whole damn room howled like a pack of dogs baying at the moon.

Jesus just left Chicago and the devil went down to Georgia—both accounted for, but absent. Comforting thought.

Weary of time-biding, she pushed the subject. "Maybe you're the one who should take care. The killer may be after you next."

Marv choked; he hit his chest with his fist. "Me? Why me?"

Their server walked up and Marv ordered coffee. Sid waited for its delivery before she answered his question.

"There seems to be a link with Caleb Hebert's disappearance. From what I understand, you're the only one left of the teenagers who hung out together. I don't know if you guys had anything to do with his death, but I believe the killer thinks so."

"What? That's impossible. No one killed Caleb."

She fixed her gaze on his dark eyes and asked, "What do you mean, no one killed Caleb? How do you know?"

He straightened in his seat and glanced around the room. The nearby tables were now empty, so he spoke loud enough for Sid to hear, but not loud enough that the others could. "It didn't affect me—so I just kept my mouth shut." He leaned forward, both elbows on the table. "I know no one killed Caleb because I was there that night. I saw what happened."

"What night? When what happened?" She decided against telling him she'd read the police file.

Marv drained his coffee cup then lifted it toward the server. After she'd refilled it, he spooned in sugar and cream and beat the liquid like it was cake batter. Resting the spoon on the table, he entwined his fingers, propped his hands on the edge of the table and stared at them.

Although impatience raged inside her, Sid held her tongue, determined to force him to break the silence.

"Okay…" He sucked in a deep breath. "Okay… The truth is…" He paused, started over. "Let me put it this way. Caleb loved Blue. Blue loved Caleb, too, but he wouldn't admit it to himself, or anyone else. I figure that's why he went into preaching."

"What are you trying to say?"

"I figure he thought God would keep him safe from his 'sins of the flesh.' He always preached about Paul's thorn in the flesh. But the real thorn was Blue's."

Marv loosened his tie and rolled up his sleeves, leaned closer to Sid and whispered. "I was too afraid to tell anyone all this when I was a kid. Later I didn't tell anybody because it wouldn't bring Caleb back." He glanced around the room, wiped his mouth, and stuck his big hands in his lap. "Caleb's death was an accident, but it was kept secret to cover up another truth. We've got a gay community here, just like any other town. People act like it doesn't exist. You don't talk about it—it ain't there. Scares the hell out of people to think someone in their midst is different than they are."

"Are you gay?"

"Me? Hell no. You ought to know that from personal experience."

Heat rushed into Sid's cheeks as she remembered the night Sam caught Marv kissing her.

"But I know lots of folks who are." Marv pulled his hands back up on the table. His voice was tight, constricted. "I didn't know he was dead. I just thought he was unconscious. Okay, here's what happened. The gang was horsing around out at the lighthouse. It was Caleb, Blue, me, Abe Collins, and Jack Agnes. Sometimes Ned Durwood was with us, but that night he couldn't come. His daddy was home from Germany and his mama made him stay home."

Marv stared at the table. "We'd brought a case of beer and no one was feeling any pain. All of a sudden Caleb walked up to Blue and kissed him square on the lips. Scared Blue half to death. He shoved Caleb, who fell and hit his head on a big rock and didn't get up. Bonin came up about then…"

"Bonin?" Sid interrupted. "The sheriff?"

"One and the same. He was a couple years older, so he didn't really hang out with our group, but we all went to the same school. He helped us put Caleb in his car and drove us back to Orange."

"Was Caleb breathing?"

"Yeah, he was groggy, but he was okay. Just dazed—you know. They dropped me off first, saying they were taking Caleb to the hospital. It wasn't until a day or two later I learned they hadn't. I didn't know what had happened, but Blue came by my house and begged me to never tell anyone about that night."

"And you never did."

"I never did. Besides, I didn't think anyone had killed him. I just thought he'd run away, humiliated by what he'd done."

Sid licked her lips and wiped a strand of hair out of her eyes. She could only imagine the pain this secret had caused Caleb's family. "Is that it?"

Marv nodded, chin tucked to his chest.

She stood, tossing her napkin on the table. Frustration amplified her voice. "You should have told me this when I asked you before. Not just because we're friends, or at least I thought we were, but—but the truth might have…" Her voice trailed off as she glanced around the room and saw all eyes on her. "I'm sorry. I can't sit here any longer; this makes me sick. I hope you're planning to pay the tab." She stumbled past the band playing a rousing rendition of *Marie LeVeaux.*

She go GREEEEEE… Another man done gone.

👁   👁   👁

Marv's revelation churned in Sid's gut all night long. The urge to see this damn lighthouse so filled her, she felt like a volcano working toward an explosion. At daylight's first peep Sid headed to Sabine Pass.

When she got there, dilapidated dwellings, abandoned cafés, restaurants, and odd businesses sat devoid of life, a sad reminder of the once-thriving community. She turned on 1st Street and drove to the dredged-out inlet where half a dozen ships sat in various stages of repair, their hulls sandblasted, naked in the bright sunlight.

Standing in the middle of marshland on the other side of Sabine Lake, the abandoned lighthouse looked like a rocket ship someone had forgotten to launch.

Determined, Sid tromped through knee-high grass along the edge of the water, circled rotting dock posts with large, frayed ropes, and tripped over rusted angle iron. Nowhere did she see a way across the channel to the lighthouse.

"A purty sight, ain't she?"

Sid wheeled toward the crackly voice and almost into an old woman standing close behind her. The woman's smile revealed one snaggletooth set in pink, glistening gums. She wore a long, pink-print cotton dress protected by a white bib apron.

Sid acknowledged the woman with a smile, hoping if she didn't invite dialogue, perhaps the woman would move on. If she didn't get inside that lighthouse, she'd spend another night without sleep. But how could she get away from the old woman without being rude?

Instead of being discouraged, the woman clasped Sid's elbow and led her closer to water's edge. "Built in 1857, she was. Pert-nigh as old as me." The crone laughed, gravel in her throat. "Saw only four years operation before the Civil War then she sat dark."

"Sounds like you know the history of the lighthouse." The conversation had just moved Sid's way.

"That lookout tower up yonder," the woman squinted, pointing to the top, " 'twas used by both the Union and the Confederates. Union fellers stole the lens and shipped it up north. Dick Dowling and his men won the battle of Sabine Pass just over yonder." The woman turned and pointed. "After the war, we got the lens back and put her back in service in 1865." The old woman flipped her apron. "You belong around these parts?"

"No. I live in Orange. I'm just interested in this area. I hear there was an old hotel here during the 1800s."

"Kate's place? Shore was—ever body round here's done heard

of Kate. Little red-headed spitfire, that's what she was." The woman squinted up at Sid, shielding her eyes with the edge of her hand. "Stood up to a whole slew of Union soldiers, she did. My kinda woman."

The old woman snickered, hiding her mouth with a gnarled hand. "Hear tell one year there was this big hurricane what destroyed the whole town. Schools were a goin' and all. Farmers were out pickin' cotton when the winds came. By six o'clock that evenin' tide water was six feet deep in the houses. Folks tied kids to the tops of live oak trees to keep 'em from drownin' and floatin' away."

Under other circumstances the tale would delight Sid, but now impatience bubbled up—brimmed over. How could she get rid of the woman?

"By midnight, what town was left was dead. Folks said the storm were pert nigh a hundred and fifty mile wide. Eighty-six people died that night right here in Sabine Pass alone. 'Bout all 'twas left was that there lighthouse." The old woman turned and nodded south. "Rescuers came up from down Galveston way. They found the keeper, his lady-friend, and two other folk, trapped in the tower. The house they'd lived in was gone. Water was twenty feet deep in places."

"Can I get inside the lighthouse?" Maybe she could kill two birds with one question.

"Need a boat from this side of the lake. Now, you can drive across into Louisiana, but you still have to wade through wet marsh. Long time ago there was a little footbridge down the road a piece. Most folk don't even know about it. I reckon you might can cross there. Take this little road over here," the woman pointed with an arthritic finger, "it winds around a heap, and it's full of potholes, but it'll get you to the footbridge."

Her tale complete, the storyteller waved and walked off.

The encounter left Sid wondering whether any of this had anything to do with the murders. Or was it Kate's way of helping her? Regardless, she had to get inside.

She climbed back into her car and bumped down the marshy coastline until she found the footbridge. The nearby grassy shoulder looked soft, so she drove down a ways until she spotted a small patch of gravel and pulled in.

The rickety crossover led her into overgrown marsh where water seeped through her tennis shoes and squished between her toes, making her wish she'd brought Martha's hip waders. If this way was better, she wondered what the trip to the lighthouse was like from the Louisiana side.

Forced to give up her visual of the lighthouse while she trudged through the towering grass, she shivered, not sure if from the cold, or from fear. She pushed ahead for what seemed an eternity.

Uneasiness prickled down her spine when she plowed through a thick overgrowth and almost fell into a beaten-down path in the bulrushes. Someone, or something, had recently been through here.

Unsure if the creepy feeling came from eyes—human or otherwise—watching her, she followed the path, checking her flank with every step.

At length, the path opened into a small clearing and there stood the abandoned lighthouse, resolute, spectacular. From a distance she'd thought the building round, but on closer inspection, saw it was octagonal, and tapered at the top. Eight concrete buttresses surrounded its base.

She looked up at squawking seagulls, her hand shielding her eyes, and then a few minutes later something flushed a covey of startled quail from its hiding place in the reeds. Did they know something—see something—she didn't?

She approached the lighthouse, but when she saw that a weathered beam of wood lay across metal brackets, securing the door, disappointment dropped to her stomach. It looked heavy, she'd never get it up.

But, resolute, she maneuvered, shifted and shoved, ramming splinters into her hands until, at last, the board yielded and one end dropped to the ground. She lifted the higher end, gave one last push up and over, and the beam banged to the earth. Reverberations pounded her eardrums and waved up through the bottom of her feet.

The heavy door creaked as Sid pulled it open. Stepping over a low ledge, she eased inside the dark, octagonal room. Light from the open door and a small window high above provided her only light. The reek of waste—human or animal—nauseated her. She turned, wanting to leave, but a force outside her own volition seemed to nudge her back into the trash-cluttered room. She tripped over a piece of rusted metal as she stepped through debris and around wooden beams piled on the floor. In the center of the room, a wrought iron spiral staircase dangled by one lone piece of angle iron. The first few rungs of steps had rusted completely off and fallen to the floor. Sid felt as if the tiniest of shudders, even her breath blowing against it, might make the whole thing crash to the floor.

A filthy mattress piled with old clothes hugged the back wall. What looked like five shriveled toes of a foot stuck out from the bottom of the pile. Heart pounding out of her chest, Sid skulked toward the toes like she'd entered some zone of twilight where nothing made any sense. She leaned over, lifted the fabric...

...and jumped ten feet when her cell phone rang.

"Annie? Oh my God, Annie, I'm so glad you called. Get an ambulance out to the Sabine Lighthouse. I've found Ella."

Twenty-Three

Sid paced the emergency room corridor battling a thick scum of remorse. If she hadn't shunned Ella the day she came asking Sid for advice, perhaps none of this would have happened. One woman asking another for help—but no-o-o, she was too caught up in her own issues with religion, so had pushed Ella deeper into the arms of her attacker. How could Sid forgive herself—let alone, be forgiven?

An orderly walked by pushing an old man in a wheelchair, and Sid's thoughts went to Dempsey. So far she'd failed him, too.

Chill bumps covered her arms. What had she missed that had brought Ella to the brink of death?

The emergency room door swung open and a young doctor walked out. "Anyone here with Mrs. Bluett?"

"Yes, here," Sid called, too terrified to move. "I'm with Ms Bluett. How is she?"

"Not good. She'll survive, but after what she's been through…" The doctor shook his head while staring at his blue-wrapped shoes.

"What can I tell her family when they get here?"

"It's going to take time, lots of it." The doctor fought back emotion supposedly trained out of him. "She has internal and external contusions, dehydration—but long term? The emotional damage will be the most difficult to heal. With the right help, I think she will."

"May I see her now?"

The doctor led Sid through automatic doors and down a hallway to curtains shutting Ella off from curious eyes. A policeman stood guard, and nodded as Sid stepped behind the drape.

Ella's pale face and ratted hair made her look like a doll left out in the rain. Her eyes were closed, her breathing shallow. Contents from IV bottles drained into bruised arms.

Dereliction of duty, the scene cried out at Sid—duty to help another woman in need.

"Is she asleep?" Sid muttered to the nurse at Ella's side.

"Just lightly." The young nurse smiled at Sid. "We've given her a sedative, though. Soon, she'll be fast asleep. Why don't you go ahead, speak to her."

Ella's eyes fluttered open. "Sid? That you? They said—you… Thank y—"

The expression of gratitude did nothing to assuage Sid's guilt. She stepped closer, and clasped Ella's cold, thin hand. "I'm *so* sorry. I should've come sooner."

"It's okay…you didn't know. He's hit me before—when angry or…" Ella's words came out slowly, half-enunciated. "He didn't like anyone to question his beliefs, 'specially his own wife."

Ella trapped Sid's eyes with hers. "He's dead, isn't he?"

Sid blinked in acknowledgment. The words wouldn't come.

"Suicide?"

"No, doesn't look like it."

"Accident?"

Sid shook her head.

"Murder?"

Sid nodded.

"Who?"

"We don't know yet."

"At least it's over." Ella's words thickened and stopped. Tears rolled down her cheeks. She closed her eyes.

Sid started to ease her hand from Ella's, but Ella squeezed it and held on.

"It's okay, honey," Sid said, softness in her voice. "No one blames you." *They damn well better not.* "If he hadn't been killed, I might never have found you."

Ella smiled weakly and drifted off into nothingness.

Her hand still in Ella's, Sid sat next to the bed. Her weary body begged her to let go, but her spirit held tight.

Later, they moved Ella to a private room. Deputies came and went, asking Sid questions, writing down information.

Ella's hand was still in Sid's when Ella's parents arrived. Sid recognized them from the photo she stepped over when she broke into the parsonage.

Grief covered the elderly couple like a shroud atop a corpse. Her father blubbered as soon as he reached Ella's side, but her mother stood stoic, like she'd erected a protective wall between herself and pain. Her eyes glistened with moisture as her quivery hand cupped her daughter's cheek. "Oh, Ella, what did I do to you?" She spoke barely above a whisper. Sid wondered if she heard the woman correctly. If so, there seemed to be enough guilt to pass around.

Sid slipped her hand out of Ella's, wanting to escape, wanting to give the parents time alone with their daughter, but her way was blocked—blocked from leaving a place she didn't belong.

"We never should've let you marry him in the first place. You were so young—just a baby. We thought he was a good man. Oh my little Ella." Her mother leaned over and rubbed her hand across Ella's forehead, smoothed down her hair.

Ella's eyes fluttered. "Mom?"

"Shh. Sleep. Yes, it's Mother. I'm here. I'll be here when you wake up. You just rest, you're safe now."

Ella's father stepped around the bed and grabbed Sid's hand between both of his. "Thank you for being here with our daughter. Are you the one that found her?"

Sid nodded and clasped her free hand around his. "I'm Sidra Smart."

"Armstrong," he said. "We're her parents. I can't tell you how much…" His words dissolved into tears. He pulled out a handkerchief, wiped his nose and stuck it back in his pocket. "You look tired, ma'am," he continued. "Would you like to go get yourself a cup of coffee or something? I'd go get it, but I… He glanced over at his daughter. "I don't want to leave her."

"No—no, of course you don't. I'm fine. But I will slip out and take a break. Can I bring either of you anything?"

"No. We're good. Take your time. We'll be here for the night."

"Then I think I'll go home and see if I can get some sleep. If she awakens, please tell her I'll be back."

When Sid got home from the hospital, all she wanted was bath and bed. She headed to the kitchen to fetch a glass of ice water to take upstairs with her. There stood Annie at the butcher-block workstation in the middle of the kitchen. A large fowl lay in a pan in front of her, its legs spread wide. Beside it, a well-worn cookbook lay splayed in similar condition.

"What to wear?" Annie asked, looking up at Sid. "Don't it always boil down to that—even when all a woman wants to do is dress a stupid bird for dinner. I'm trying to create something different with this dang fowl—but I'm stuck." She stepped over Chesterfield, sprawled on the rug in front of the sink. He hissed up at her as she tossed a spatula in the sink. "Oh calm down Chesterfield. Nobody's gonna make you move your lazy butt." She grimaced at Sid. "That fat cat gets fatter and lazier every day. I swear he thinks he's king of the hill."

Any other time, Sid would have agreed with Annie, but today her zombie brain stayed in idle.

"How's Ella?"

"Huh? Oh." Sid shrugged her shoulders. "Physically, I think she'll be okay." She pulled a chair out from the kitchen table and sat with her forehead propped on her hands. "Emotionally, it'll be long time."

"Looks like it'll be a long time before you're okay, yourself."

"I'm just so ashamed, Annie. I should've listened to her when she came to my office that first time. There's no excuse."

"There dang sure is. You been doing some healing yourself. Religious wounds go deep—deeper than any knife plunged into your heart. And they cut to your soul. Be patient with yourself, young'un."

Sid stared at the table. "I'm clueless now. If the preacher killed the others—who killed Blue? Sometimes I think I'm made for this job, then other times I think I'm in way over my head. But if I don't get to bed soon I'll be asleep here on the kitchen table beside your pan."

"Then I'm going to worry about this bird tomorrow." Annie flipped the cookbook closed, picked up the hen, pan and all, and shoved it in the refrigerator. "You head on up, me and Slider will go for his evening walk."

Sid glanced over at the dog, who'd just walked into the kitchen. He looked at Sid as if he couldn't believe his ears. Annie? Take him for a walk? Too weary to argue with either of then, Sid headed upstairs, flopped on her bed. Soon, blackness crowded out conscious thought.

She awoke with a start and glanced at the clock.

Midnight. Slider lay upside down in the chair, moonlight dancing on his belly.

When she'd been this confused on her first case she had driven out to Millersfield Farm and received inspiration. But where would she go this time? Surely not the farm. Maybe Sabine Pass—not to the lighthouse again, but where Kate's house had sat. At dawn's light, she'd head out. With that resolution she drifted back into a fitful sleep.

👁   👁   👁

As the first sun ray came through her window Sid slipped out of bed, dressed in blue jeans and sweatshirt, left a note for Annie, and she and Slider headed out to Sabine Pass.

When she spied the lighthouse across the lake she thought about Clarence Clark's restoration project. Maybe he could accomplish that now. She hoped so, else the memory of what happened to Ella would fester inside the place.

Parking the Xterra near the site where the old woman said Kate's Catfish Hotel had stood, Sid switched off the engine. She and Slider exited and paced waters edge, each stepping carefully through weeds and brush. Cold wind blew across the water. She yanked the edge of her sleeves over her hands and crossed her arms over her chest. Trying to put herself in an altered state, she stared across the lake and forced all thought out of her mind except that of Kate's diary. She let it flit behind her eyes and heard Kate cursing out Union soldiers for taking her horse and cart to fight against Kate's friends and neighbors.

But who fought a war today? And if they did, how did it tie into the murders?

"Sorry, Kate, if you're trying to give me a message, you're going to have to hit me over the head with it, because I'm not getting it."

Horse and cart—horses—carts—soldiers—uniforms—the only men she knew in uniform were Quade and Sheriff Bonin.

👁   👁   👁

Sid had never heard of anyone staking out a sheriff, but her experience with Quade, on her first case, led her to rule him out. She went with the sheriff. That night, Sid parked across the street from the sheriff's house beneath a large pine tree that protected her from the soft glare of the streetlight on the corner. With no moon out, the shade was even deeper than usual.

The night seemed endless. She unwrapped a tuna salad sandwich she'd brought from home and nibbled away, glad for something to do other than sit. Before she'd eaten half of it, an older model dark sedan eased down the street with its lights off, and parked a block away. She watched, curious to see who would get out, but when no one did, she decided it was probably teenagers coming home, making out in front of their parent's house.

Another hour passed, and her rear was numb when the sheriff walked outside, climbed in his car and drove off. Sid switched on her motor and followed, checking the built-in compass on her rear view mirror. They headed east.

Bonin's car crept down the street. At one point he braked, red taillights glaring. He stuck his arm out the window and signaled to a man in shadows. The man approached the car, accepted a package handed him by the sheriff, and then walked back into the dark.

The sheriff drove further.

Soon, Sid had no idea where they were. She glanced at the clock on the dash—two in the morning. She'd never seen this part of town even in daylight.

She punched the automatic door lock again just to reassure herself.

Traffic was light—most sane people home in bed—when the sheriff made a second stop. Again, he passed a small package to some mysterious person appearing from the shadows.

But the night took on a whole new level of sinister when the same dark sedan she'd seen parked in front of the sheriff's house cruised past her, and then unobtrusively circled back behind her, reappearing in her rearview mirror a few minutes later.

"Who in hell is that?" Sid adjusted her outside mirror.

So she wasn't the only one watching the sheriff.

Or was the guy watching *her*?

Spooked by that thought, Sid made a u-turn at the first cross street and, varying her path, headed home, paying diligence to every car she passed and those that followed her. If, indeed, the dark sedan showed up again, she decided, she would circle back and drive straight to the police station. But she didn't see it again that night.

The next morning she stopped by George's office unannounced, hoping he had time to talk. She didn't dare tell him she'd been shadowing the sheriff, not yet at least, nor that someone else shadowed him as well—or her.

George ushered her to a chair, his hand at the small of her back again. Chatting all the while, he headed to the coffee pot while Sid took a chair in front of his desk.

After he poured Sid a cup, he opened the cabinet, pulled out a flask, and poured a glug of amber liquid into his own cup.

"One of these days, I'm going to have to try some of that in mine."

"Anytime, you just give me the word. I quit offering, don't want to make you no alcoholic."

She leaned back and propped her feet up on a nearby chair. "Not much chance in that. I'm not easily addicted—except maybe to dark chocolate. Now, what can you tell me about the east side of town?"

"East side? Never heard it called that before."

"Really? What's it called?"

"Early part of my life it was called the ugly N-word-town. Some of the locals still call it that amongst themselves, sick as that is. Then again, prejudice goes both ways, don't it." George shook his head and tsked. "When you say east side, you talking about the projects?"

"Hmm," Sid nodded as she sipped. "I guess so. Wanna take a ride through that area?"

"You're not serious. Now?"

She grinned at George over the edge of her cup.

After they finished their coffee he led the way outside. "Knowing you, if I don't go, you'll be going by yourself, and I'd feel a heap worse about that. No telling what kinda trouble you'd get yourself into."

They climbed into George's pickup truck and headed down Cordrey Street. After a couple of turns, George broke the silence. "There're several different projects around town, but they basically all look about the same. Most of them are gated, supposedly for safety, but that don't keep the problems out, more like, it fences them in, I suppose."

A few minutes later, George pointed to rows of two-story brick buildings that looked a cross between a seedy motel and apartments. "Look here, this here is one of 'em."

Every unit looked identical. Sidewalks snaked between the units to an unkempt grassy area with a dilapidated swing set. Some of the apartments were two story, like townhouses, others single story. Most homes had the windows open. A few had screens, although most of them were ripped or bent.

"And just when were you in this part of town?" George asked. "Most white folk don't feel safe here."

A shrug of her shoulders was all the answer she allowed.

"From what I hear," George continued, "this is a high drug area which, of course, leads to more crime. Some folk make a feeble attempt at playground equipment, but a kid's toys and his imagination seem to be all they have to keep themselves occupied—that and dodging bullies and bullets." George drove slowly through the area, his head scanning left and right.

One yard stood out from the others. Sid nodded towards it. "Looks like a few residents beautify or personalize their place. Look at those flower pots and little yard ornaments by that front door."

"Yeah," George explained, "but unless they're elderly, or pretty high up on the food chain, that stuff gets damaged or stolen pretty quick. There's a social structure inside the gate, and everyone in here knows who falls where."

An ambulance sat in front of one apartment, the emergency light twirling. George indicated it with a nod of his head. "They respect EMS and police, but they watch to make sure the authorities do their jobs. If they think their folks aren't being taken care of, they have no problem yelling and pushing EMS people. After a shooting or major fight, tensions are so high that if EMS breathes wrong, they're on top of 'em."

"But why would they react that way to emergency teams? They're just there to help. Police, I can understand that a little, since some folk don't trust them—at times, for good reason. But EMS?" Sid shook her head. "That doesn't make sense—at least not to me. I guess you have to live here to understand it."

"My guess is, the majority of these people don't want to live here, but they just don't know any other way. It's survival of the fittest every day. Then you see the ones who don't care. Maybe life has them calloused." He lifted his hand, palm up, "I don't know," and then dropped it back on the steering wheel. "The daytime hours seem pretty normal, but when the sun goes down, it's a different world entirely."

George spoke as if the area had an entity all its own, set apart from the rest of the town—and the world. "When drugs and alcohol start flowing, the disturbances begin. They come out in the dark and pretty much disappear in the light. There are mixed races here, but in each project there is usually one predominant race. The insides of some of the units are what you would expect—dirty, old broken down furniture, cracks in the walls, bare light bulbs and rust-stained sinks. Then there are a few that when you walk in, you'd have no idea you're in the projects. The walls are painted a nice color; the place is clean, decorated, candles, nice furniture." He turned to Sid and explained. "Now I don't mean Ethan Allen, but decent furniture. You know? These people have no other choice—it's either here or the streets. They're not the people with drug problems. These are good people in a bad environment, trying to rise above the circumstances."

"Makes you want to give them a hand or something." Sid felt moisture brimming her eyelids.

"There's one little elderly lady I give a couple of dollars to every now and then to tide her over till her next government check comes in."

So George did have a generous heart.

"Her son watches me while I'm in that complex and makes sure I'm okay. He's told me on more than one occasion that if I ever need anything, or anything taken care of, to let him know, because I help his mom."

Sid shuddered and looked around. "Do you see him here—now?" A tingle ran down her neck, across her shoulders and down to her fingertips.

"See that guy standing over in the shadow of that doorway?"

George nodded. The guy nodded back ever so slightly.

"Derreck Jones. He has my back when I'm in this area. I know he's watching me from the time I come in until I leave. When I see him around town, he makes a point to tell me he saw me and the circumstance, what I did, how long I was there. That's his way of letting me know he's got me covered."

Sid sat up straighter. "Must be a good feeling—knowing someone's got your back." A premonition ran down hers.

Twenty-Four

That night, as Sid repeated her vigil in front of the sheriff's house, a light rain fell, blurring images and buffeting sounds. After an hour or so, she dozed, drowsy from the constant drip of rain on the windshield. When she roused, all the lights in the sheriff's house were dark. The car still sat in the driveway. Evidently Sheriff Bonin had called it a night.

Just as Sid started her motor, the same dark sedan she'd seen the evening before cruised by, slow-like. The driver leaned forward peering through his windshield toward the sheriff's house, then drove on.

Sid shifted into drive and pressed on the gas, headlights off. "Sid, you're asking for a whole heap of trouble," she muttered as she followed a safe distance behind the sedan.

This was one damn puzzling mess. Even the thought of the curse word skipped her mind back to Sam and his over-obsession with such words. She'd tried to be perfect in his eyes, thinking she'd earn those proverbial *stars in her crown*. Idiot, she thought, shaking her head.

Fifteen minutes later, Sid realized she'd followed the driver back to the same neighborhood she and George had visited earlier that day, which did not improve her nerves. The thought of home and bed felt mighty good.

The driver parallel-parked at the sidewalk then climbed out and shut the car door.

Sid switched off her headlights and eased to a stop half a

block behind him, keeping an eye on the guy's retreating back. She opened her bag and fingered the cold, hard Glock that Quade insisted she carry loaded. Reassured, she snapped the bag closed, reached up and switched the dome light to the off position. One hand stilling her heart, with the other, she turned off the ignition, dropped the key into her pocket, and eased out. The neighborhood and the moonless night added to her apprehension.

With brisk, silent steps the man headed toward an apartment.

Sid followed, stealth-like, hiding behind shrubs, watching for movement, listening for untoward sound.

Just as he approached the apartment's small concrete porch, the cell phone in Sid's pocket rang.

Dammit. She rammed her hand into her pocket and punched the Off button. *Not now, Annie.*

The man altered his steps without looking back then darted around the side of the apartment. Why had he run? Why hadn't he just gone inside and locked the door? Or turned and attacked her?

Senses heightened, she tiptoed to the porch, telling herself what an idiot she was to be there.

A deep groan came from inside the apartment.

Oh God. Dare she go inside? Run? Could she? Was someone hurt? Dying? Had the man tried to lead her away from whatever was inside? Or had he entered through a back door—or window—and been hurt?

One thing for sure, it was none of her business. Furtive, she glanced around the neighborhood. Not a soul in sight. Her best bet was to leave while she still could. Weak-kneed, she turned.

There was the groan again.

Instinct kicked in; Sid reached for the doorknob.

No, this is stupid.

Her pulse throbbed in her ears.

The groan grew more urgent.

But what if…

She turned the doorknob, eased the door open, and peeked inside. The first thing she saw was the man she'd just followed. He must have entered from the back. Even in the dim light of a small table lamp, something about the man looked familiar—but what, and from where?

Now, he stood frozen—staring, but not at Sid.

She nudged the door open wider and followed his gaze to a single bed rammed up against the back wall. A young woman lay in crumpled sheets, writhing in pain, her legs spread wide, hands gripping a metal headboard.

Sid looked from the woman to the man, and then back again at the woman, whose black skin glistened with beaded moisture. Her eyes were slits, pleading, begging. No wonder the groan had sounded familiar. The woman's belly was swollen, and between her legs, a small determined head fought to enter the world.

When Sid stepped inside, the man started to lunge at her, but stopped, glanced back at the woman, indecision riding high on his shoulders. After what seemed like an eternity, he shrugged. "I don't know why you followed me lady, but do what you have to. I've got to help my sister." He knelt beside the bed and grabbed the woman's hand. "Tell me what to do, Sis."

Sid hesitated for one cold-stone second and then moved into action. "Towels, we need clean towels and fresh water." She spoke sternly, shoved the man aside. "Go to the kitchen and—and boil something—and call 911."

"But…"

"But nothing. Let's get this baby here. Then we'll talk." Sid pushed the man toward the kitchen and then called after him, "Where's the bathroom?"

He pointed down a short hall.

She sprinted to the bathroom, scrubbed her hands, grabbed a handful of clean, folded towels, and ran back to the bed.

"It's okay. You're going to be okay, honey." Sid moved deftly, like she delivered babies for a living, while her heart felt like the pedals on Lance Armstrong's bicycle.

"You ever delivered a baby before?" the woman cried, near panic.

"Next to it." Sid spoke calmer than she felt. "I've had a couple, and I've watched a baby being born on TV." She laughed. "We're gonna do just fine, Ma'am."

Pots and pans banged in the kitchen. Water ran.

The woman went rigid as a new wave of pain consumed her body.

"Breathe, don't forget to breathe." Sid sat on the foot of the bed and spread the woman's legs wider. "The head's crowning. We're almost there! Push!"

In the midst of the contraction the woman ran out of oxygen. She stopped pushing to catch a breath, and the head slipped back up into the birth canal.

With no idea what to do next, Sid leaned back and took a deep breath. *Trust the process*, she told herself.

"What's your name, sweetie?" She rubbed her hand over the woman's swollen leg.

"Rhoda."

"Okay, Rhoda, here's what I want you to do. When you feel the next contraction coming, I want you to take a deep breath and push. But this time, when you need to breathe, don't let up on your push. Keep the pressure here in your pelvic area." Sid placed her hand on the woman's lower abdomen. "Don't relax here. When you do, the baby slips back up."

The woman nodded. Sweat dripped off her face.

"Hold the pressure—take a quick breath, keep pushing. We're almost there, sweetheart. Hang in a little longer."

Sirens wailed in the background.

The contractions wouldn't wait, and with the next one, Rhoda followed Sid's instructions. After a couple more hard pushes, a dark, bloody, squiggling mass slid out of Rhoda and into Sid's waiting hands.

"It's a boy, Rhoda," Sid choked the words out as she swabbed the inside of the baby's mouth with the corner of a thin towel.

The baby gasped once and let loose with a bellow.

The man tore into the room from the kitchen. "A boy? Oh my God, he's here." Awestruck, he stepped over to the bed and stared at the tiny bundle.

Being careful of the cord, Sid wiped the baby's face and laid him atop Rhoda's stomach.

The siren stopped. The man ran to the door, threw it open as the paramedics walked up. "He's here. The baby's here already. Hurry."

"Then there's no need to hurry," one of the paramedics said, laughing. It was the same two women who had shown up when Blue was murdered. They walked over to the bed. One took the baby, the other attended to Rhoda. "Looks like you did a fine job, ma'am. That's a healthy looking boy. He sure has good lungs."

They all chuckled with relief at the screaming baby.

"Let's get things wrapped up here, and we'll transport them to the hospital. Sir, you want to accompany us? Maybe your friend here can meet you there."

He looked at Sid.

She nodded. "We can talk later."

"You know where I'll be."

"By the way, what's your name?"

"Jones, Derreck Jones."

👁   👁   👁

"Why were you stalking the sheriff?" Sid sat in the hospital cafeteria across from Derreck. Both of them held steaming cups of coffee.

"Ma'am, I'm not real sure you want to know."

Sid stared into his black eyes.

"No offense lady, but you don't look the type to get yourself messed up in a pile of shit. This here shit's been piling up for decades."

Sid said nothing. Nor did she blink.

Derreck looked around the room, then back at Sid. "Before you got to the hospital I made some calls, else you and me wouldn't be having this conversation—just wanted you to know that."

Who had he talked with? George?

"I'm not right sure you ought to get yourself involved in this but…" He scooted his chair closer to Sid. "You ever heard of selling your soul to the devil? Well, this sheriff done sold his a long time ago. Whole neighborhood knows what's going on—but can't nobody do nothing to stop it."

Another man walked over to their table—tall, good-looking in a rugged kind of way. He wore faded denim jeans, and a dark-colored t-shirt that showed through an unbuttoned red flannel shirt. His black complexion was scarred from acne, but instead of marring his looks, the scars seemed to enhance a character built from adversity. After pulling over a chair, the man sat beside Derreck.

The temperature in the cafeteria was cold, but both men's dark skin glistened in the overhead lights. Nodding solemn-faced at the newcomer, Derreck said, "This here's Lee."

If Sid hadn't been alert, she would have missed the slight elbow punch Lee gave Derreck just as another man walked up to the table.

"Hedge." Derreck and Lee spoke in unison, voices tense.

The room no longer felt hospitable.

Derreck introduced Al Hedge to Sid, who shook her hand, but his eyes darted away.

"Am I interrupting something?" Hedge asked, looking at Derreck.

"We were just here talking about personal stuff. Can I get with you later, cuz?"

"Sure, sure." Hedge huffed, and walked off, then glanced back at them as he stepped into the hall.

"Who is he?" Sid asked.

"My cousin a couple of times removed. He runs the Men's Club, a gay bar out in Bridge City. The only guy I know running one that ain't one himself."

"I don't trust him." Lee sighed, leaned back in his chair and crossed his arms over his chest.

"Okay, let's start over." Derreck shoved aside the coffee, clasped his hands in front of him, squeezed, then released them, tapped his fingers on the table. "What I'm about to tell you has been going on a long time. My old man was a victim. He's still in Huntsville prison because of the guy, and he ain't even gay, just the daddy of one."

Lee picked up the conversation. "Someone is planting drugs in gay men's cars."

"You know who's doing it?" Sid scooted forward in her chair.

"Not sure who it is." Derreck picked up the tale. "But it's getting planted—that we know for sure. Then, when that guy gets stopped by the authorities for any reason, real or made up, they find the drugs and the guy goes to jail. It's that simple."

Sid straightened in her chair. "Quite a system someone's got going."

"Check and see how many gays get arrested in this town compared to others." Derreck looked Sid in the eye. "We've been trying to find out who's doing it."

"Is that why you were following the sheriff?"

Derreck looked away then back at Sid. "If it is him, this town's got a bigger problem than folks know."

"Could there be any connection between this and the murders that's been happening?" Sid knew she was grasping at straws, but she felt desperate for any new clue.

Derreck raised his eyebrows.

Lee shrugged. "Don't rightly know. But I do know the preacher was gay."

"Reverend Bluett? How do you know that?"

Derreck looked at Sid, then down at his hands twisting on the table. "Blue was a good man, ma'am, knew him all my life. If he could've just been free to be himself. But you can't be who you ain't. God knows, he tried. Being a preacher made him feel better about himself, but you know," he looked at Lee, then back at Sid, "it ain't who you are, but what you are that marks you in this town. Guilt ate him alive. Abe Collins was gay, too. He was another one of 'em what hid it by marrying."

"Is everyone in this town gay?" Sid asked.

"More than you might think," Derreck answered, shrugging again.

Now it was Lee's turn to scoot his chair closer to the conversation. "Pardon me, ma'am, but I should tell you this. The sheriff and Mrs. Collins 'ate supper before they said grace'."

"Excuse me?"

"Like—living in sin—you know? Sex?"

"Oh." Sid felt herself blush, finally understanding the colloquial phrase.

Lee whispered, leaning toward Sid. "I got this cousin; Maynard's his name. He's a deputy with the sheriff's department. He's known about Bonin and Mrs. Collins for years, but he had to keep his mouth shut. He told me the preacher was there at the Collins' early that morning, and the sheriff knows it 'cause he picked up evidence at the crime scene." Lee twisted in his chair and lowered his voice. "If it came out about the preacher and Abe, then other stuff might come out about him and Cherrie. This way, the sheriff walks away clean."

Now they really had Sid's attention.

"Cherrie Collins was still alive when the sheriff and my cousin, Maynard, got there," Lee explained, "but Maynard says the sheriff sent him out to the patrol car to get something. Just as he stepped back on the porch, he heard the sheriff calling Mrs. Collins a pushy bitch. By the time Maynard got inside, the sheriff was piling her body on the bed."

But how was Ned connected to all that, Sid wondered.

As if Lee read her mind, he offered. "After they found Ned dead, the way we figure it, the sheriff just made him the fall guy. Wrong time—wrong place sort a thing. I figure Ned saw the bloody mess, panicked, and took off."

"He must have seen the sheriff's car there. Why would he run?" Sid asked.

"Not necessarily," Lee replied, "not the way the house and the drive sit in relationship to the backyard."

"Will your cousin testify in court?" Sid asked.

Lee shook his head. "Probably not."

Pushing it a little further, Sid asked, "Will he talk to me?"

"I don't know, but I'll ask. Want me to call him?"

Wide-eyed, Sid stared, nodded.

Lee scraped his chair across the tile floor, sending goose bumps down Sid's arms. He headed to a pay phone in the corner, turned his back and dialed.

"The baby doing okay?" Sid tried to make small talk with Derreck while they waited for Lee's return.

"Doctor said he's doing fine. Can't thank you enough. This baby's really important to my sister. Her husband got killed a couple of months ago in a random drive-by shooting. This is all she's got left of him. I don't know what I would've done if you hadn't been there."

"You did look a little panicky," Sid teased, glancing toward the pay phone and the conversation taking place.

Just then, Lee hung up the phone, and headed back to the table, nodding. "Maynard said tonight, 'round ten—in the projects. Knows a place that'll be safe, or least he thinks it'll be. Take care, though. Folks watch for outsiders coming in, and you'll sure stand out. It's a different world than what you're used to. Want I should pick you up?" Lee offered.

Sid swallowed a lump in her throat. "That would be great."

They agreed on a meeting place, shook hands and Lee left.

Before Sid left the hospital, she and Derreck went up to the nursery and ooh and aah'd over the baby. Sid promised to come see mother and newborn when they got home. She drove out of the hospital parking lot intent on tracking down George, but her cell phone rang just as she flipped open the lid.

"Ms Smart? I'm the adjuster from your insurance company.

I need you to meet me at your burned-out office."

"Can't it wait? I'm kind of busy at the moment."

"Yeah, it can wait, but I can't get back to you for months. I'm heading out to Florida to work on damage done by the hurricanes. I'll be here a couple more minutes then I'm out of here." A click sounded, then dead air.

Damn. "George, you'll just have to wait." Sid flipped the phone shut, stuck it on the dash and turned her car around.

By the time she left the adjuster, George's office was shut and locked. She tried his cell phone but only got voice mail. Well, she'd tried.

👁   👁   👁

Lee stopped in front of a ratty-looking apartment and turned off the motor. "Nervous?"

"That's an understatement," Sid laughed, but she felt like two tribes of army ants battled just beneath her skin. George would kill her for doing this without him.

Lee waited in the car while she walked toward the front door. Trash littered the ground, empty beer bottles and cans, food wrappers. Sid's heart pounded louder than her footsteps.

The apartment windows were open, screens ripped and bent. Cockroaches blatantly crawled across her feet as she stood at the front door of the unit. She yelped, frightening a feral cat that darted from a pile of trash.

She tapped on the door. A man in deputy uniform opened it. Without a word from either of them, Sid slipped inside. The deputy locked the door and motioned her toward the back of the apartment.

They picked their way across a brown shag carpet crisscrossed with extension cords. Faded curtains hung loosely over haphazard blinds. In the far corner sat an ancient TV set, and on top of it, a can of bug spray.

The man reached the kitchen ahead of Sid and flipped on the light.

The stove, counter and table stood in varying stages of crustiness. Undeterred by harsh lights, or their presence, roaches crawled around in paper plates, cups, spoons. A beat-up refrigerator sat beside a double sink.

Outside, Sid heard laughter and talking, giving her a sense of normalcy. Her heart sank when Maynard walked over and shut the door, but it sunk even further when she saw what lay behind it—a thin paper plate covered with bits of dried food and omnipresent roaches. Beside the plate sat a plastic Cool Whip container half-filled with water, cigarette butts floating on top. Near by, a litter box overflowed onto the cheap linoleum.

Sid dug her thumbnail into her index finger, hoping the pain would take her mind off of her churning stomach. The thought that vomit in the room would only provide more food for the roaches helped not one bit.

The deputy stuck his hand out. "Maynard, ma'am, but I'd just as soon you forgot my name, or that you ever talked to me. You know what I mean?"

"What name?" Sid shook the man's hand, as moist as her own.

"Sorry to have to meet here, but there's not many places safe enough. This here belongs to a bro, and as you can see, he don't clean much. Fact is, he don't even know we're here. It's better that way." The man looked around the room. "I'd offer you a chair, but..."

"No, that's okay, I'll stand," Sid squeaked, hoping he'd hurry.

Maynard looked Sid square in the eye. "I'm here 'cause Lee asked me to meet with you—tell you what I know about the sheriff. I'm taking a big risk, but I trust Lee with my life, so if he says you're okay, I'll take his word. But ma'am, you need to know you're treading dangerous waters."

Sid cleared her throat then, "I heard you were at the Collins place the day of the murder. I want to know what you saw, what you suspect, and what you know to be true."

"Whew, tall order. If the sheriff finds out I'm talking to you, you know I'm dead."

"I'm afraid you're not the only one."

Silence filled the room. The only audible sound was insect feet scratching across paper plates.

Maynard rubbed both hands across his bald head, turned and paced the small kitchen. "Anyway, the way I figure it, Cherrie found out about Abe and the preacher's affair…"

"Wait, what do you mean," Sid interrupted. "Abe and the preacher were having an affair? How do you know that?"

"Let's just say I know, and leave it at that, okay?"

"Okay."

"As I was saying, Cherrie caught 'em in the act, grabbed a kitchen knife and swung at Abe, caught him right in the heart. After he fell, she came after the preacher, who we figure grabbed the knife and swung in self-defense, panicked and ran, thinking he'd killed her, but Cherrie wadn't dead.

Me and the sheriff was riding round on patrol when she called him on his cell phone in a panic. Said she'd killed Abe then played dead after her and Blue struggled over the knife. That the preacher had run off thinking he killed her, and knowing she'd killed Abe.

When we got there, the sheriff told me to stay outside. But then I seen Ned walking across the railroad tracks toward the house. I headed up to tell the sheriff."

That part of the story varied a little from what she'd heard at the hospital. Had the sheriff sent Maynard to the car, or left him there? She made a mental note.

"Before I got up the steps to the front door, I heard 'em arguing. Cherrie was saying the sheriff had to leave his wife now, and marry her, but he sounded fed up. They struggled, and in no time, Cherrie lay dead on the bed with her husband. When I told him about Ned coming, we hightailed it to the patrol car. Sheriff talked about how lucky he was Ned had come up." Maynard stopped to take a breath.

She'd held her breath, too, and exhaled.

"I figure Ned panicked, ran out and got himself killed by the train," Maynard continued. "Probably wasn't paying close attention after what he'd seen. As far as the sheriff was concerned, all the better."

"Do you know anything about drugs stashed in cars of gay men?"

"Ma'am, you sure 'nough don't make this easy." Maynard blew through pursed lips and stared at the floor. He shuffled his boot against faded linoleum, but when he looked up, truth spread across his face like a kid threatened with the woodshed. "I don't know who's doing it exactly, but I sure as hell know someone is."

"But you have an idea." Roaches and deteriorating cat feces seemed of little consequence at the moment. Small beads of sweat covered Sid's top lip. She wiped her hand across her mouth and then swiped it on her sleeve.

"Yes'm, I have an idea, all right, but..."

"You think it's the sheriff?"

Maynard laughed. "I think so, but I'm not positive. One thing I do know, though. I'm glad he don't know I'm gay."

"Why is that?"

" 'Cause he sure don't like 'em."

"But how does he know who's gay and who isn't?"

"Ma'am, that's another thing I wish I knew."

Sid and Maynard said goodbye, both wishing the other well.

But the next morning when Sid picked up *The Orange Leader*, Maynard's picture was plastered across the front page. *Local Deputy shot dead in line of duty.*

Everything he'd told Sid was now hearsay.

👁   👁   👁

It was late afternoon before Sid got to George's office and found him with his head stuck in a file drawer digging through folders. "Hey you, got a minute?" She called out, surprising him.

"Hey, sha. Yeah, give me just a minute to get this file back in straight." He shuffled the papers in the manila folder and crammed it in the drawer. "Now." He sat and plopped his big, ugly shoes on his desk. "What can I do you for?"

Sid recounted Maynard's story from the night before, and the information she'd gotten from Derreck and Lee. George listened, nodding his head every few minutes, sometimes staring off in the distance.

"Ain't that Maynard guy the deputy that got shot to death last night?"

"I'm afraid so."

"And now, you have no one to back up what he told you." He slammed his hand down on his desk. "Dammit, you can put your boots in the oven, but that sure don't make 'em biscuits. I figured something like this was going on—heard rumors, but never knew for sure. How'd you get wind of all this?"

"Delivered a baby." Sid sat with a smug grin on her face.

"You did what?" George's feet thudded to the floor as he bolted upright.

"I caught Derreck Jones following the sheriff, so I followed Derreck. Didn't know it was him at the time. When he went home, I trailed him into this apartment and found his sister in hard labor."

"Well, I'll be damned, Sid, you're something else." George walked over and refilled his coffee cup. "It all makes sense." George blew air through pursed lips, ambled over to the window.

Then he stiffened.

His voice soft, but his words stern, he whispered, "Out the back door, Sid. No questions. Just go. Now."

Sid jumped as if she'd been prodded with a hot poker. She darted to the door, grabbed the knob and tried to turn it, but her sweaty hands slipped off.

She wiped her palm on her pants leg and grabbed again.

The door stuck, swollen from humidity; she pulled harder.

George scuffled behind her. "Hurry," he demanded.

One more yank, and the door opened. Slipping through the exit, she took one quick glance over her shoulder and saw George shove her handbag underneath his desk, heard a commotion in the front office, and then George's words, "Sheriff, now what do I owe the pleasure of your company?"

Forcing her body to move slower, when all it wanted to do was flee, Sid snuck around the end of the building. The sheriff's patrol car sat alongside hers. She rammed her hands down into her pockets for her keys then realized they were in her handbag inside.

She charged down the side alley, through an older housing addition until she reached a railroad. Afraid she'd be seen if she walked on the tracks, she eased down and crept through tall weeds, with no idea where she was, or where she was going, or when she'd get there.

The sun dropped below the horizon, making her path even more difficult. She tripped over an old bicycle tire and later, a discarded mattress.

Was she over-reacting to the sheriff's visit? George's tone indicated otherwise.

Across the tracks, a Catholic school stood vacant, kids and staff long gone. She made her way to the back courtyard, slipped through a double-wide gate, and flopped down beside a vending machine. The concrete walk felt damp, but the warmth of the motor eased the stiffness creeping into her bones.

This was crazy—a woman her age being chased by the sheriff.

Hunkered down, she leaned against the wall, pulled her cell phone out of her pocket and dialed George.

"Sid?"

"George? You okay?"

"I'm okay. He just left. Where are you?"

"Some Catholic school on the other side of the railroad tracks."

"I know where you are. Wait for me, I'll be right there."

Ten minutes later, she heard wheels crunching on the driveway, but she waited until she heard George softly call her name before she emerged from the shadows.

"Get in, quick."

Once inside, George u-turned and drove out of the parking lot and headed toward I-10.

"Hell, Sid, you've sure stirred up a hornets nest." He glanced over at her, and then in his rear view mirror. "That damn sheriff thinks the sun comes up just to hear him crow. Sounds to me like you're on to something. Question is, now what the hell do we do with it?"

"You're asking me? You're the authority here."

Both of them laughed, nervous, not funny.

"I wonder how he knew I was at your office?"

"Your vehicle ain't easy to miss, sha." George glanced over at her. "Most detectives drive a car—or in this town, a truck—that blends in with all the others. But no, not you; you have to drive a big yellow Xterra as bright as a billboard lit up at night."

"Okay, what do I do now?"

"It's *we* Sid, not you." George took the Bridge City exit.

"You going to your house?"

"Yep. Thought I would. Don't know where else to take ya. Damn sure can't take you home."

"But won't he be watching your house?"

"He ain't after me, he's after you. You done stirred up some mighty powerful trouble."

"Double back—take me out to Ben's."

"Hillerman? Okay, I can live with that," George said, making another u-turn. "Oh, I brought your purse, it's there on the floor."

When they reached Ben's house, Sid slipped out of the car under cover of dark, and rang the bell.

Twenty-Five

Annie hung up the phone, thrilled that Sid had called to report she was spending the night with Ben. She collected Chesterfield and draped him over her arm while she pulled Slider by his collar across the kitchen towards the back porch where she'd placed a warm blanket and a bowl of water. "You'll be okay out here for the night, buddy," she said, defending her actions to the dog, who stiffened his legs as she dragged him across the doorjamb.

Back inside the kitchen she reached into the cabinet for the second half of the cat's daily dose of Phenobarbital. He'd been seizure-free for six years; she sure didn't want to mess with that. She opened the bottle, pulled out a pill and pushed it down the cat's throat. "Good boy," she smiled down at him as she rubbed under his neck. Accustomed to the procedure, he offered no resistance. That done, then she turned out the lights and headed upstairs, the cat still in tow.

Just as Annie stepped into her bedroom, the phone rang. She snatched it up thinking maybe Sid needed her.

"It's Maggie, honey. Is Sidra there?"

"Sid? No she's out gallivantin' as usual." She wasn't going to reveal Sid was sleeping at Ben's. But why on earth was Annie's oldest friend asking for Sid?

"You sittin' down?"

"Oh, for God's sake, Margaret Ann, tell me what you got to say. You don't have to be so dang melodramatic."

"Uh, I was hoping Sid would be there with you. It would

make this easier. But, well, it's Frank, baby," Maggie choked on her words. "Walter found him at dusk out in the middle of his pasture surrounded by his Jerseys. Looks like he'd gone to bring the cows in for the night."

Annie's chest tightened. "What're you trying to say? He's okay, right?"

Chesterfield yowled. Annie dropped him to the floor and he scatted out of the bedroom.

"He had a heart attack, sweetie, he's—there's just no easy way to say it. Honey, Frank's gone."

Annie leaned against the wall and slid to the floor, the receiver still at her ear. "Where is he?"

"They've taken him to the funeral home. Weren't no need to take him to the hospital. Coroner said it looked like it had been quick. He didn't suffer much. Heart just quit." The line grew quiet. Then, "Annie, honey, can I come get you? Call Sid for you? You got to let me do something." Pain radiated through the phone line.

Why didn't she feel anything? Her husband of umpteen years had just died, and all she felt was numb. "No, no, I'm okay. I'll call Sid, and we'll be right there."

"We'll handle things on this end 'til you get here. You're sure now. You don't need me to come get you?"

After reassuring Maggie one more time, Annie crawled to her feet and straightened her nightgown. Just as she laid the receiver on the cradle, Chesterfield hissed behind her. "Its okay, Chessy, we're…" She turned to pick up her cat, but stopped when she saw the sheriff in her bedroom doorway, in a standoff with her cat. Come to break the news, she figured, and she just hadn't heard him knock.

👁 👁 👁

The next morning Sid opened her eyes to Ben, still asleep. She watched his chest rise and fall with each breath. With all his brown hair, including morning stubble, he reminded her of a hibernating bear—but more like a teddy than a grizzly. She turned over and glanced around Ben's bedroom. Condensation covered the windows, giving the outdoors an ethereal quality, making her want to snuggle underneath the sleeping bear.

Instead, she got up, showered and dressed, and by the time she heard him in the shower, she'd found the makings for coffee. Soon as the coffeemaker stopped dripping she poured herself a cup, meandered to the back window, and stared out at a titmouse perched on the birdfeeder.

She didn't hear Ben walk in until he hooked his arm around her waist and pulled her to him. She felt him, fully aroused against her.

"Morning, you. Sleep well?" he asked, nuzzling his chin on the top of her head.

"Mmm. Hated to get up." She set her cup on the table and turned into his arms. The warmth of his white terrycloth robe felt soft against her cheek. She snuggled into it, twining her fingers in the still-damp hairs of his chest. "Let me guess," she smiled up at him, "your shower wasn't a cold one."

"No way. Not when I have you here." With his parted lips just off of hers, he spoke in her mouth, pulling her tighter against him.

She gulped in a breath when he ran one hand around her neck and slid the other one down to her buttocks. He pressed his lips against hers, soft, urgent, tasting of mint. She denied herself a moan of pleasure. In such a short time, the man had learned just how to kiss her, how to set her afire with his touch—and that left her way too vulnerable. When she'd left Sam she promised herself she'd never let that happen again.

"Every night I lay awake planning what I'd do when I saw you again," Ben whispered in her ear. "When my doorbell rang last night, I never dreamed it'd be you standing there."

"Was the rest of the night as you'd planned?"

"Only a beginning my love, only a beginning." He caught her eyes with his, clutched the bottom of her blouse and pulled it over her head then kissed her ear. "Got time?"

His hot breath on her neck sent chills down her body. She quivered with her need to have him inside her.

He took her hand in his and headed to the bedroom. "I've been thinking," his words were slow, cautious. "I'd like for you to sell The Third Eye and get a job that isn't so dangerous."

Passion washed out of her like a forest fire doused by a tsunami. This was exactly what she'd feared would happen. "Let me go." She yanked her hand out of his, stalked back into the kitchen, and snatched up her blouse. When she tried pulling it on, she found one sleeve wrong side out. "Damn it, you got the whole thing twisted."

Ben walked over. "Here let me help."

"I don't need any help," she spat through clenched teeth. "I can put on my own damn blouse."

But the blouse was against her too, for after straightening the sleeve, she tried pulling it over her head and a button tangled in her hair. She yanked out a couple hairs as she fought her way through the garment.

Meanwhile, red-faced Ben stood across from her with his hands on his hips.

"What the hell's going on, Sid? Why are you so upset?"

"I don't need a man telling me what to do."

"I'm not trying to tell you what to do, dammit, it's just... I don't like the idea of you risking your life every goddamn day!"

"This is my job—my business."

"That's the point. As long as you run the detective agency…"

"This isn't going to work, Ben."

"What do you mean, it isn't going to work? Can't you open some other business—or get a job or something? Anything that doesn't put your life at risk every waking moment."

"I spent the first half of my life taking no risks, doing what I was told, but no more." Irritation heated her cheeks, which pissed her off royally. She snatched up her bag, "Now, please take me to get my car."

"Mind if I put on my pants first?" Ben snarled then turned and stomped, barefoot, down the hall. The set of his shoulders, and determination in his step still argued his point. She knew his stubbornness, knew he wouldn't give an inch.

Neither would she.

They drove in silence, both of them staring straight ahead. She saw him glance her way when she fidgeted with the engagement ring around her finger. She stuck her hand under her thigh.

The parking lot in front of George's office was empty except for Sid's vehicle. Ben shoved the gear to park, dropped his hands on his knees and huffed.

"One thing you've got to know about me, Ben." Her words came out so hot that Ben leaned away from them. "I won't put up with a man telling me what I should and shouldn't do. And I won't put up with over-protectiveness. Until you're willing to accept that, there is absolutely no chance for us."

She yanked the door open, grabbed her handbag and slid out of his car and into hers without a word. Back stiff, head high, Sid started the motor, turned the vehicle, and drove off, refusing to glance Ben's way.

She headed home to change out of the same clothes she'd worn traipsing through weeds and across railroad tracks. Discounting the bitter taste of swallowed tears and the sadness in her chest, Sid shoved her thoughts elsewhere, anywhere other than Ben.

Traffic on Sixteenth Street was light this early in the morning and gave Sid time to notice all the businesses she'd ignored before. Fast food restaurants, doughnut shops and older small homes now converted into offices, all spaced between red lights at every block. As she sat at her fourth stoplight in a row, she tapped her fingers on the steering wheel and stared at the light. Tears brimmed the edge of her eyelids. She swiped them away, pulled out a tissue and wiped her nose.

"Sidra Smart, get your mind off Ben and on this case. Think." She banged the palm of her hand on the steering wheel to staunch the tears. "You can do this."

Who did she know that she hadn't checked out?

The guy at the hospital—Hedge, Al Hedge—he'd acted strange. They said he owned a gay nightclub and wasn't gay, himself. That, in itself, seemed unusual.

When the light turned green, Sid made a sharp u-turn and headed to Bridge City.

Someone must be fingering gay men for Bonin—had to be—else how would he know who was gay and who wasn't? You couldn't just pick them out in crowd. Well, yeah, sometimes you could, but not always.

The Men's Club hugged the shore of the Neches River. The gray-colored structure blended into the background. A thick coat of paint on the windows blocked all light, both from within and without. Plastered on the front of the building, a simple black and white sign announced the name of the place.

Sid crossed traffic, turned left into the gravel and grass parking lot, and stopped beside a rusty Ford pickup truck. She'd hoped to find the place empty, for she'd gotten good at this B & E stuff. But the front door swung open without noise or difficulty.

"Hello?" she half-whispered, peeking around the door. No one answered. She stepped inside. Neon beer signs cast a soft enough glow to not bump into anything.

The place looked like any other bar before it comes alive with lights, action, and alcohol. Tables were positioned randomly around the room with chairs turned upside down on tabletops. With no one leaning on, or standing behind, the bar, it looked forlorn, useless. At the end, a large glass fishbowl overflowed with white matchbooks. Sid took one out and ran her thumb over the black raised letters, *The Men's Club*. She flipped open the cover. Designated lines provided space to enter a guy's name, height, age, and of course a telephone number. She closed it and stuck the matches in her pocket.

A poster of a nude man holding a bottle of beer hung on the wall behind the bar next to an announcement of an upcoming drag show. She'd never seen a drag show before and wondered if they were anything like the womanless weddings her dad took her to when she was a kid. If so, she was missing out on a lot of fun.

She'd decided no one was there until she saw a dim light shining under a door in the rear. When she stepped that way, her foot stubbed an empty beer bottle, and it clattered across the floor.

She froze in place and waited.

The room exhaled, or was it her, when no one came charging from the office. She inched closer and put her ear to the door. The male voice was in the midst of a one-way conversation—either talking to himself or someone on the phone.

A clammy skin advised her not to interrupt.

Irritated that she couldn't make out what he said, she cracked the door open.

Al Hedge sat with his back to her, fidgeting his chair left and right, a telephone to his ear. "…pretty busy last night, yeah. Didn't see any new ones come in—not any we don't already know of."

The person on the other end must have said something because Al Hedge paused, then gave a colluding laugh. "Yeah, I know what you mean. So you got her, huh?" Another pause, and then, "Well, I hope this works 'cause this put us in over our necks. We screw this and we're both up shit-creek. And I'm not even talking about your election and our business. Maybe after things calm down, we better do like we done before and lay low for a while." Then, "Okay, keep me posted." He hung up the phone and stood.

Sid stepped away in a panic. Winding around tables and chairs, she slipped out the front door expecting a blow on the head, or a shot in the back.

By the time she slinked to the car, her knees felt like rubber, and her nerves like a tightly wound jack-in-the-box. She cringed with the rumble of tires on the gravel parking lot, relieved when she pulled onto the paved road, and headed home.

After her heartbeat slowed enough to hear her own thoughts, she wondered what the hell was going on. Who was he talking to and who did the other guy *have*? Hedge had said *she*. Well, they weren't talking about Sid. Ella? No, that had been Blue, and that news had already made headlines. No one had Ella now except Ian.

It didn't make sense.

The twenty minute drive home wasn't long enough to answer all the questions raging through her head, so she pulled into the driveway behind Annie's car, got out and walked down the sidewalk to The Third Eye. She unlocked the door and went straight to her computer.

It took a minute to boot up and open her browser. She typed in Orange County Appraisal District, then scrolled over to Appraisal Role Search and clicked on By Street Address. When the form came up, she typed in the street address of The Men's Club. On the black, white, and orange web page, the only owner listed was Alfred A Hedge. Sid logged off.

Pulling her dirty shirttail out of her slacks, she headed toward the kitchen. "Annie, you here? Slider?"

She pushed her way through the kitchen's swinging door and checked her watch. Annie would never be caught sleeping this late. She always had the laundry on the line by eight o'clock. Maybe that's where she was, outside. Sid walked around the butcher-block island to the back door and opened it to a sleeping dog. When Slider heard Sid, he scrambled to his feet and lunged around her legs to get inside.

"What in the world are you doing outside, baby? Did Annie put you out here? Where is she? Do you know?"

Slider looked up at her as if to say he didn't know—much less care—where Annie or his antagonist had gone.

She stopped long enough to feed the starving dog then headed for the laundry room, continuing her search.

Annie still viewed getting her laundry on the line before anyone else as a competition, despite the fact no one else in the town even hung laundry outside. She refused to use the dryer, preferring, 'the fresh smell of sunshine on my sheets and towels'.

In the laundry room she found no clothes, and no Annie.

The house took a shuddering, uneasy breath.

"Chesterfield?"

Maybe they'd gone for a drive.

No, Annie's car had been parked in front of Sid's.

After she checked the whole downstairs and found neither Annie nor the cat, Sid headed up, now convinced her aunt must be ill.

It took a minute to recognize the orange ball lying in a heap at the head of the stairs. "Chesterfield?" She charged the rest of the way up the stairs, two rungs at a time. When she reached his side she saw streaks of dried blood across the cat's fur. His eyes were closed, his breathing shallow.

"Annie?" Sid darted down the hall to her aunt's room.

The bed was made, but slightly disheveled, the shattered bedside lamp lay on the floor.

The house exhaled again, louder this time. It's breath smelled of dank salt water and rotten fish.

Twenty-Six

Dizzy—if Annie could just open her eyes, maybe the room would stop spinning—but—heavy.

A badge floated by, and somewhere way off in the distance, a hiss.

Images thrashed around in her head like tentacles of a sea creature caught in a net. A ringing phone floated by, and she tried to answer it then realized she had no arms. Frantic, she struggled.

It was Maggie—had to talk to Maggie.

Husband.

The fog in Annie's head began to clear.

Oh, no, not…

Grief smothered her like a hot blanket. A tear surfaced, slid out the corner of her eye and down her temple.

But before the salty drop reached her hairline, she sunk back into a drug-induced sleep.

When next she opened her eyes, the sun lightened the room. She lay on a rickety cot in a room that rocked, her hands tied behind her back. On a small table in the middle of the room, a coal oil lamp burned, revealing a small hunting cabin with weathered wooden beams and rough-hewn walls. Odd paraphernalia lay scattered around the room. Annie's nose twitched from a fishy smell; she twisted around and rubbed it against the canvas cot. Rhythmic sounds jarred a memory. She stilled her breath. All she heard was the ragged breath from a heap of clothes on a cot across from her until the soft lap of water filtered in between the snores.

We're near water. Annie bolted straight up on the cot.

Water?

The spin of the room hadn't been in her brain. The whole dang building swayed. "We're not near water, we're *on* water. This is a house boat," Annie whispered.

👁   👁   👁

The red taillights of the car glowered at Sid as the neighbors drove off with Chesterfield cradled in the woman's lap. They'd wrapped him in a thick towel, nuked in the microwave, before transporting him to the vet.

Sirens wailed in the distance—louder every minute—while Sid waited in the front yard, her arms wrapped around Slider. Both of them shivered. She couldn't wait inside; the house felt as empty as her heart. First the fight with Ben, now Annie was gone.

Both irritated and thrilled when she saw Ben's car trailing the incoming cruisers, she rubbed down the goose bumps on her arms.

Cars screeched to a stop, doors flew open, and officers jumped out. Sid tried to focus on Quade walking her way, but Ben reached her first. He didn't say a word, just grabbed her and held her tight. The tension he'd demonstrated earlier that morning had vaporized into the humid air.

All she wanted to do was to let go, sink down into Ben. Instead, she stiffened, clenched her arms to her side, determined not to yield, wanting so badly to let go.

"What happened?" Quade asked as soon as he reached Sid.

How in hell did she tell him she'd slept at Ben's last night—how great the sex had been, and how she'd felt this morning when Ben drew the damn line on the floor. How she hadn't even been here when her aunt was kidnapped? And even her time with Ben wasn't worth it now.

Ben released her, but stood clasping her hand as she recounted her discovery of Annie's disappearance—what she found when she got home, how she'd not come home the night before—refusing to look Ben's way, stuttering in the process of the telling. Quade glanced at Ben who stared at the ground like a kicked puppy.

"I'm contacting the FBI on this one," Quade announced to the group. "Kidnapping with intent to blackmail, or to hide another crime, is a federal case." He turned and headed toward his officers.

Quade gave instructions, pointing toward the house, back at Sid. He stared at the ground, and shuffled his boot through the wet St. Augustine grass, splattering heavy dew up on his khaki uniform pants.

He walked back to Sid and asked her to meet him at his office. He'd be there as soon as he finished. "My guess is, this is a ploy to get at you. Annie's just a decoy."

👁   👁   👁

After answering every question Quade could think of, Sid had been excused. She walked out of the police station, crawled in her car, and sat twirling the engagement ring around her finger. There was no way she could concentrate on Ben's proposal with Annie missing, especially now that she knew his opinion about her running The Third Eye. Why had she even accepted the ring in the first place? She shook her head and pushed aside thoughts of Ben.

Where in hell do they have Annie? It had to be Hedge, and whomever he was talking to on the phone. That's the only thing that made sense.

She backed the car out and headed down the street with no idea where she was going. She passed her burned-out office site, and pictured Annie the first day she'd shown up, all smiles, eager to help. How could she have been so resentful of the woman? Despite Annie's incessant phone calls, she'd actually been a lot of help.

Sid just drove, paying little attention to her surroundings, tears rolling down her cheeks. She surprised herself when she ended up in the parking lot of Blue's church.

Old habits return under pressure... She sat and contemplated whether or not to make a request of the God she'd put on hold.

"You okay?" The question, accompanied with a knock on the passenger window, startled Sid out of her zombie state.

Before she could respond, Blue's secretary Priscilla—the holy woman—jerked open the passenger-side door and slipped inside.

"You okay? Can I help?"

"No, I'm okay, just a weak moment," Sid swiped her eyes with the backs of her hands and forced a smile, not willing to be the woman's good deed for the day.

"I know what you mean. I've been having a lot of those since Pastor got murdered, and then all that news about what he did to his wife... Have you heard from Ella? I tried to get in to see her, but they said no visitors."

"Ella's okay."

"Good."

"Have they found out who killed Pastor yet?"

"No, not yet."

Priscilla's perkiness had vanished. She still seemed keyed up, but recent events had taken their toll. Her hairdo wasn't curled quite as tight, and even looked a little imperfect. The fur stole was gone. She still wore the diamond pendant necklace, but it hung just a little crooked.

"Tell me Priscilla, how have you handled all this about your pastor? Must be difficult when God's representative falls off a pedestal, and even more so for those who kept him up there." Sid bit her tongue a little too late. "I'm sorry," she added, "that wasn't nice."

"To tell the truth, I feel like my world's fallen apart," Priscilla fiddled with the straps on her Dooney & Burke handbag. "Everything I believed has been shattered. I've not told anyone this, but—I was in love with Pastor."

"I know."

"It showed?"

" 'fraid so."

Laughter, sadness—even a little sarcasm—slipped out of the woman. "I tried not to be, but he just seemed so—so perfect. Always talking about God and all. You know? Had the answers to anything. Sometimes I felt like he knew everything there was to know about God. Kind, gentle, helpful. The perfect man. Then, after he died I heard he was one of those homosexuals." Priscilla shuddered. "To think..."

"Yeah, I rather suspect that caught you by surprise. It did me, too, and if you recall, I was married to one of those perfect men, too. Not gay, as far as I know, but a minister." As soon as the words came out, Sid wished she hadn't said them. She'd not intended to reveal her pain.

Priscilla raised her eyebrows and opened her mouth, but before she could ask any questions, Sid waved her off. "Never mind that, right now, my aunt's missing, and I'm worried sick." She paused, fully expecting Priscilla to offer to pray.

Instead, she perked up and asked, "Missing? As in wandered off? Can I help?"

Taken aback by the offer, Sid's first reaction was refusal, so she patted Priscilla's hand lying on the console between them. "That's okay, thanks."

"I mean it. You've got to let me help you. We women have to stick together." A smile belied tears glistening in the perfectly made-up eyes.

No sooner did Sid shake her head, saying, "No, that's okay, it's too dangerous," than a DVD replayed behind her eyes, a rerun of Sid almost shoving Ella out of her office that first day, and then of Ben's coercive voice saying *I don't like the idea of you in danger.*

"A look-out might come in handy," she said, and then confided to Priscilla what she had been told about the sheriff. How he set up gays, and of her suspicion he'd kidnapped her aunt to silence Sid.

Priscilla stared straight ahead, her mouth open.

Oh, God, this was too much for the woman. Sid hushed, sat in silence and stared out the windshield, wishing she'd never taken the woman in confidence.

After a long pause, Priscilla roused. "Not that I don't believe you," she patted Sid's shoulder, "but it's hard to—to believe this is happening in our small town."

Another long pause while Sid agonized over the revelation she'd shared with a woman she barely knew.

"You think the sheriff had anything to do with Brother Blue's death?"

"Can't prove it, but it's possible."

"Then I want to help." Priscilla persisted.

"Why?"

"Guilt."

"For what?"

"My superior, judgmental nature."

Sid's own guilt tapped her on the shoulder. She'd been no better than those she'd judged. Swallowing hard, she looked at the woman beside her. Now wasn't the time or place for Sid's confession, but maybe someday...

Priscilla leaned across the seat and hugged Sid before she knew what was coming. Startled, she pulled back at first, but then returned the gesture. Before Priscilla left, she promised Sid she'd tell no one about their conversation, or Sid's suspicions.

"I'll be calling you as soon as I know what my next step is," Sid called out as Priscilla shut the car door.

After she left the church, Sid stopped at the animal hospital, relieved to learn the cat would be okay. The doctor wanted to keep him there for observation and monitoring, but his wounds didn't look fatal.

Next, she headed home. She didn't care what Quade said, she was going to sleep in her own bed.

They had their bait—Annie—now they'd wait on Sid.

Normally, she felt like the house breathed in sync with the

ticking of all the clocks—the heartbeat of the house, Annie called it—but now the house seemed as breathless as a graveyard.

In the kitchen, she glanced at the cat's empty bowl. Poor Chesterfield, she'd treat him better when he returned. She picked up the bowl and set it in the sink, promising herself she'd wash it tomorrow.

Double-checking the doors and windows, and taking her Glock with her, she and Slider headed to the stairs. Kate hadn't shown up in a while. Hopefully tonight wouldn't change that. Sid was in no mood for ambiguity or subtlety.

But, as if her thoughts generated paranormal behavior, when she started up the stairs the house started breathing again.

Stock still, her hand on the banister, Sid sucked in her breath, held it, and listened. There it was again.

She tried to shake off the spooky sound by breathing in and out herself—slow, deep, loud—then headed on up.

Halfway to the second floor, she glanced to the top of the staircase. A shadowy figure stood there, waiting. Encased in black, from the gown, to the black veil, the figure now looked just like the woman in the picture at Dempsey's.

Slider's hackles raised, and a low growl emanated from the back of his throat.

"Annie, is that you?" Sid froze. Her hand squeezed the rail. Should she go up—or run? Not sure she had the strength to do either she blinked, hoping the apparition would turn into Annie.

It didn't. Sid pointed the gun.

"Kate?" God she felt silly—stupid. Yes, she had seen a ghost before, but she'd never been convinced it had been one. Instead, she'd told herself she'd been half-asleep.

This time she couldn't do that.

The woman turned and glided across the floor, beckoning Sid to follow. The long filmy black veil flowed behind the apparition as she headed towards Annie's bedroom.

Sid didn't know whether to follow or to call 911. Nothing in her prior life had prepared her to see a ghost, much less follow one—quite the contrary. But then again she'd never lived in a ghost-active house before, either.

"Stay here if you want to, Slider, but I'm going up." Heavy foot followed heavy foot as she moved up the stairs and down the hall, the floor squeaking under her weight, frightening her even more. Then she realized the floor hadn't squeaked a moment before—when the figure had swept past. Sid took another step, listened for the creak—reassurance she was awake and physical. Solid.

The figure—Kate—rounded the corner into Annie's room, but when Sid stuck her head in, the woman was gone, and the lamp still lay on the floor.

But no Kate.

Damn. Sid didn't know if she felt lucky or disappointed.

"Okay, Sid, you're losing it," she yelled, desperate to hear a human voice.

She left Annie's room and headed toward the dog, relieved whatever she thought she'd seen was gone. As she passed the bathroom, she heard a faucet dripping. Just as she stepped inside to tighten it, the drip became a downpour. Water shot from the faucets of the shower, the tub, and the lavatory. The commode ran, as if it had just been flushed.

"What the hell?" Sid turned off the knobs and watched the water swirl out of the respective bowls while her blood felt like it curdled in her veins.

Kate was trying to tell her something—but what?

She stumbled to her room and collapsed, face-first, onto the bed next to Slider, who'd all ready crawled under the covers. Confusion clouded her brain as she lay there moaning, eyes squeezed shut. After a few minutes, she rolled over onto her back, one arm on her forehead, and stared up at the ceiling. Tears rolled down the side of her face and into her hairline.

Was Kate trying to lead her to Annie—tell her where the woman was? Did it all have to do with water? That maybe Annie was near water?

Sid was going out of her damn mind.

She slipped Ben's ring off her finger and laid it in on the bedside table, and then pulled down the covers. Doubting she'd sleep, she left the lamp on, and curled into Slider's warm, real, body. Instantaneous, inky darkness engulfed her.

👁   👁   👁

Sid squinted at the clock beside the bed as she snatched up the insistently ringing phone. "Sid? It's Marv. Did I wake you?"

"Well, yeah. Are you at the office this early?"

"Had some work to catch up on. Sorry to disturb you, but listen, I'm wondering if you might come by the office first thing this morning."

Sid wracked her brain. What else was on her schedule? Oh my God, Annie was still gone. "I guess so. It'll be a while though, I'm not up and dressed yet. What's this about?"

"I'll tell you when you get here." Marv said, and then Sid heard the dial tone. Foggy-headed, she wondered, did she still have Marv's name on the list of suspects, or had she marked him off?

She crawled out of bed, staggered to the bathroom and made quick work of her daily grooming routine. While she made the bed, Ben's diamond glistened at her from the nightstand. She switched off the lamp, hesitated, then picked up the ring and pushed it on her finger.

On the way to Marv's office, she called Quade to see if there had been any new leads on Annie's disappearance. But even before he told her, she knew by the sound of his voice that there wasn't.

She walked into Marv's office and greeted his assistant who, without explanation, escorted Sid into Marv's office.

He'd gone out for a couple minutes, the assistant reported, but had emphasized that he wanted Sid to wait in his office. The woman walked out and shut the door.

Sid wandered the office, irritated that she had to wait on

him after he'd rushed her to get here. She checked the bookshelves, peeped through the blinds. She had better things to do than fritter time away waiting for Marv. Why in hell did he call her then leave?

She sat in his chair and twirled around, picked up a pen near a folder stamped 'Confidential' and bounced the pen on the shiny desktop, tap, tap, tap.

Mindless, irritation growing, she flipped the corner of the file, glanced down and saw the name on the folder—Alfred A. Hedge.

Twenty-Seven

"Least you can do is untie my hands so I can wipe my own ass." The little modesty Annie had was now gone. Sitting on a slop jar in front of a Gabby Hays-look-alike stranger had a way of doing that, she figured.

"Oh shut your bitching, woman. Here." *Gabby* handed her a wad of cheap toilet paper. "I tied 'em in front, now. What do you expect, a one-way ticket outta here?" Unsupported by toothless gums, his lips flapped as he talked.

"That would be nice."

Sarcastic laughter boiled out of his throat. He hobbled to the opposite side of his cot and sat with his back to Annie. An unbuckled overall strap swung loose down his back.

Locking away her grief over Husband's death, Annie sat doing her business. No way in hell would she tell this codger about it, for she knew he'd make light of it—use it against her. She'd always been called a strong, stubborn woman. Well, this was one time she had to use those things to get her through this. Sid was coming. Annie just had to buy Sid time. "What's this all about?" she asked. "Why'd those guys bring me here—and why are you here keeping me prisoner? Don't you know that's a federal crime?"

"I just do what I'm told."

Tight-lipped old coot. Her stomach growled from hunger. She'd heard about women who couldn't eat right after their spouse died, but nothing had ever effected her appetite. "How about some food?" Annie wiped, put the lid on the granite slop jar and returned to her cot, sitting carefully so as not to tip it over. "You're gonna empty this stuff out ain't you? Or do we have to smell my pee all day? And where can I wash my hands?"

"Shut your yap, woman. Food'll be here directly. If you don't shut up, when it do get here, I'll eat it all me self."

Annie lay back and sighed. Her stiff joints ached from the humidity. "You're a hopeless case, that's all I gotta say." She put her bound hands over her eyes. "You ought a be ashamed, treatin' a helpless old woman this way."

"Helpless schmelpless." He laughed, choking on the phlegm in his throat. " 'bout as helpless as a rattlesnake. I seen the way you been lookin' 'round, checkin' out this place." He threw the words over his shoulder. "Never you mind. We ain't goin' no where till we're told to."

"Who's telling tell you that, those men what took me?"

"I said never you mind."

Footsteps clapped against the deck outside the door. "I'm a gonna open this door, but if you wanna keep seein' daylight, keep your trap shut." Gabby struggled to his feet and walked to the window stiff-legged, one hand on his hip. "It's 'bout damn time." His arthritis-deformed hand fiddled in his pocket, pulled out a key and unlocked the door. A boy no more than six or seven walked in carrying a large wicker basket.

"Grandma told me to bring this." The boy looked at Gabby, then over at Annie, propped up on her elbow.

"Who's that? What's she doin' here? Is she tied up?" The boy's big brown eyes stretched wide.

"No, she ain't tied up. She's just holdin' that there rope. And besides, it's none a your business. Now, go—git. Git outta here. And don't forget to tell your grandma I said thanks, else I'll never hear the last of her bitchin'."

The boy turned and scurried to the cabin door, pausing a moment to look back at Annie. He threw warning words over his shoulder as he ran out.

"Grandma said tell you a bad storm's headin' this way, and

that you better get off this boat and get home."

Gabby closed the door and turned the key. Soon, the boy's footsteps faded into the moans of a growing wind.

"Hey, old man, you gonna let me eat some of that food?" Annie swung one bare, varicose-veined leg off of the cot, then the other. Grunting, she pushed up and sat with her bound hands in her lap.

The smell of fried chicken and biscuits filled the room. Annie was so hungry she'd swear her throat was cut.

Gabby took the kerosene lamp off the table and handed it to Annie. "Here, hold this."

Annie opened out her hands and held the lamp as best she could. The cool glass soothed her dry, aching hands. If she weren't so starved, she'd throw the dang thing at him.

Gabby lifted the basket lid, pulled out a red-checkered cloth and spread it across the table. Next he pulled out a platter of fried chicken, a pan of biscuits, a jar of jelly, and a pile of corn on the cob.

Annie licked her lips.

He took the lamp from her and sat it on the edge of the makeshift table next to the food, and then started untying Annie's wrists. "Here, get somethin' to eat and quit your bitchin'."

Her hands tingled as circulation returned. She rubbed first one wrist then the other as she plopped herself down in a weathered, straight-back chair. Then they both grabbed a piece of chicken and chomped hungrily.

"Chicken's good." Annie tossed the bare drumstick into the basket on the floor, wiped her fingers on the tablecloth. "But it's got a touch too much salt and it's a might greasy."

"Well, I'll be sure to tell the dang chef," Gabby said as he gummed off a leg bone, smacking between bites.

"And the biscuits are heavy and sickly pale—no crust at all. You gotta put grease in your pan, put the biscuits in, then flip 'em over in the grease. That way, when you bake 'em they'll take on a nice brown color and have a crispy top and bottom. These are too thick and doughy. Biscuits should be nice and thin."

"You're lookin' a gift horse in the kisser, woman."

"I know, I know. And I'm thankful for the food, don't get me wrong. But I sure could teach that woman about cookin'."

"Maybe you'll get a chance to do just that. Then of course, maybe you won't." Gabby gobbled his food like a pig gobbles slop, pushed his chair back and stretched his arms over his head. "Nap time. Here, get back over to the bed." He grabbed her by the elbow and pulled her up from the table.

Before the decision to do so registered in her brain, Annie swung around, brought her knee up as hard and as fast as an old woman could, and jammed it in his groin.

She'd seen them do that on T.V.

"Jee-sus Christ." Gabby yelled, grabbed himself, and slid to the floor.

An ostrich trying to fly wouldn't look any more awkward than Annie felt, flapping her arms and stepping high-footed over the moaning heap on the floor. Headed to freedom.

Some tidbit flitted around the edge of her brain, but for the life of her, she couldn't remember what it was until her hand snatched the doorknob.

The key.

👁   👁   👁

"You sure you want to get involved in this?" Sid didn't even bother with polite greetings when Priscilla answered the phone.

"Where do you want me to meet you?"

"I'm sitting out front."

"Out front? But I'm not even dressed."

"That's okay, I can wait."

"But what do you wear to a search-and-rescue?" Priscilla asked.

"Clothes." Sid was already regretting her decision to let the churchwoman get involved. Knowing Priscilla, she'd come out wearing spike heels and her mink stole.

"Do I have time to fix my face?"

Is it broken? she almost asked, but remembered the pressure she'd been under to achieve perfection while married to *Pastor*, and squelched the question. "Put on your make-up, and come on. Hurry, before the weather gets worse."

By the time Priscilla got to the car, Sid had fielded an out-of-town call from George who admonished her to take care. The thing was, she'd taken care all her life, and had gotten nowhere by doing so. If only someone would wish her success instead of safety.

"Okay, where to first?" Priscilla's face looked as pinched as her voice sounded.

"You sure you want to do this?"

"I'm sure. I just don't know *what* to do. You think our hair will get mussed up?"

"Probably." Out of the corner of her eye, Sid saw Priscilla pat her un-mussed hair.

"The weather report says a pretty bad storm is heading this way." Unease tinged Priscilla's voice.

They both buckled up and pulled their belts tighter.

"I have no clue where to start," Sid admitted, cranking the motor. "All I know is it has to do with water, and I suspect, Adams Bayou." No way in hell was she ready to explain her source on that.

Priscilla blurted, "Pastor always said…"

Sid stiffened.

"I've really got to stop that don't I?"

"I really wish you would."

Both of them grew silent as Sid drove away from Priscilla's well-manicured neighborhood. The wind picked up, squealed through the tiniest cracks of the car windows.

"This storm is looking bad," Priscilla said, finally breaking the silence. "We don't usually have this kind of storm so early in the year. I don't know what's happening to our weather patterns.

It's downright scary."

Sid heard, but ignored the comment. Weather or no, she was looking for Annie. "You familiar with Adams Bayou?"

"Yeah, it's the bayou that flows through Orange. My husband takes his boat out and goes fishing. Sometimes he takes me, but I don't touch the smelly things. I take a book and a pillow." Priscilla leaned forward and peered out the windshield. "But you really think we should go out there in this weather? The bayou may rise over its banks."

Blowing wind and rain—butterflies in her stomach—none of it mattered. Annie did. "I read where people have houseboats out there. We're looking for one named Misty Babe. Ever seen it?

Priscilla nodded. "Name sounds familiar, but I'm not sure what it looks like."

Following Priscilla's directions, Sid drove until the road changed from black-top to an unpaved line of potholes strung together by an occasional patch of gravel. Her wheels splashed muddy water out of the holes and onto the windows. Useless windshield wipers only spread the mud. Sid peered through a small spot cleared by washer fluid.

Anxiety built in her chest until she felt like an elephant sat on it. What if all this was for nothing? She glanced over at Priscilla's white-knuckled hands gripping the dashboard. The woman's eyes bugged out.

This was too much for Priscilla; Sid should never have brought her out here. She rolled her window down part-way so she could see the bayou on her left.

Boats lined the shore, rocking and tossing in the troubled water. They passed small fishing boats tied to trees, and fiberglass or aluminum house boats that looked like they'd seen better days. A pontoon party boat fought with its moorings.

But no Misty Babe.

At length, Sid ran out of potholes and gravel. Dead End, the yellow and black sign announced.

"That's it. End of the line. It's not out here." Priscilla sighed with relief, pointing. "You can turn around right over there."

"We've got to walk the rest of the way."

"Walk? In this weather?" Priscilla looked at her like she'd suggested a flight to the moon. "Don't you think we'd have found it by now? There's nothing further up river."

"You can stay here. I'm going." Sid pushed her door open against the driving wind and rain, and stepped out.

Priscilla climbed out the passenger door and sloshed around the front of the car. "If you're going, I'm going," she yelled above the weather.

Single file, Sid in front, they wended their way over cypress knees, and through pine needles floating in ever-larger puddles of water. Priscilla clung to the back of Sid's shirt, her shoes knocking up against Sid's heels. Both of them staggered against the wind.

A cluster of wet Spanish moss from a low-hanging branch plastered Sid's cheek like a wad of rain-soaked spider webs. She shuddered, brushed off the creepy thing and kept going, fueled by the thought of Annie held captive. But by the time they reached water's edge the creepy feeling had crawled down her quivering legs.

Following the bank of the river for a half mile or so, they crossed over more cypress knees, tree roots, broken branches, sodden leaves and brush, past abandoned canoes, and small trawlers.

"It's not here," Priscilla hollered. "That was the last one. Let's go back."

"A little further—around this bend." Sid pushed harder, desperation and disappointment settling in her chest. "We can't stop, Prissy, not yet, we..." The wind slammed Sid's words back down her throat.

"It's no use, Sid. She's not out here. They must've moved the boat someplace else. We need to go back."

Rain pelted Sid's face, disguising her tears. She reached behind her, grabbed Priscilla's hand and charged on until her foot caught on something.

All of a sudden, a tangle of hands, knees, elbows, and feet tumbled after the other. Trees and river and sky blurred into one. Jumbled questions zipped through Sid's mind until she hit mushy ground, Priscilla on top of her.

"What the hell was that?" Sid called out, looking up at Priscilla. Her ankle throbbed.

"A tree root, I think. Let me look." Priscilla slid off Sid, sat up and they both squinted in the rain. A giant Pond Cypress hovered over them. "Yeah, see that big root right there," Priscilla pointed. "That must be the tree they call The Survivor. It's over twelve hundred years old, my husband said."

Sid rolled over and sat in the watery mess. "I don't care what its name is—look, my ankle's already swollen twice its size." She crossed the throbbing ankle over her other leg and rocked. "I swear the root wasn't there a minute ago—it's like it reached up and snagged my foot." Sobs broke off her bitter words.

"Here, let's get you back to the car." Priscilla grabbed her hands and pulled. Half-way up, their wet palms slipped. Sid's world spun again as she fell backwards, full length, into the mire.

The rain had lessened, but Sid was already soaked to the skin and bone-cold. Her ankle hurt like hell. Rain dripped off her hair and into her eyes.

Water, Sid. Water.

The sound of fast-running water penetrated her misery. Faucets in the bathroom—pouring down the drain.

Lost in the noise of slapping water, at first Sid didn't realize the sound wasn't in her head. She clambered to her hands and knees, found her now mud-coated gun, and slipped and slid through sloppy mire. She rounded The Survivor tree and, head down, charged toward the sound of slapping water like a bull after a wet red cape.

Near hysteria, Priscilla yelled at Sid's retreating backside. "Stop, where are you going? Come back."

Sid ignored her. Scrambling through heavy underbrush,

brambles scratched her face, caught at her long-sleeved blouse, and pricked her fingers. The vague feelings of pain spurred her faster, like that point in childbirth when she tried to hold back the pain until she realized moving into it was the only way through.

Soon as she rounded a small bend in the bayou, there sat a weatherworn, rough-hewn boat rocking in the water, waves lapping at its sides. A rope moored the boat to a tree jutting out over the water. A makeshift ramp led from bank to boat. Near the path leading to the boat, an alligator waddled toward a duck squatting in the cattails. The duck quacked once, then silence.

The houseboat bobbed in the churning water like an empty bottle bobs on the ocean.

It fit the description she'd read in Al Hedge's client file on Marv's desk. Since that day at the hospital when she'd been introduced to Hedge, she'd known he hid from the truth.

Misty Babe. Red, peeling letters on the boat's bow confirmed Sid's find.

She motioned Priscilla to wait. "Down, down," she whispered, signaling with her hand.

She swiped the back of her hand over her mud-soaked face and stepped onto the ramp, gun ready. Pain shot through her sprained ankle as she hobbled down the ramp and stepped onboard just as a gust of wind slammed into her. She caught herself against the side of the cabin and froze, waiting. But when confronted by nothing but the howling wind, she slid her feet over the rough-planked deck to a filthy four-paned window.

Peeking around the edge of the window, she looked inside and saw an open basket on a barrel-bottomed table, cots on either side. Annie, still in her nightgown, lay tied on one of them. An old man in striped overalls lay sprawled in a chair, snoozing. No one else seemed to be on board.

She returned to the ramp and fought her way back to shore. "Here," she whispered above the wind, handing her wet cell phone to Priscilla. "Head back to the car, call Quade and tell him we've found Annie, but we might need some help."

Priscilla stared blankly, her eyes tense slits. "What's his number?"

Exasperated at having to explain the obvious, Sid whispered, "911," and then demanded, "Do it."

The woman snatched the phone and splashed back the way they'd come.

Sid watched until Priscilla was out of sight then sucked in her breath and returned to the floating prison. She stepped down three short steps to the cabin and tried the doorknob. Locked.

"Open up." she raised her voice above the storm, banging on the unpainted door.

The door cracked open. A wizened old man stuck his head out. "Whatcha want?"

Sid shoved the door open and charged past the man to Annie, still on the cot.

"Sweetheart, you okay?" Sid asked, making quick work of scanning the room. When she saw no one else, she bent over the fragile-looking face of her aunt who had a gag stuck in her mouth.

Relief replaced Sid's heartache when Annie opened her eyes and nodded, her eyes crinkling at the corners, her skin glistening in the humidity.

Sid glowered at the old man. "What the hell do you think you're doing?" She stashed the gun in her pants pocket, yanked off Annie's gag, and then started untying her aunt's wrists.

Annie licked her cracked lips, cleared her throat. "I knew you'd come, Siddie."

"You cain't just barge in here and take her away," the gravely-voiced man cried, his eye on Sid's pants pocket.

"And just why can't I?"

" 'cause if'n you do, they'll…"

"You're right, Pops—they will." The rough voice came from the doorway. "Easy as catching ducks with a duck call." A smirk played across Al Hedge's face as he strutted further into the room. "I knew taking the old woman would get you here."

"Annie had nothing to do with any of this. It's all me. Let her go," Sid yelled just as the brunt of the storm hit. The boat rocked wildly, knocking her off balance. She caught the edge of the table and hung on, but watched, horrified, as her Glock slid across the floor out of reach.

Hedge stumbled, moved toward her, his voice elevated over the storm. "Oh, she'll go all right—straight to the bottom of Adams Bayou—right after you. Alligator meat for sure."

Footsteps thudded outside the door, and then Sheriff Bonin charged down the steps into the cabin, holding up Sid's cell phone. "Look what I found."

So it was Bonin after all.

Her heart thudded with lost hope. She'd dropped her gun, Priscilla was dead, no one was coming to help. Her loved ones scudded across her consciousness—Chad and Christine—Ben. Even Sam.

Before she could calculate her next move, a sudden wind surge hit the boat from another direction, tearing it loose from its mooring. Waves tossed the rickety craft away from the dock as if it were a matchstick.

Aware of Bonin and Hedge heading toward her, Sid scrambled away, fighting chairs, a tipped over barrel, cots, whatnot. When she reached Annie, sprawled on the undulating floor, her once-white nightgown, now a sodden dirt-brown, Sid leaned over and whispered in her ear. "I'm going to try to hold them off. When I do, you head for the door."

Annie nodded.

Sid turned and Bonin was on her, grabbing. She spread her legs, gathered leverage and shoved into him, and they both fell. "Go." Sid yelled. "Don't look back. Run."

Annie moved stiffly up the steps.

"Move." Sid ordered. "The car's to the right, keys under the seat. Hurry."

Bonin scrambled to his knees and grabbed Sid's ankles just as the waves slammed the boat back against shore. She twisted free and tumbled on top of him, snatching at his shirt, clawing at his face and eyes.

"After the old woman, go." Bonin shouted at the old man, who limped to the door, hand on his hip. "You better go help him," Bonin yelled at Hedge. "He'll never catch her. I've got this one."

The two men headed off the boat after Annie.

Waves flung Misty Babe out into the middle of the bayou. Rain pelted the tin roof. Water poured in through the open hatch. All the while, Sid struggled against the sheriff. They banged into tables, floating cots, baskets.

Keep your head above water, his hands off your throat, someone advised Sid.

A quick, hard shudder shook the vessel. The portside began collapsing. First the sides, then the ceiling fell in on them, and then the whole houseboat fell apart and started floating off.

Survivor instinct told Sid that both she and the sheriff were now at the mercy of raging floodwaters. She thrashed, splashed, fought to tread water, her ears, eyes, nose, throat—everything filled with the muddy liquid. The storm-filled sky and the murky flood waters melded into one pulsating, breathing, aphotic being out to claim her. She sputtered and spit, forced her eyelids open.

Where was Bonin? She didn't see him.

And then his hands locked around her neck.

Wild, arms flailing, she twisted and clawed.

Still he held on.

One of them gulped for air, but Sid wasn't sure if it was Bonin or her. His hands tightened around her throat and he shoved her beneath the water.

All need gone now except for air, and she had none. Easier to just let her lungs fill with the water of life. Just let go, breathe it in.

Her muscles relaxed, let go.

But just as she did, an ethereal voice wrapped itself around her thoughts of resignation. "I'll see you in the lower regions of hell first—and you may burn it down if you damn well choose."

Kate?

Sid roused, clawed, shoved, and pried at the death grip on her throat.

A hand closed around her arm and jerked it toward Bonin.

Sid fought against the force, but it pulled Sid's hand down, down, and then squeezed it shut around something soft and round hanging between Bonin's flailing legs. Instinct tightened her grip while she scrambled around with her other hand for anything that floated—anything to get her head above water.

Bonin's voice, muted by the water, choked, spit, cried out.

The inkling that she had his manhood in her fist penetrated her water-clogged senses. Claw-like, she squeezed tighter, then tighter again, her hand now a vise.

She fought to get her head above water and gulped in great breaths of wet air until a radiating pain shot up her arm, and the battle pulled her back under.

All the while, Bonin thrashed beside her, still an anguished prisoner of her fist.

Finally, she felt him slip deeper into the black, churning river, pulling her down with him.

The sound of far-off, vague voices penetrated her senses. Were they real? Or were they fabricated within her mind—like the force around her hand?

The earthy taste of the brackish water settled into resignation—acceptance. She felt the ease of relief as she stopped the struggle.

The roiling water forced her and Bonin deeper, still her hand squeezed his scrotum.

But then dismembered fingers pried her fist off of Bonin's crotch, and she sensed him sinking to the bottom.

Within the blackness of her mind, Sid felt an amorphous figure shove her hard, fast, up toward the surface. Her lungs fought against the pressure, begging the figure to let her go, to let her suck in the primordial liquid forced out of her at birth, to return to the embryonic state where nothing mattered.

"Fight, woman, fight," the woman's voice shouted.

Startled out of her death spiral, Sid viciously kicked her feet. A torpedo-like spin shoved her up through trash, tree limbs, a floating body.

She broke the surface gasping for air. Dirt-filled water poured out of her nose and mouth.

Certain her rescuer was in the water with her, she swung around grasping for an arm, anything solid.

The dirty water and low-hanging trees gave witness—she was alone.

Light rain pelted her face. Wind, now only a slight breeze, tripped across the water.

She heard voices in the distance. They loomed closer and closer until they crashed through the palmettos and underbrush. Quade and his officers thrashed through the water, yelling her name.

Sid dogpaddled toward them until strong arms gripped her like a vise and sloshed her toward shore. They slipped and slid their way up to solid land. Then winded, she, Quade, and another policeman all lay back in the mire, gasping.

"This one thing I've got to hand you, woman," Quade said, still struggling for air, "You're not deficient in the guts department."

Epilogue

Sid stood next to Annie's bed in ICU. Her dearest friend, Maggie, grabbed Sid's hand and squeezed it tight. "Thank you, Sid. If ya'll hadn't gotten Star Flight out there when you did, she wouldn't've made it. And thanks for riding with her to Houston. She didn't know nothing, but I know she felt you by her side. It means a lot to me." Tears welled in Maggie's eyes and rolled down her cheeks.

"If it hadn't been for me, she'd never have gotten herself in that mess in the first place."

"No, now don't you say that. Annie did what she wanted to do. That was good for her, despite the kidnapping and near-drowning. What's the doctor say?"

"That she's a tough old bird. She's doing fine. Proud of her adventure—and especially proud of her picture in the newspaper." Sid held her belly, laughing.

"Thanks for letting me stay here till she's discharged. I do want to drive her home. We got Frank's funeral arrangements to make and all."

"No problem. Thanks for looking out after her. I've got to get home and check on Priscilla. Thank goodness Sheriff Bonin wasn't a good shot. I'm just thankful she got that call into Quade before Bonin saw her." Soon as I check on her and file the police report, I'll come to the farm and help get everything ready. It's going to be tough on Annie. She and Uncle Husband were married a long time."

"Well, I'll be there for her. I know you will too. She'll make it. As you said, she's a tough old bird." Maggie walked over to Annie's bedside, checked on her then came back to Sid. "What time's your flight back to Orange? Can I take you to the airport?"

"Thanks, I've called a taxi. It should be here soon. I've got to head downstairs and wait for it. Give Annie my love when she wakes up. Tell her I'll see her soon."

Sid arrived at Houston Hobby Airport with only minutes to spare. After she boarded and settled down for the brief flight to Mid-Jeff airport, her thoughts went to Ned. Dempsey would be relieved to have his son's name cleared. But as a result, now the whole town had to heal. A church was without a pastor. A county was without a sheriff. People had suffered discrimination, false imprisonment, and some even died because of who they were—or what they did—or what they knew—like Jack Agnes. People held the weapons, but prejudice was the killer.

If it hadn't been for Marv's courage to break client confidentially by leaving the file on his desk, she'd never have seen the legal document showing Sheriff Bonin as Al Hedge's silent partner of the gay nightclub. That made it easy for Hedge to provide the sheriff an ongoing list of who was gay and who wasn't.

Nor would she have learned of Bonin and Hedge's pending litigation with the Catholic Church, or that Father Benedict sexually abused Hedge when they were kids. And how he'd made his alter boy, Bonin, watch—over and over and over.

How Hedge and Bonin had agreed to trust no one who was gay, and to do everything in their power to rid their town of those who were. Family loyalty—Marv's record showed—forced Hedge to insist Bonin leave certain people out of the scam, but other than that, anyone was fair game.

Hedge's file told how Father Benedict wouldn't let Bonin close his eyes or turn away. "Bonin, you're missing all the fun," he'd say. "Open your eyes. Look, look how much fun this is." When he was young, Bonin had confessed to Hedge he'd thought there was something wrong with him because Father Benedict never had sex with him.

But then, when they turned sixteen, Hedge and Bonin had taken a solemn oath to never go back to church again. Their mammas cried, saying how they'd failed to teach their sons right from wrong. Hedge's old man beat him until Hedge grabbed the belt and pitched it in the trash. Both of them swore they'd never let a man do that to them, or any other man, again.

Then, that night at the lighthouse, Bonin walked up and saw Caleb lying on the ground. The gang recounted to Bonin, Caleb's actions toward Blue. They loaded Caleb in the backseat, dropped off everyone but Blue and Abe, drove out to the swamp and buried Caleb. No one was sure whether the boy was alive or dead when they had tossed him in the hole.

But whose hand had that been around hers in the water? Was it Kate's—or was it the deep part of her own soul fighting against prejudice and injustice? And if it was Kate, why did she care about the case?

Sophia.

Her old landlady—there was the connection. Sophia had tried to tell her Kate was helping Sid that last time she'd gone to visit the crone. Kate was Sophia's ancestor as well as Dempsey Durwood's. Kate helped Sid so Sophia could let go and cross over.

Tears welled in Sid's eyes, thinking about the thin red line connecting women to each other.

The flight attendant came on and announced their descent as the sun shafted through the window and sparkled off of Sid's diamond. Twisting the ring around, she watched the colors of the rainbow glisten and shine on the perfect marquee cut.

She needed to get used to the look and feel—and the idea—of it, before she landed and faced Ben.

Marriage to Sam had meant the loss of self, the expectation of submission, of maintaining a certain weight, age, belief system, personality.

She'd never go back there again. She loved who she was now—for the first time in her life. Before, she'd always tried to be what others thought she should be. Now, given enough time and running space, she literally felt like she could fly.

Then there were the expectations. How did a woman and man live together and maintain reasonable expectations of the other? Did he pick up his shoes? Did she pull the cover when she turned over in bed? What about freedom? Freedom for herself. To curse when she wanted to, and fart as the need may arise. She refused to 'look the part' of a D.A.'s wife. She'd done enough 'looking like' the preacher's wife. And no way in hell would she believe the same as he—or pretend to.

No, she'd put on the ring too quickly. First, she and Ben had to get some things settled.

She hadn't meant to divorce Sam, it just sort of happened as she took one step at a time. Maybe if she'd learned how to speak up before it got that far, things would have turned out differently—then again, perhaps they wouldn't—Sam's commitment to his denomination superseded all else. With that measuring rod, she would forever fall short of his expectations and forever be doomed to a burning hell.

She couldn't live that way. She *wouldn't* live that way.

But she didn't know Ben that well yet, so the question was, could Ben accept without compromise who she was? She'd give him a little more time—but only a little.

She stepped off the airplane, walked through the passageway and straight into Ben's arms.

And breathed.

THE END

Honoring the real Catherine (Kate) McGill Dorman

Kate McGill Dorman
BORN OCT. 7, 1828
DIED DEC. 24, 1897

In this work I have featured a fictional ghost named Kate Dorman. Although the ghost is a figment of my imagination, there once really lived a Civil War heroine named Catherine McGill Dorman, better known as Scrappy Kate. Information for the fictional diary in the story comes from true accounts of her life.

Often, American women heroes get overlooked in history books. Historian W. T. Block, on his web site at www.wtblock.com, has insured Kate, and her contribution to her community, is not forgotten.

When I first became acquainted with Kate through Mr. Block's writings, something stirred within me—such as stirred within Sid Smart when she saw Kate's picture on Dempsey Durwood's sideboard—and that something, I believe, wanted me to help keep both Kate's memory and her spirit alive as an inspiration to women today.

I believe that 'something' was Kate, herself.

I honor you, Kate, and hope my work pleases you.

For more information on Kate Dorman, visit historian, W. T. Block's web site at www.wtblock.com.

Don't miss the first novel in the Third Eye Mystery Series by Sylvia Dickey Smith:

Dance On His Grave
ISBN-978-1-60318-006-1

Sidra Smart's adventures continue:

An excerpt from the next story in the Third Eye Mystery series, slated to appear in 2008.

Rachel's breath came in quick short bursts as her feet pounded the dirt road running alongside Adams bayou. She loved to run, loved the feel of her long blond ponytail swishing across her shoulders, the wind tickling her face.

Early morning sunlight speckled through the treetops ahead of her, creating a lacy, dancing pattern of sunlight and shadow. It reminded her of the shadows in her own life she'd just come through, and of the new sense of direction she'd found since she'd screwed her head on straight. Running made that happen. Running had helped free her of the demons she'd carried inside—unworthiness, fear of abandonment, being judged by others. Soon she'd turn eighteen, her dreams waiting to be fulfilled...

👁   👁   👁

Two men, both dressed in black pants and short-sleeved polo shirts, crouched low in the bushes ahead of the on-coming jogger. Neither moved, or said a word, responding to the other in hand signals. Dark curly ringlets dangled down into the collar of the larger man with tattoos down both arms. He gripped a large canvas-looking bag with both hands. The other man, skinny, nervous as an over-wound top, held a syringe. They watched the girl approach, dollar signs behind their eyes.

A thing of beauty she was. She'd bring a good price on the open market.

THE THIRD EYE
INTUITIVE INVESTIGATIONS

Author
Sylvia Dickey Smith

Sylvia Dickey Smith was born and raised in Orange, Texas - the land of Cajuns, cowboys, pirates and Paleo-Indians. She entered this world backwards - feet first and left-handed - and has been described as doing things backwards ever since! At seventeen, with a year of high school to go, Sylvia married a "preacher-boy" and soon thereafter became known as the preacher's wife. Years later, she and her family lived on the island of Trinidad, W.I. for a few years, where she developed a love for other cultures, races, religions - she virtually found her voice.

At age forty she took her first college course, and in less than six years graduated with honors from the University of Texas at El Paso, earning a B.A. in Sociology and a M. Ed in Educational Psychology. Sylvia founded her own business conducting management effectiveness training, individual and marriage counseling, and assertiveness training for women. She also facilitated therapy groups for sexual offenders on parole, and for adult survivors of sexual abuse. For several years she served as an adjunct professor, worked in the field of rehabilitation, and directed operations for a long term care facility. Currently living in Round Rock, Texas, when Sylvia isn't writing she's busy scheduling and conducting writing workshops and promoting her books around the country.
Visit Sylvia's website! www.sylviadickeysmith.com

Printed in the United States
113782LV00001B/62/A